THE ENTANGLED PRINCESS

A Clean Medieval Romance

THE BITTER KINGDOMS SERIES BOOK 1

SHANTAL SESSIONS

The Entangled Princess: A Clean Medieval Romance (Book 1)
Copyright © 2018 by Shantal Sessions

Cover art by
DARK IMAGINARIUM Art & Design

The characters and events in this book are fictitious. Any similarity to real persons, living or dead, is coincidental and not intended by the author.

All rights reserved. Without limiting the right under copyright reserved above, no part of this publication may be reproduced, stored in or introduced into a retrieval system, or transmitted, in any form, or by any means (electronic, mechanical, photocopying, recording or otherwise) without the prior written permission of the both the copyright owner and the above publisher of this book.

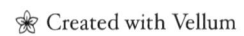

❦ Created with Vellum

*For My Husband
Gene—
Who told the story first.
Je t'aime toujours.*

A NOTE FROM THE AUTHOR

Imagination is a wondrous thing. I remember holding hands with my future husband as we hiked the trails of the beautiful Wasatch Mountains. Ideas percolated. What began as a fairytale in my mind as I breathed in fresh air, blue skies, picturesque forests, and meadows grew into a story of star-crossed lovers on opposing sides of a great war. Disputes among European countries during the Middle Ages helped shape the plot, where interrelated royalty, betrayal, treachery, murder, battles, and invasions were commonplace, all in pursuit of obtaining the power and wealth of a throne. In my book and in history, two great armies met on a muddy battlefield, intending to end a war fought by their fathers and grandfathers. The Battle of Agincort, which Shakespeare immortalized in *Henry V*, is inspired by that horrific conflict. While the places and characters are fictional, the battle from which I drew inspiration is very real. As a result, this book contains some PG-13 type violence and less than twenty biblical swears.

The battle is important to the plot, but the romance is heart of the story. Love blossoms in the most unlikely circumstances. I became interested in action, adventure, court intrigue, and how characters, so much in love and fighting for just one chance to see their beloved again, would respond to such challenges. They buck the system in many ways, very ahistorical, but fun to write. As the grandpa in *The Princess Bride* says to his sick grandson before beginning the book, there is "fencing, fighting, torture, revenge, giants, monsters, chases, escapes, True Love, miracles..." I'm pleased to inform you this book has some of those, too.

Happy Reading! -Shantal

I
THE PRINCESS

Always in the deep, silent darkness before dawn, before the light of the sun turned black into grey and shed its blinding shadows, Meg stole quietly away from the castle. She was used to walking in the dark, but this time she stumbled as a loose cobblestone pitched her forward. Catching her balance, she straightened her cloak and kept walking.

"Why must you do this?" Lady Byron scolded Meg from behind as she huffed, trying to keep up. "It's the middle of the night, it's cold, these alleys are quite disreputable, and the soldiers..." She trailed off, her voice quavering. "They rake you with their eyes."

Meg almost laughed. "They can't even see me in the shadows. Besides, I'm wearing a cloak. It's impossible to rake me with their eyes." She turned toward her chief lady-in-waiting and saw from the light of a nearby lantern that her brows furrowed with fear.

"They can tell you're a woman and that's all the encouragement they need. They smell like a pigpen. The stench could back a buzzard off a corpse." Lady Byron sniffed haughtily and tightened her prim lips. A woman of forty or so years, she was unnaturally thin and prematurely wrinkled. Stern and rigid, she looked as if she had a knight's jousting lance attached to her backside.

"Lady Byron." Meg stopped, placed a hand on the woman's shoulder, and looked her in the eye. "I know the only reason you've started coming with me is that my father has entrusted you with my safety. He puts the onus of my behavior on your shoulders, although he does not know that I frequent the city without guards, a little too often, shall we say?"

"It's utter nonsense and sheer folly," Lady Byron pressed with a shrill, vexed tone to her voice. "But if I can't tie you to your bed to keep you from sneaking out, you'll just have to endure my presence."

"An annoyance I can easily bear... Look, Lewin's candles still burn," Meg said as she grabbed Lady Byron by the hand and pulled her along toward the cottage.

As they walked through the threshold into the kitchen area, Meg saw no one. A fire crackled in the hearth. Flour dusted the butcher block, but no one was home. Meg ushered Lady Byron toward the fire so that she might warm up, but turned toward the cellar door when she heard the stairs squeaking. She hadn't remembered that they squeaked so badly, screeching like the old, rickety wheel of a cart.

The latch clicked and the door cracked open. Someone pushed and it swung wide thumping against the rough rock wall. A teen boy stepped into the kitchen, munching on an apple. His attention focused on the door to the cottage, he hadn't bothered to check near the fireplace. A second boy caught Meg's eye as he stood in the doorway to the cellar. He stopped dead in his tracks, staring at her in wide-eyed shock. Both held several loaves of bread in their arms. They were thin, tousled, and grime-ridden. One boy wore only a vest and a pair of homespun breeches held up by a rope belt. The other had on a long-sleeved tunic and breeches with a work apron slung over his head that tied the front with back panels at his waist. Neither of the boys had shoes on their feet.

"You pilfering wretches!" Lewin roared as he walked in the door with his wife Melinda. "You'd better run!" The boys dropped their loaves and darted to the opposite side of the butcher block, where Meg and Lady Byron stood watching the antics. Meg didn't know whether to try and protect herself and Lady Byron from the troublemakers or admire them. The boys were far too fast for Lewin and dodged his grasp. One hurdled over the table. The other skidded under the table and across the floor, and together they ran into the night. Luckily, they didn't knock over Melinda on their way out the door.

"Filthy little mongrels," Lewin griped, panting and frustrated, hands on his hips.

"You do keep a rather large collection of bread, cheese, and fruit in your cellar. It can't possibly be a secret." Meg shrugged and gave him a crooked smile. "I'm sure the days you bake, the aroma attracts every guttersnipe and vagabond for miles."

"Oh, my lady. Forgive me. My father will kill me for acting like a crazed boar in your presence."

"He'd give it a good belly laugh, don't you think, Lady Byron?" Meg elbowed her chief lady-in-waiting.

"Yes, I think Cooksey would rather enjoy it," Lady Byron agreed with a small, shy smile. "We should tell him upon our return."

"Please don't, ladies." Lewin bent down to pick up the loaves that fell to the floor. "My father takes pride in being the king's head cook all these years, and he expects me to live by a certain decorum. He doesn't want to be embarrassed. Truth be told, I've got to make a living and those thieving rascals don't make it easy."

"Don't listen to him for a second. The war is making him rich." Melinda walked toward a table and pulled cloths off dough rising in bowls near the fire.

"What are you doing out and about in the middle of the night? Should I alert my father that his princess is getting into mischief?"

"I think a report of that nature would fall on deaf ears," Meg said, smirking. "If anyone hides my secrets, it's Cooksey. I'm stuck in the castle all day and must hide from my brother William, the tormenting monster, so I might as well get some air at night. I take the tunnel just outside the castle wall to an abandoned apothecary. It still smells like an herb garden. It's perfectly safe," she rationalized when she saw their expressions of disbelief.

"She's tempting fate," Lady Byron said acidly.

"I suppose that's why you've come along then, Lady Byron, to keep her out of trouble?" Lewin asked.

"I'm testing my skills," Meg interrupted. "My one good brother, John Paul, taught me how to escape a man's iron grip among other things, like how to wield sword and shield, javelin and pike, bow and arrow. When he returns to the castle from doing father's work in the field, he instructs me on battlefield strategy and the history of war as he would a young prince. It annoys William horrendously. Of course, that's one of the reasons I do it. Since I'm clearly trained as well as a man, I think I'll taunt one of the castle guards, get him to attack, and see if it works." When Meg waggled her eyebrows, Lady Byron looked as if she might faint.

"She's either the smartest girl I know, or the luckiest. Heaven knows she'll not act like a royal on my account," Lady Byron lamented and primly pressed a winkle out of her dress.

"My lady, what am I going to do about these children stealing my food? I can't even walk out the door any more. It happens nearly every day," Lewin grumbled.

"I guess you're going to have to feed them," Meg quipped thoughtlessly as the words tumbled out of her mouth.

"I'd go broke. That'll never happen."

"Why not?" Meg protested, wondering if she could gather extra resources from her father, get people to help, and feed the city's hungry children. Maybe she could get her ladies-in-waiting and some of the nobles' wives to make clothes for them, too. It would be the most wonderful thing in this war-weary world to set up places around the city, her beloved Tirana, where the people could find some relief. She would talk to her father about it.

"Here you go, my lady." Melinda handed her a thick slice of bread slathered with honey butter. "I assume that's why you've come."

"And the company," Meg insisted. "But yes, this is divine. Thank you."

"She eats like a sparrow and often faints," Lady Byron chided, but then she softened her features and looked kindly toward Meg. "I'm glad to see you taking an interest in good food."

"How can I eat when so many go without? It doesn't seem right."

"Come sit and eat then," Lewin encouraged as he walked toward a small sitting area in the cottage.

A noise in the street captured Meg's attention. She rushed to the window to see a small detachment of soldiers from her father's army in the street. They were not on alert or disciplined. This was a band of unruly men, drunk, stumblin2g, laughing, but they held their weapons at the ready as the made their way toward the castle. They flanked a cloaked and hooded prisoner, someone who looked far too small and delicate to cause any trouble. It made Meg wonder who would require an escort of this nature. It didn't appear to be official. Meg couldn't imagine why the guards would act in such a manner. Was this her father's bidding? It didn't seem likely, but she'd talk to him about this, too.

"Come, Lady Bryon," Meg said and raised her hood over her head. "I want to find out what these men are up to."

"I'm not going to get in their way. They're too drunk to tell the difference between royalty and criminals right now," Lady Byron snapped.

"Fine."

Meg turned on her heel and walked out the door. Lady Byron huffed disagreeably and followed in her wake. Paying more attention to the ties on her cloak than to her steps, she tripped on the stone steps of the cottage and careened face first into a very solid chest. A man's chest. One of the guards had fallen behind along with his comrade. When Meg looked up, his face showed outright alarm. He placed his hands on her shoulders, as if she were a delicate vase full of flowers, and pushed her upright so that she could stand without leaning on him. He stepped back, his gaze lingering, completely unabashed for holding her glance. Meg should've found it unnerving, but instead, his focus put her at ease. A strange mix of softness and intensity lit his light blue eyes, not indecent ardor, crushing neediness, or even squinty dismissal, like she'd seen in the eyes of other men. Meg realized she quite liked his eyes and admiration. Heat rushed to her cheeks.

Having entirely lost her words, she looked down and found a grave interest in her boots. When Meg ventured a look toward them, his comrade tried not to smile and looked away. The one with the eyes, well, he couldn't seem to look at her again, either. The silence was insufferable. She couldn't bear it.

"Thank you for using your ... chest ... I guess it is, to prevent me from shattering my teeth on the cobblestones, sir. I'm grateful."

"Uh ... of course ... It's my privilege to help a lady in distress."

"Especially one with perfect teeth," his comrade whispered out of the side of his mouth.

The soldier cleared his throat and scowled.

"And lovely eyes, I might add. A glorious creature to be sure." He mumbled the last part, but Meg still heard it.

"That's enough." The guard gave his friend a frustrated sidelong glance.

"So, you find my features akin to a fine horse? How charming..." Meg arched her brow in accusation and gave him a withering look. The guard with the nice eyes raised a hand to his lips to stifle a laugh, but his shoulders shook gently with laughter. His friend looked caught off balance by her remark, his mouth agape with a little crinkle between his eyebrows. Meg whirled in the opposite direction and left them behind, dragging Lady Byron by the hand.

2
A DILEMMA

Meg sat near her father on an overstuffed pillow on the floor, close enough that he could touch the long tendrils of her hair. King George Edward Longbourne reclined in a great wooden chair in his chamber, facing a giant blaze. With his scruffy grey beard, stringy hair, and eyes that could barely see past the drooping folds of his eyelids, he looked smaller than she ever remembered him. He looked like a child pretending to be king, sitting on an oversized throne, dressed in clothes that were too big, his feet just touching the floor.

"They're gaining momentum, Meg," her father said. "I can feel it when I breathe. It's as if their presence puts a toxin in the air."

"I cannot believe you would say such a thing, Father. There is always hope," Meg argued. She looked into his careworn face, the travail of the kingdom mirroring abominably in every scar and deep crevice.

"But is it not so, my dear?" he asked after much reflection. "Have not my spies warned for months that the enemy is preparing a new offensive? I just received word from several field commanders that the Edmiran army has broken through the outposts. The location of the breach was executed with fine-tuned precision, one that would give them access to the most practical route into Tirana. I feel like I've opened the gates and ushered them in myself. We will have to realign our forces." He rehearsed the strategy, his brows colliding in concentration. "I'm sure we'll hold them back for a while, but our army will be hard pressed."

"The invader appears to have the advantage, but we cannot let that demoralize us. We've always been able to get away, Father. You forget that." Meg patted his hand reassuringly.

"But not turn them back, not in almost a hundred years. That is what we must do to win," he said in a defeated voice. "I do not know if I have it within myself to turn the tide. I have long prayed for a miracle. You know that, my child."

"What about Commander Kane?" Meg stood up and faced her father with enthusiasm. "Perhaps he is your miracle."

"Commander Kane has proven to be shrewd and immovable, a wall of stone, full of grit and thickness of purpose." The king held his hands clasped, his forefingers steepled against his beard. "He has provided Asterias's defenses with much-needed victories for some years now. Because of him, the invader has paid dearly for every advance. It doesn't matter. The war goes on with no end in sight. Then, there is this man they call the Wolf Knight," he said, his voice laced with exhaustion.

"Nonsense, Father. That's just a beast from a fable." She paced the room in front of the fire, kicking up dust and the scent of rosemary from the rushes on the floor.

"The legend may be nonsense, but the man is real enough, I assure you." He tapped a fingernail on a stack of papers on the small table beside his chair. "Report after report comes of his unending strength and brutality. He's become an unconquerable hero and legend in the Edmiran army. Our own people succumb to the stories. They are terrified of him, as if he were some sort of specter that could summon the power of evil against them."

"I can't believe that he's fiercer than any of our knights.

What about John Paul? I've heard nothing but glorious tales of his cunning and bravery."

"Listen to this." He waved one of the papers at her, ignoring her protest. With a bit of scowl, she sat in the chair beside him. "Many years ago, the Edmiran army entered Asterias again. The army marched through the mountains instead of landing by sea, which is a toilsome job in itself, and joined forces with a company of carpenters that had already sneaked through the border. The first force had been living in the forest long before my spies ever realized they were here, building catapults and other horrible tools of destruction. The Wolf Knight was just a lowly member of the cavalry at the time.

"Before long, a great battle ensued and it was not going well for the Edmirans. We charged, outflanked them, and pressed toward the middle for the final push. We were so close, almost had their commander in our grasp. Several of our soldiers thought they saw the young soldier go down in a great sword fight with one of our most revered knights. They never used the catapults except to burn the field with the carcasses of flaming pigs."

"That's ridiculous." Meg tapped her foot on the stone floor as she looked angrily into the fire.

"It's not ridiculous, Meg. You see, they used the catapults for just that purpose, not to maim my forces, not with pigs anyway, but to create chaos, to make it harder to hear and see and even breathe on the battlefield. That's when a young man on horseback, whom we all thought was too gravely injured to mount a horse, charged through a ring of fire and smoke, leading a fresh army behind him. The pelt of a gigantic white wolf spread across his shoulders and trailed down his back, floating on charred, black air, threatening and intimidating all who saw him that day. He has been known as the Wolf Knight ever since."

"What can I do, Father?" She leaned forward and tried searching his eyes. He was sullen, his head bowed, with his eyes lost in the folds of his swollen eyelids. "I want to help, to be of comfort to you, and to be of service to our people. I have an idea if you'll allow it."

"Anything you want. Just name it, dear girl."

"Are you sure, Father? I want to use some of our reserve grain to feed children in the city. The war has made it difficult for them to get enough food. They're starving. Cooksey could help me find people to get the wheat into the right hands, people who'd be willing to make the bread and distribute it. I think it could work, but it would divide our stores for the army."

"How do you like your new horse?" the king asked, ignoring her proposition.

"You know I love him," Meg answered, puzzled by the abrupt change of subject. She decided not to turn the conversation back to dividing the kingdom's precious reserves. She'd take the idea to Lord Cronmiller, Asterias's prime minister, and get him to sign off on the deal. Her father had said yes, after all.

The king's face crinkled into something of a smile, as if stretching his skin from cheek to cheek was a daunting effort, but he nodded appreciatively. "I can see you sitting atop that beautiful bay right now. You know, I commissioned our master of horse to find just the right animal for you," he added, a tiny, mischievous twinkle in his eye as he pointed a finger at her.

Meg recognized a shadow of his former self and it felt as if someone had wrapped their hands around her heart and squeezed. *How I miss you, Father.*

"I knew a bay would be perfect, especially one with a black mane, tail, and stockings. I couldn't be more delighted."

"And a puff of white on his snout," Meg added, enjoying the banter. "That's why I named him Golden Cloud. Thank you for giving him to me, Father. I loved mother's horse, but the mare was getting a little old. I fear I've driven Hopkins and his groomsmen mad with my constant demands to ride on the castle grounds. Come riding with me, Father." She grabbed his hands and searched his eyes. "It would do you good. We could go out onto the plain together. I would love to ride at full speed through the lush hills and have the wind streak past, hair and cloak fluttering behind."

"Tsk, tsk, tsk," he waved a finger at her, smiling a little brighter. "You sly little devil. You know the rules. You're not to leave the city, even on horseback accompanied by guards. It's too dangerous. Maybe when we've won the war."

"You've been saying that for years." Meg pouted at him like she did when she was a little girl. "I've never ventured onto the plain and felt the breezes from the verdant meadows, or waded my feet in the ocean, or inhaled the rich pine scent of the forests. You're purposely depriving your daughter of a well-rounded life."

"Just stay out of trouble, dear girl." He patted her hands and shifted his gaze back to the fire. "I cannot talk anymore," he sighed. He pushed the papers off the table and they scattered on the floor. "The war is all I ever discuss with anyone who walks through that door. I just want it to go away, Meg. I've never wanted anything more in my entire life, except wishing your mother right here beside me."

"I love you, Father," she whispered. Meg knew deep down that he had given up, but she could not. She would not sit near the throne and watch it crumble. Feeding the children was only the beginning. She would look for other ways to cheat Edmira and bring victory to her father and to Asterias.

Standing up, Meg kissed her father on the forehead and left the room. As she shut the door to the king's apartment and passed by his guards, she saw William and several of his entourage trying to entertain a young girl in the great hall. He had placed her at one of the large tables that ran the length of the hall. They surrounded her, trying to engage her in conversation and encouraging her to drink some wine.

The child would have none of it.

She clasped her hands and held them between her knees. Her eyes were downcast, lost in the folds of her gown. When she looked up, her eyes darted around the table, like a skittish animal caught in a net. Spooked and jittery, she lunged out of the grasp of every person who tried to touch her. With the anguish and pleading in her eyes of a frightened prisoner walking to the scaffold, she looked toward Meg as if she were her only salvation. She seemed far too young to be a courtesan for William, but she was quite lovely. That was reason enough to suspect William's motive for bringing her to the castle. The last time Meg had sneaked out of the castle, she remembered seeing the city guards escorting a prisoner of small stature. It struck Meg at the time. She wondered how such a little person could've caused so much trouble and gotten arrested. Seeing the girl made perfect sense. They kidnapped her and brought her here for William. Meg wanted to spit in his eye.

"What are you doing here?" William growled when he saw Meg.

"Just walking to my chamber, brother," she said, a little startled that he would be so belligerent with her in front of others. Meg caught another glimpse of the terror in the girl's eyes and resolved that she must do something. If her father could assign her nothing more, she could take care of this.

Movement drew Meg's attention to another man sitting on a bench under the tall, sculpted windows across the hall from William and his friends. She hadn't noticed him before. He seemed to be waiting for her to emerge from her father's chamber. Tall enough, but shaped like a bull, Godwin Brantley, the Duke of Breckenridge, was one of William's oldest friends. Her brother called him Bran. From the southern reaches of the kingdom, his lands had not felt the trauma of the war as much as the north. John Paul told her that the duke profited from the war by selling goods from his province to the army for grossly exaggerated fees. Meg already disliked him and had no desire to spend any time with him, but her father had asked her to be respectful and genteel to the nobility.

"My Lady Marguerite," he called as he hurried to walk with her. "May I speak with you?"

"My Lord Breckenridge." She greeted him with a false smile.

"I would be honored if you would sup with me tomorrow eve, as I shall be dining with the king. I have news from the great lands of the south."

She stared at him, unmoving like a doe in the forest, waiting in silence until danger has passed. Meg wished that she'd had the presence of mind to have an excuse already formed just for this purpose. She would not allow this man think that he could court her. Suddenly, her mind conjured the man with the sky-blue eyes, the guard she bumped into on the street. He crouched behind a bush in the forest until he saw her. Then he stood and walked toward her, smiling. Meg caught herself blinking, trying to shake out of the vision. A sudden, unexpected ache gripped her heart. She realized she'd never see him again.

"My lady?" prompted Breckenridge.

"Oh ... I have already promised my ladies-in-waiting that ... that ... I would treat them to a sumptuous banquet tomorrow evening as they have been so good and gracious to me. I am sorry, my lord, but I cannot break my promise, now, can I?"

"A feast for only you and your ladies? In a time of war, when we have all been asked by the king himself to spare as much as we can for the army?" He raised his eyebrows and wrinkled his forehead, the creases reaching all the way to the middle of his balding head.

"Yes, my lord," she replied irritably as she turned her back on him.

3
JOHN PAUL AND AN IMPROPER PRINCESS

The fire crackled, the cushioned chairs promised comfort, and the soup steamed, but Meg couldn't countenance satisfaction. She paced in front of the fire, one hand raised to her lips as she gnawed on her thumbnail, wondering how she could free that poor young girl out of William's grasp. Someone tapped on the door and she knew it was John Paul coming to sup with her. Her ladies-in-waiting guessed as much, too. They lined up to greet him, tittering nervously, smoothing their gowns and shawls. Lady Byron soothed them into quiet dignity as she opened the door.

"Thank you, Lady Byron." He walked into Meg's apartment, his beautiful wolf-like dogs following behind him. They circled her apartment, sniffing, clicking their claws on the stone floor, and then curled up near the fire. "Ladies." He gave a nod in their direction and smiled. He sauntered up to Old Addy, the nursemaid and storyteller Meg never had the heart to dismiss, and kissed the top of her hand, as would a gallant knight. The woman blushed and called him "quite a naughty lad," as she had ever since he was boy. Meg chuckled under her breath. Of course, he would charm them. Who could resist the playful, dancing eyes, the mischievous smile, or the mop of golden blond hair streaked so beautifully by a summer sun?

John Paul stood quite formally for a moment, but he looked toward her and ambled over. He gave her a slight bow, kissed the top of her hand, and held it as he led her to a chair.

"Sister, how are you this lovely evening?"

"I am well. Will you join me, brother?" She couldn't help smiling at him herself. "Our meal is waiting."

"Yes, delightful. Thank you." He looked directly at Lady Byron, dismissing Meg's ladies. He took a seat as Lady Byron herded the women away so that they could have a private conversation. "They are rather hard to get rid of, aren't they?" he said, picking up a goblet of wine.

"They are rather taken with you, John Paul. Most women are," she replied, tipping her own goblet to him in a toast.

"It's more of a burden than you would think," he said, his face posed in mock seriousness as he took a sip from his cup.

"Poor John Paul. I'm sure you suffer greatly." Meg tried not to laugh.

"I don't want to be rude," he protested light-heartedly. "You have the same problem, my dear sister."

Meg furrowed her brows and pursed her lips. "I'd rather not talk about that," she said, still bothered by the Duke of Breckenridge's invitation to dine together. She glanced behind her to see if her ladies had busied themselves. It was not often that she could speak privately with her brother. She had to devise the circumstances. "There is a young girl in the castle. I think that William…"

"Hannah," John Paul said.

"What?"

"Her name is Hannah," John Paul affirmed. "And don't worry about William." His glance told her to drop the subject. "I've already talked to him."

"I'm not worried about William," she snapped.

"Meg, I warn you now. You will not pry into our brother's business." John Paul leveled a steady gaze at her, speaking more sternly than she ever recalled. "I have expressed my concern regarding the impropriety. He agrees that it does not suit him. He was taken with the girl's beauty, and that's all. I must give him a chance, as a gentleman, to abide by my request. Now, that's the end of it. Do you understand?"

Meg nodded. She understood John Paul's predicament, but could not abide by it. Let William turn a young girl into a whore? Hardly.

"What about the war?" She changed the subject to something they spoke of often. "Tell me what you think father and his ministers will do now that the enemy has broken through our outposts once again. You've been to enough of these meetings, listened to enough reports from the field to fill a granary."

He chuckled and sipped his wine.

"Please, brother. I must have your opinion."

"I think they will send out spies," he shrugged, "and try to gain more intelligence before they make a final decision on where to draw the battle lines."

"That's it?" she replied.

"That's what all this will come to — another battle, and one in which we can win again decisively. The trick is getting all of the Edmiran army out of the boundaries of Asterias, even if we do win."

"If we win?" she repeated, getting a little shrill. "But what about knights in shining armor on splendid steeds with their banners unfurling and trumpets calling and the king himself leading a massive army into battle with a trick up his sleeve?"

"Oh, Meg. You've really got to stop reading so much," he laughed. "That's all romance and glory, not the reality of war. And what about Father? Can you see him leading anymore?"

"No, I'm afraid not," she sighed. "He's so ... beaten. He's certainly not a young man anymore."

"Nor does he have the heart for it."

"There must be something we can do."

"Trust that father and his advisors are inspired and will come up with a brilliant plan."

"Oh," she sighed heavily. "I had a feeling you would say that. I'm much too impatient. I can hardly breathe with the anticipation of what will happen next. And I worry so much for our people."

"As do I."

"If the war reaches the city, it will be awful. You should hear the stories that Old Addy tells of past battles."

"Tragedy is the name by which war is known among its noncombatants, for they are the ones who feel the presence of death and its attendant sorrows."

Meg recognized the quote, delighted to know that John Paul read some of the same books she did.

"You're not the only one who reads." He cocked his brow and winked at her. "Forgive me, sister, but why is this so interesting to you? Why do you need to know all the details of decision-making? It's not proper, you know." He offered a rakish smile as some of his long blond hair fell over one of his beautiful green eyes.

"Because I'm a woman?" she finished for him sarcastically. "You're all so predictable. Why is it that I should not be involved in making decisions?"

John Paul looked at her, his face a sea of calm, but then his lips trembled. His cheeks crinkled as he descended into uncontrollable laughter.

She swatted his arm, and he almost spilled wine on his breeches.

"You saucy little wench," he shouted, jumping to keep his drink from spilling on his clothes. "It's fine, ladies," he called to all six who had inched closer. "You may go back to what you were doing."

When he sat back down, she whispered mischievously, "If I

am of so little value, then why does Father allow me to learn and train as men do?"

"Because all you have to do is smile and bat your eyelashes and he cannot say no to you."

She raised her arm to swat him again, but he was ready for her and caught her arm. An unfortunate problem for John Paul, she thought, having to restrain his sister from clouting someone in the jaw. He'd already saved her numerous times from William. She should've been smart enough not to retaliate when he got drunk and threw his punches.

"No, it's so that I may be as prepared as my two brothers in case..."

"Counting on our demise already, dear sister?" He wrenched her arm a little more with a bit of a wicked grin. When she grimaced, he let go.

"No, not at all," she said, defeated. She slumped in her chair. "Honestly, I do not want the throne. The law prevents a woman from inheriting, anyway. It would go to some distant cousin or nephew as it stands right now if you and William were murdered in your beds. Look at what it has done to our father and his father before him. It's just ... I don't know."

"What?" her brother prompted.

"I just really hate sewing. I must call upon the stars for patience whenever I put a needle in my hand," she said more loudly than she should have.

They laughed together and began their meal. Meg took another cursory glance between the chairs and noticed that her ladies could not believe their ears. They seemed scandalized by her comment. What was she to do? Out of rebellion and stubbornness, she had never learned how to do what the court expected of her. Her life would've been very different if her father had sent her away to be schooled in arts and manners, as he should've done if he'd wanted a proper princess. War prevented so many of the usual traditions.

Meg noticed Lady Byron's sour expression as she fingered the ring of keys fastened to her sash, as she stood glowering behind the ladies.

Poor Lady Byron. She would never have her proper princess, either.

4
POTENTIAL FOR TORTURE

A captain in the Edmiran army, Nicholas Greenwood Sheppard, rose before dawn and trod quietly through the encampment toward the stabling area. The cooks and smiths stirred under their tents and awnings, clucking at their underlings to gather firewood and fetch water from a nearby stream. The thick, moist air produced a heavy layer of dew. Pockets of fog here and there, backlit by amber light, contrasted nicely to the clutch of trees still black from the morning shadows.

Just past fires stoked by sleepy squires, he found his horse and beckoned him. The animal approached and nuzzled Nicholas on his cheeks, neck, and shoulders, puffing warm breath that smelled of hay.

"It's good to see you, too, Zander, defender of men." Nicholas spoke softly to the animal, rubbing his snout, and patting his huge neck. "I'd rather ride alone with you any day over most men, but you know that, don't you?" He sidled through the short, rickety gate of the make-shift stable, running his hand along the destrier's spine. He bent to check the quality of the horseshoes. It had been a long journey back from Tirana.

His commander sent him to the city to scout for a possible

mission to assassinate the Asterian prince. William was an easy target. As far as Nicholas could tell, the man was a swine. He'd already heard of his reprehensible behavior in taverns and brothels. Some tales had him getting away with murder. There wouldn't be much mourning for him, but it would take their minds off the war for a while as they planned a state funeral. In the meantime, if he could get close enough to Commander Kane and take him out of the picture, then Asterias would stagger for the fall. It worked in theory, he thought to himself. He hoped to weaken their beleaguered monarch even more, to have him negotiate with Edmira under more trying circumstances.

"How are you today, you fine wee beastie? Now, let's talk about the important things in life, shall we?" Nicholas said playfully. "Did you sleep well or were you dreaming of those beautiful fillies that we saw on the way to camp, manes flowing in those high mountain meadows? I don't blame you, lad." He ruffled the horse's mane. "I dream of a pretty girl, too." Nicholas hadn't expected the jolt to his heart when his eyes met hers. He stared. He shouldn't have, but she almost fell face first into the street before tumbling into his arms. She got his blood moving, a lovely woman to be sure, but there was no room for women in a time of war.

Tallying his supplies and things he must do for the mission back to Tirana, Nicholas realized he'd forgotten to sharpen his knives. He headed toward the grindstone and began his work.

"Mighty Mother Earth!"

He heard Luke, his second-in-command, yelling from behind him and turned to watch him approach. "What a waste of manhood. This blasphemous war! Look at yonder noble fellow bent over the grindstone, willing to sacrifice his potential, his manhood, for something called victory. Who will care in a hundred years? Who will remember?"

"Good morning, Luke."

"May he outlive his passions and his foolishness, and may I join him!"

"Amen to that!" Nicholas thumped him on the back.

"So, laddie, we're going to scale a wall," Luke began, as if he were discussing the simplest of tasks. He folded one arm across his chest, the other raised to his chin. "A rather altitudinous one, if I do say myself. In addition, there will be guards." His voice was matter-of-fact, but bordered on the humorous. He stomped closer to Nicholas and put his face close to his, his eyes showing mock alarm. "Do you recall that I'm an old man with greying hair and must use a lens for reading? I'm lucky to heft my leg over my horse's arse."

Nicholas crimped his mouth and tried not to laugh. Luke was anything but old. Ten years older than Nicholas, Luke had a bald head and fully bearded face, hardened features, and squinty, fierce brown eyes. He always knit his eyebrows together and wrinkled his forehead in stern concentration, except for when he cracked jokes or told stories. During those times, Luke simpered and smirked, which often led to a wide, infectious smile as the skin at the edge of his eyes crinkled into his cheeks.

Luke was neither large nor small, but wiry and strong. He could do anything a younger man could do, except that he complained that he couldn't, loudly. In a past life, Luke made an honorable living as a master teacher before violence stole his wife and daughters away from him, yet Nicholas did not believe that Luke joined the army for revenge. He could not continue to torture himself with their deaths and missing them so much. He needed a distraction.

"Yes, Luke," Nicholas said. He patted him on the back as if he were a frail old man. "There will be guards. But those young waifs King Colestus has sent us will have no trouble climbing up that wall like sticky little insects. You and I will take a bit more time, but my guess is Goodman, our man on the inside, will follow through, so no worries."

"No worries?"

"It's foolproof," Nicholas baited.

"Nothing ever is, laddie."

"Consider it an adventure."

"I'm getting too old for this," Luke sulked.

∼

"Now is the moment of truth, laddie." Luke sat down next to Nicholas and leaned back against a huge rock. It took several days, but they'd traveled the distance from the Edmiran camp, down a long canyon on high trails that sagged perilously toward a rushing, rocky river. Bitter winds chased them out of the canyon and across the plain. In the dead of night, they hid themselves in a great boulder field just outside the wall surrounding Tirana. "We'll pull ourselves over the top of the wall, be discovered, and die."

"We'll see," Nicholas sighed impatiently. "I trust Goodman, but he is taking longer than I expected."

"You know what they do to prisoners of war," Luke said, his voice nonchalant as he adjusted the rope and bow that he wore across his chest.

"I don't want to hear it, Luke," Nicholas said, his eyes darting to the spaces between the notches in the wall.

"They'll torture us for information," Luke continued matter-of-factly, his voice rising above a whisper. "They'll tie us to the rack and pull on our arms and legs until our joints pop and we can no longer use them. And then they'll drag us to the scaffold, because we cannot walk, since they will have dislocated our leg bones from our hips and knees, and then they'll hang us. And when our vertebrae are suitably cracked, but we have not yet died, they will cut us down and disembowel us. You and I will live to see our innards cut out before our eyes."

"Hail! Down below," a youthful voice bellowed from above.

Nicholas tackled Luke and tumbled into the shadow of the rock he'd been sitting on. They fell onto an unforgiving slab of stone, muscles and bones punished, ears straining for more sound, breathing hard in anticipation of being caught.

"What the...?" Luke began in a forceful whisper.

Nicholas put a hand up to silence him and checked to make sure his men had plunged into darkness. It was a moonless night. Seeing anything in the depths of the shadows from that distance would be nigh impossible. Still ... stranger things had happened.

Some Asterian soldiers had gathered and leaned over the edge of the battlements searching for possible trouble, their voices echoing through the night. Finally, Nicholas heard another guard yell, "Nothing to see here. Move on!"

Nicholas exhaled and turned his head in both directions to watch his men pop their heads up to see what he would have them do. Once they gathered around, he planned to tell them that he would cancel the mission. Nicholas feared something terrible had happened to Goodman. They could not get over the wall without a man on the inside.

Goodman was one of the captain's boy soldiers and not any older than Nicholas when he went into the army. Nicholas had placed him the care of an Edmiran spy so that he could help them get over the wall when the time came. The corporal still had freckles sprinkled across his nose and cheeks, along with a certain boyish negligence that left grime on his face, if not a bit of stubble growing along his jawline.

"Sir, I think it's Goodman," said one of the boys. He stared up at the top of the wall with ogling eyes, pointing.

They all turned around and looked up. Sure enough, Goodman stuck his head through one of the notches in the battlements. If Nicholas didn't know any better and could see up close, he'd swear Goodman was grinning.

"All right, men. You know what to do. Let's hop a fence."

～

THE PALMS OF HIS HANDS BURNED AND BLED. NICHOLAS FELT like he'd placed them over a fire and could not pull them away. He'd done what he could to protect them, wrapping them in several thick layers of leather. He wore fingerless gloves over them, but it was not enough. He reached the top of the wall, pulled himself through one of the notches in the battlements with the help of a couple of boys, and fell onto the sentry walk, exhausted.

Nicholas allowed himself a few moments to catch his breath before he got up and patted Goodman on the shoulder for a job well done. The timing had been perfect. The sentries were at the outer end of their patrols and had not come back to the guard tower yet.

"You know your orders, men," he said in a muffled voice as the young soldiers gathered around him. "It's a cold, dark night. It will be easy to hide in the shadows as the guards walk back along the ramparts and return to the posts. Make your way into the city down separate sets of stairs. Do not go together. If any one of you gets caught, I want them to think you're just curious lads with nothing better to do. Let the Asterians worry about striplings slipping through their patrols.

"You are my support tonight as I try to gain access into the castle to assassinate their prince. You are going to be my eyes and ears while you're in Tirana and when our spy Claymore sends you out as camp followers with the Asterian army. The Edmiran army is now much closer to the capital city. Many destitute women with children seek jobs to do for the Asterian soldiers for a bit of coin. You will fit in perfectly. Make friends with the people and learn what you can. Even though you are playing the part of children, do not be deceived. It is a dangerous job. I need as much information as you can find. It may help us win the war. If anyone finds out who you are, they will kill you, but they will try to find out who sent you first. Your most important job is to safeguard that information with your life. The enemy cannot know."

Nicholas emphasized the words in a forceful staccato, but then his voice softened. "You are vitally important to the success of this mission, but I want you all to return to the Edmiran camp when the time is right. Stay safe. Claymore will give you notice. Off with you now," he said, gesturing with his head for them to follow Goodman.

"Yes, sir," Goodman whispered as he shepherded the crew away and pointed out various routes to take. Nicholas anxiously watched as his band of boy soldiers disappeared into the night.

❧ 5 ❦
SPINNING WEBS IN THE DARK

Nicholas hissed. Sharp thorns from nearby rose bushes jabbed and scratched him as he scaled the rope to the balcony. He was rather astonished by them, so thick and tall, clinging to sturdy trellises. Realizing he might be seen, he stepped deeper into the shadows of the balcony, closer to the princess's arched, shuttered doors. Nicholas gathered the rope and grappling hook as he took in his surroundings. The balcony jutted out from the castle wall in perfect symmetry, a half circle of stone with carved, elegant pillars and railings that supported graceful arches overhead, well placed to view the spectacular garden.

He tested the door to see if it would squeak. It did not. As quiet as a specter, Nicholas entered the bedchamber of the princess as Claymore suggested, the spy's intelligence sure that the princess's balcony and private room remained unguarded. Scanning the room, he noticed a few candles guttered, sputtering low light. From a window adjacent to the bed, the gentle breeze nudged curtains hanging from the sturdy four-poster bed's canopy. Nicholas was curious about this young woman. Even the men in his army spouted tales of her great beauty, but the white, airy curtains veiled her completely. A thin candle stood in its holder upon a table next to the bed. Near the door to her chamber, the page of a book propped open on the table fluttered by the delicate draft.

Taking quick steps toward the chamber's thick wooden door, Nicholas first hid his rope and grappling hook behind a heavy dresser. He tested this door, too, checking to make sure the hinges would not object. The door inched open without a sound. When it opened more, the hinges squeaked horribly, as if someone were yanking long, stuck iron grating from mortar and stone. He froze in the doorway, wondering if he dared to look over his shoulder to see if she had awakened. He could just imagine her poking her head through the curtains and calling the guards.

The princess shifted under the covers. She must've been dreaming, because he heard her gasp and mumble. Nicholas checked to see if the curtains were still closed.

Nicholas let out a breath he didn't know he'd been holding.

Determined to make no more noise, he sidled through the narrow opening of the door and left it slightly ajar so it would not squeak again. He saw no one in the apartment, but he spotted nearby doorways in which he believed the rest of the princess's ladies-in-waiting slept. He couldn't have women up and about, screaming at the top of their lungs if they saw him. Nicholas unstopped his water pouch and moistened the sleeping pellets he bought from the underground market in Edmira. He decided against using the vapor on the princess. He didn't want to risk disturbing her again. One by one, he walked to each doorway, and slid the pellets under the heavy wooden doors. He could already smell the faint scent of perfume.

"Sweet dreams, ladies," he whispered.

Nicholas walked to the door of the princess's apartment and contemplated. He would surely find a guard on the other side. Darkness and stealth had allowed him to evade the guards protecting the castle wall. Fortuitous circumstances allowed him to sneak through the garden and breach the princess's balcony without encountering anyone. That's where his luck ended. The poor lad on the other side was not going to like the questions hurled at him when the castle awoke in an uproar tonight, Nicholas thought grimly as he moistened the last of his pellets and slid them under the door.

∽

Meg ran. How could they turn on her like this? She was trying to help, always trying to help, but they caught her. Their grimy hands pulled and tugged, ripping her gown and grasping for her jewels. Bereaved women yanked at her, shrieking like wraiths, demanding news of their loved ones.

Meg felt her breath catch in her throat and panicked, the high-pitched screams still ringing in her ears. Wait ... she thought in confusion, not quite emerged from the grogginess. Was that her door? She'd asked the chamberlain to fix it a thousand times. Meg turned and lay on her side, her erratic heart hammering in her ears. She peeked through the curtains, wondering if Lady Byron had come in.

How on earth? Her eyes bulged and she froze in a panic.

She fell on her back, breathing hard. Did the man with the beautiful blue eyes, the one she'd been thinking about for so long, really walk into her room?

Impossible ... but there he was.

She stared at him through the tiny opening before he left her chamber, candle light from a table illuminating his face. Meg hadn't considered what he did outside of helping with the enterprises that Cooksey and Lewin had helped her set up throughout the city. She wondered before how a soldier could justify to his commanders spending so much time carrying bags of flour, shoveling manure, spreading hay, fixing wagons, soothing any animal into performing its duties, and generally being a good citizen. Maybe his presence in the castle was part of a fact-finding mission for the army? Maybe they were testing security measures? Her head spun with the possibilities.

Soaked with sweat and getting cold, Meg swung her legs out of bed, walked to her wardrobe, and found her cloak. Shrugging into it and trying to tie it, her trembling fingers fumbled at the job. His presence here was worrisome. What if he was not as he seemed? What if he were here to wreak some appalling evil upon her father? Somehow, she felt compelled to embark upon the most frightening act of her entire life. With her heart leaping, Meg cautiously peeked through the opening of the door and walked through.

∽

CURSE THE GODS! NICHOLAS THOUGHT, SHAKING HIS HEAD with a sigh. He hoped to catch Prince William alone and use surprise and stealth to attack him. He wanted the prince's blood to pool on the cold stone floor in silence. If he hadn't used all the sleeping pellets, Nicholas thought, kicking himself, he could still get the job done.

A man sat with Prince William in cushioned chairs that faced the fire in the luxurious antechamber just opposite the great hall. Set behind a long wooden bench, he could see the men through small perforations at the top of a screen.

"Your sister rejected my invitation to dine, Will. And she lied, contriving a silly excuse about a feast for her ladies." The big man pounded the arm of the chair slightly, bouncing his meaty palm once before he wrapped his knuckles around the end, tightening his hold, a mere whisper of his forceful grasp. Unabashedly bald and powerfully built, the man had all the trappings of a wealthy landowner and knight, perhaps a duke, but Nicholas did not know him. He would send his boy soldiers on a mission to find out.

The prince, on the other hand, looked large, but not necessarily strong. His spies told him that William favored the king in stature, with auburn hair and brown eyes. He might've been handsome, Nicholas thought, but the man sitting in front of the fire was overweight and rumpled, reclining lazily, never putting his goblet down. Rumors of his fondness for spirits not embellished obviously fueled his foul deeds, and etched themselves into his countenance.

"I am not surprised, Bran, old boy. My sister thinks she can say no to every suitor and my father indulges her."

"Does the king really mean for the princess to marry for love? I'm certain I've never heard of anything more ridiculous."

"He loved my mother," Will said, shrugging. He swirled the wine in his goblet before drinking. "He still pines for her, the old fool."

"It's not the way of the world." Bran leaned on the arm of the chair opposite the prince, shaking his head. "Men marry for money, to inherit great lands, and to improve their status in the world by creating alliances. If he must lay with his wife to produce heirs ... Well, I suppose it must be done. I'd rather lay with a woman of more sordid ways." He became still, savoring his thoughts as if he chewed on a piece of delectable meat. "Dark, sultry mistresses are more to my liking."

"I must admit, I can't see why men fall silent in Meg's presence," the prince said, bewildered. "She's plain and uninteresting to me."

"Ah, Willy." Bran chuckled and bounced his palm on the arm of the chair again. "As her brother, you cannot possibly see it, but she is by far the loveliest lady in the land. Any man would be a fool not to think so. I'll make a deal with you, William." Bran clanked his goblet on the table between them. "A king's ransom for the girl."

"You've got my attention." The prince sat up straighter in his chair and looked the man in the eye. "The treasury is running dangerously low, as it does when we prepare for a new offensive."

"If your treaty with King Colestus succeeds and he gets the girl, obviously I would have no claim on her."

"But?"

"But if it doesn't, I would like to offer you a monumental amount of money in exchange for allowing me to take your headstrong sister off your hands, and I want autonomous rule."

"Hmm..." The prince contemplated the offer. "The southlands would still be part of Asterias, and you would pay homage to the crown, but you would rule that province." William leaned back into his chair and sipped his wine. "That would take a load off my mind, especially when I inherit the throne, knowing that the southlands are in good hands. As it is right now, my father and I never know for sure who is loyal to us and who isn't. I've never been averse to parceling off the country to the right men who are loyal and willing to pay for the honor, using the funds to fuel the war effort, but the king would never accept those terms."

"He doesn't have to. I think he'll be dead by then."

"I think you're right. He says often that he's not worthy to live and his health is declining." The prince paused, giving his friend a perverse smile. "It will happen soon enough. No need to hasten his demise."

"Consider me your man, William." Bran put a collegial hand on the prince's shoulder and stared at him earnestly, pressing his point. "In exchange, I will make sure you get everything you've ever wanted, glory in battle, women in your bed, wine in your belly, and Asterias will finally have a king who knows how to rule with a mailed fist. In this, the country is desperate. Too much has run amok in the kingdom." He settled back into his chair and stretched his legs out. "War is a dark and beautiful thing." He turned his head in profile, offered a perverted smile, and gestured for a toast. "It always casts shadows that allow us to spin our webs unseen."

William laughed boisterously, raised his goblet, and gulped his wine.

Nicholas could not have imagined gaining such crucial intelligence. He had planned to sneak into the castle, slit a throat, and be gone. Not only did he now know who the enemy presented to the scene and the actors in the show, but who directed their actions from behind the curtain. He would never have guessed it was not the king nor his sons. He knew of various ministers, but none of them seemed as heinously capable at scheming as this foul beast.

Believing that he had enough intelligence to take back to his commander, Nicholas prepared to sneak out of the castle. He checked through the perforations of the screen one last time to make sure the men still faced the fire before he took a couple of steps toward the door. His skin suddenly prickled, raising the hair on his arms and the back of his neck. He became vitally aware of his surroundings. The air seemed charged, as if in the aftermath of a lightning strike. He stood straight, lowered the hood of his cloak to improve his peripheral vision, and scanned every possible hiding place nearby. He could see no one. Just then he felt a small but noticeable wisp of air. When he turned to see where it came from, he saw the door to the antechamber closing.

Holy Mother! Could this mission get any worse? Someone had seen him and knew an intruder was in the castle. How long until the alarm sounded?

Unsheathing his dagger, he checked one last time to make sure the men were still occupied with wine in their cups and slipped silently through the doorway. In the shadows outside the antechamber, Nicholas hid behind a pillar and scrutinized the great hall, searching for the culprit.

The scrape of heels walking on stone and the echo of a voice from a distant hallway made his stomach clench with tension. The castle guards were coming. He needed a place to hide. Frantically searching for a suitable spot, Nicholas felt a gentle tug on his sleeve from behind. Expecting a fight, he spun around to face a cloaked figure. A hand reached from folds of dark cloth and beckoned him to follow.

He hesitated. He could trust no one.

Noticing that Nicholas did not follow, the figure walked back toward him. In that small amount of time, he thought a woman was under the cloak. Still wary of treachery, Nicholas stood defiantly still. The figure stopped in front of him, closer than he expected. Definitely a woman. But who? Facing him askew, she slowly turned her head, and it was as if the world melted. Time ceased to be. Only she existed in that moment. A slight intake of air caught in his lungs. Nicholas stood in wonder, blinking.

Was it really her?

The cloak hid most of her face, but what he saw was exquisite. Porcelain skin graced delicate features, eyes the color of clear green pools in the forest, and lips so full and lovely. It was the woman he'd admired for so long. The woman he'd been dreaming about since they ran into each other on the street.

Looking around to make sure the guards had not yet appeared, Nicholas swallowed hard and gained his composure. He followed her into an alcove, hidden by a luxurious dark curtain. Both tense, they huddled close to the curtain, waiting, listening for the guards to make their rounds of the great hall. Once the guards left, tension in the air evaporated, as if a dangerous storm had swept away.

Sensing that immediate danger had passed, he loosened the grip on his dagger. When he heard someone sniffle behind him, he whirled around, ready to fight.

6

A QUIET MAN

"What are you doing here?" Meg whispered as she peeked through the curtain, unsure if the guards had left. "Is this an exercise for the army? A mission to prove that the king needs more protection?"

When she turned toward him, his eyes widened. He opened his mouth to speak but then clamped it shut, frowning.

The girl William had taken from her family kept sniffling. Once Meg realized someone inside the castle might be able to get Hannah out, she bolted for the girl's chamber. It was foolhardy, but she had to try something. Hannah struggled to keep her emotions intact, crying quietly, and using her dress to mop up the moisture.

"Will you not answer me? All I have to do is scream and twenty men-at-arms will come running."

Physically intimidating, obviously a warrior, he looked as if he'd delivered many a brutal blow. What she'd found so attractive about him, his height, build, and strength, he lacked in presence. The soldier was quiet. His emotions seemed to bubble beneath the surface, as if he had a million things to say which were caught within a constricted throat. As she studied him,

Meg could see the machinations of a busy mind behind those beautiful blue eyes.

He swallowed hard and cleared his throat. "I'll report to my commander as soon as I clear out. Unmolested, I hope," he said tentatively. He crooked a curious brow at her. When they met on the street, he'd only spoken a couple of short sentences to her. Meg hadn't remembered the lovely, lilting quality of his deep voice. It reminded her of liquid silk, rich and smooth, like the castle's best store of fine wine.

Suddenly, Hannah sneezed as the door to the antechamber thunked open. They froze in silence, listening to see if William and the Duke of Breckenridge had heard. The men sauntered into the vestibule. Meg dearly wanted to peer through the curtains to see which direction her brother headed, but the warrior stepped in front of her and Hannah, shepherding them behind him, poised to fight. She hoped William would not go to Hannah's door and pound on it as he did every night, begging her in a drunken stupor to let him in. Then William fell and laughed hysterically, the heavy thud of his body hitting the stone floor.

"Will, you randy old fool," the duke chastised the prince endearingly, as if he were a naughty child who was not really in trouble. "I know you like to drink. The tales of your tavern dwelling and brothel hunting have spread far and wide. All the stars above know I've been on enough escapades with you to fill the sheriff's logs in every county of Asterias. Stealing the blushing maiden out from under their noses while they tried to sneak her out of the city was one of our better conquests, if I do say so myself. But warts on a witch's tit, man. You cannot hold your liquor, you drunken sot." He must've picked William up by his tunic. Meg could hear the ruffling and dusting of fabric.

William snorted and continued to laugh. "Who says I'm a drunken sot?" he yelled absurdly. "I'll have his head!" Meg could hear him fumbling around his belt, reaching for a sword that was not there.

As they walked toward the great hall, Meg finally dared to peek through the opening of the curtains. With their arms draped over each other's shoulders, they staggered, singing bawdy songs, their loud voices echoing long after they'd walked into the hallway that led to Prince William's chamber.

Meg sighed with relief, clasped her hands under her chin, and gave the warrior the hint of a smile. Despite her lightened mood, the warrior cast worried glances between her and Hannah.

Meg took a deep breath and exhaled, trying to gain courage for what she hoped would happen next. "Will you help me?" she asked.

The soldier said nothing. His brows shot together in firm concentration. Sheathing his dagger, he folded his arms across his chest and tightened his jaw, staring at her.

She could hardly stand the interminable silence. How many seconds had passed? He simply would not answer.

Tension surged through Meg's body, her pulse racing, her breathing rapid. He was so close. She could smell a musky hint of him, worn leather, sweat, and smoke from a campfire. Yet he smelled fresh, too, like he'd spent hours riding through a pine forest.

Admittedly smitten with the look of him, Meg admired the clean lines of his nose and jaw, sculpted cheeks, and expressive eyes and brows. His skin looked like it had been kissed by the sun. Lines of worry took shape at the corners of his eyes. And the rasp of his whiskers... She'd fantasized for an embarrassingly long time about running her hand along the line of his jaw and tumbling into the depths of his eyes. Under different circumstances, she would've stared into them forever, but she didn't have time to bask in dreams.

"I am your humble servant," he finally said in a courtly manner. He bowed his head a little, but she saw the corner of his mouth twitch.

"I know how to get out," Meg whispered as she grabbed the girl's hand and pulled her to her feet. "Follow me."

"Wait." He put his hand on her shoulder. "As grateful as I am to you for showing me out..." He raised an eyebrow and cocked his head, offering a wry smile. "It seems a bit cumbersome bringing the girl. Might she stay here?"

"Of course not." Meg shook her head impatiently. "You're going to take her home."

"I'm going to do what?" He brought a hand to his face and scrubbed it as if he needed to wake up from a bad dream.

Meg led the warrior and Hannah from the great hall to the hallway that led to the kitchen. Before they entered, Meg stopped and gestured for quiet as she peeked around the corner. She wanted to make sure that no one nibbled on biscuits as she often did, her late-night pastime. A large kitchen, its walls and floor were constructed of huge limestone bricks while its ovens and tall fireplaces were built out of rock. Thick slab tables rested in the middle for cutting meat and chopping fruits and vegetables. Everything looked in perfect order. The food was put away, the fires were out, the pots and pans cleaned and placed on tables or hung to dry. Sure that the kitchen was free from staff, Meg gestured for them to follow her.

They stalked silently across the floor, down the narrow servant's steps, and into the kitchen garden. The warrior walked straight to the gate. He searched the grounds for signs of trouble and tested the hinges on the gate to make sure they would not squeak. They inched along the outer wall to where large trees and bushes threatened to encroach upon open grounds outside the kitchen. When Meg was in the cover of shadows, she raced for the rusty iron bars that led through the castle wall and to the ruins that used to be the stables.

"An ancient tunnel leads from this ruined stable," Meg said, trying to catch her breath, "to the cellar of a deserted apothecary in the city. I use it all the time. No one else knows about it, as far as I know, so please keep it secret. And don't come back, I beg you. It would lead to nothing but trouble." Meg nervously glanced through the trees toward the castle, hoping that William had not noticed his prize was gone. "Go quickly! Please!"

"What about you?" The warrior seemed reluctant to leave. He placed his hands on his hips and leveled a stern gaze at her. He looked up through an opening in the trees and sighed heavily. "It isn't right leaving you here."

"I know how to hide."

"I will bloody well kill her!" William roared from the roof of a nearby tower. "Where is she?"

"I beg you, leave now, before he raises all the guards in the castle to search for Hannah. Right now, they think him drunk and maddened."

"Who are you?" he asked desperately.

"No one that matters."

The warrior tightened his jaw and nodded, steeling himself against her answer. He gestured for Hannah to come forward and descend the stairs. Hannah stared pitifully at Meg, much like she had the first night Meg saw her in the great hall, her expression becoming more alarmed with every step.

"Don't worry, Hannah," Meg said encouragingly. "I trust him. I've seen him doing good things. He'll take you to your family. Tell them they must leave tonight, in case the prince comes back for her."

"You have my word," he promised. He turned Hannah toward him. Placing his hands gently on her shoulders, he looked her squarely in the eye. "I promise to get you home safely."

Hannah shuddered and nodded as she looked back toward Meg.

"I will keep your secret," he said, looking at Meg. "No one will ever enter this tunnel."

"Thank you." He owed her nothing, and so his promise was a most unexpected and welcome surprise.

Suddenly, Hannah refused to descend the stairs, staring at Meg with those woeful eyes.

"Hannah, dear girl," Meg soothed as she crouched near the

opening to get closer. "You must be brave. It's either through the tunnel or back to him." She gestured with her head toward the tower where William still bellowed. "You will find flint and steel on the bottom stair to light a torch. As soon as I see light from the opening, I will shut the door and cover it. Now, go!"

Meg watched the warrior descend the creaky wooden stairs into the tunnel. He stopped for a moment and looked up toward her, his eyes pained. It seemed he dearly wanted to speak. Instead, he looked down and shook his head in disbelief. Meg ached inside, watching him go. She desperately wanted to ask his name or when she might see him again, but the guards would be searching the woods soon. They had gotten close to becoming acquainted, only to have the opportunity thwarted, like water cascading over the cliff for the fall, never to have the chance again. He took a few more steps and glanced at her once again. The last thing she saw before she closed the door to the tunnel were his pained, beautiful blue eyes.

7

BESTING MEN

As soon as the warrior and Hannah were deep in the tunnel, Meg closed the door to the entry and covered it with dirt and debris. William still shouted from the top of the nearest tower, wildly pitching his gaze toward the woods and ordering his guards to search the castle and grounds.

"Bring the girl to me!" William yelled into the cold night air, the sound of his voice penetrating through the trees.

Behind her, Meg heard the clinking of mailed shirts and footsteps rustling fallen leaves and twigs. She turned and saw two guards moving toward her quickly. Meg ran through the brush, falling, tumbling, and scratching her elbows and knees with the guards hard on her heels. The ancient drainage ditch was so close. Arms outstretched, she tried to throw herself into the ravine, but she tripped and fell spectacularly. Meg thought she had outrun them for a brief, blissful second, before she found herself being lifted by the scruff of her neck.

The guards dumped her unceremoniously on the ground, legs spread out before her, blood pooling on the fabric of her dress near her knee. Her hood still covered her head as she panted into her chest.

"What have we here?" one of the guards said, annoyed, his voice brusque. "A vagrant trying to get into the castle?"

"No, you idiot," the other chided. "It's the girl that has run away from the prince."

They each grabbed her under the arms and pulled her up from the ground. Meg spied a thick fallen branch, grasped it, and hid it under her cloak. She slouched as if she were unconscious and kept her head hidden under her hood.

Before the guard could pull back her hood, Meg swung the branch and hit him straight in the face. He doubled over, howling in pain as he tried to stanch the flow of blood from his nose. The second guard backhanded her with a mailed fist. He missed her face and hit her shoulder, but the force sent her spiraling to the ground. On her belly, she tried to crawl toward the ditch. The guard yanked ruthlessly on her leg. Meg kicked with all her might, scuffling with him, doing her best to give him a swift kick in the groin. Scrabbling away, she stood up and ran. He caught her by the left arm. Still clinging to the branch, Meg swung with her right and clubbed him on the knee caps. He finally fell.

Knowing that the guards were not subdued for long, Meg raced to the ravine. Scampering to the bottom, she sprinted toward the iron grating, one bar rusted, and slipped through. When William wasn't looking toward the forest, Meg ran to the base of the tower from which he still shouted commands. Skulking in the shadows, she scuttled along the castle wall down the hill, sneaking behind the stables and smithy's forge to the ground floor of the castle. Amazingly, Meg found a door to one of the servant's quarters unlocked. She hustled inside and startled two valets awake, but they were drowsy and probably drunk. She bolted through the room to a door that led to an inner hallway. Once inside, Meg heard her brother's clamor echoing from the kitchen wing and raced to her own chamber.

Slamming the door behind her, Meg bent over her knees, panting. When she caught her breath, she realized that her ladies had not stirred from the commotion and wondered why. Usually, one or two of them stayed up late or couldn't get to sleep at all. Even now, how could they not have heard her brother's blaring, all the commotion going on inside the castle, and the guards yelling outside? How long would it be before William pounded on her door?

Meg still held Lady Byron's keys, the ones she'd stolen to unlock Hannah's chamber. Grasping handfuls of her hair, she closed her eyes and held her breath, trying to determine how she would put them back. William must not find evidence of her involvement. Meg couldn't tie them back onto Lady Byron's sash, so she decided to slip into her lady's bedchamber and hide them in a drawer, as if Lady Byron had tucked them there herself. Hopefully, William would not demand that Lady Byron produce her keys. It might take her a terrified minute to find them under his glaring command. Meg ran as fast as she could to her own bedchamber, stuffed her cloak and bloodied dress behind a wardrobe, and slipped into a nightgown. She ran her fingers through her hair and quickly pulled on a luxurious robe.

Just at that moment, William hammered on the door. Meg flew into her apartment, but slowed to a graceful walk as she took deep breaths and tied the sash around her waist. Lady Byron lurched to the doorway of her room, her hands clinging to the jamb, catching her balance as her eyes struggled to focus. Meg's ladies tumbled out of their bedchambers mumbling to each other about the uproar, shrugging into robes, and wrapping warm shawls around them. They seemed so slow to react, their heads and shoulders drooping like spring flowers trying to push their heads through wet, heavy snow.

"My lord." Lady Byron answered the door. Now composed, she curtsied and allowed Prince William and the Duke of Breckenridge to enter the princess's apartment.

William barged directly toward his sister. He stopped within a few inches of her, stuck his face close to hers and raged, almost a whisper. "Where have you been?"

Expecting to be bowled over by his infamous temper, Meg was not quite sure how to respond. She stood straighter and jutted her chin defiantly. "As you see, my lord," Meg gestured with her hands toward her ladies. "We have been awakened by the commotion." Lady Byron lit a candle and Meg could see that they had lined up as always when beckoned. She almost wished they could be kept in the dark. Meg felt blood dribbling down her wounded leg and her shoulder throbbed abominably.

"What? No sumptuous feast tonight, ladies?" The duke cocked his head to the side and offered Meg a leering smile. His eyes danced with the quixotic pleasure of seeing her caught, a cat toying with the mouse.

"Pardon me, my lord?" Lady Byron asked as she took her place next to the princess.

"The princess herself told me," the duke explained, "that she would be entertaining you all with a feast this very night. She said that you had all been so ... let me find her exact words ... 'good and gracious' to her and that she wanted to reward you for your service."

"Well, as you can see, we have finished," Lady Byron said. "We supped earlier this evening with the king, not much in the way of a feast, you know, as we're conserving for the army. He enjoys himself so very much here with the musicians, the view of the garden, and his lovely daughter. It's a shame you weren't here to enjoy it with us ... my lords." She finished and bowed her head. Meg detected just the hint of a triumphant smile.

Undeterred, the duke leaned against the mantle of the fireplace, fiddled with the leather bracer on his arm, and looked around the apartment as if it were his own and could only imagine the changes he would make to it.

"All of you!" William roared, pacing in front of them with hands behind his back. "I want to know where the princess was tonight, and if I don't get a satisfactory answer, there will be consequences."

They all curtsied low and bowed their heads in terror-stricken silence.

When he got to Meg, he looked her up and down with disdain and sneered. For a frantic moment, she thought he'd seen the blood coursing down her leg. She could feel it now and was sure some of it must've seeped on to the floor.

"Just tell me where you were, Meg, and I will leave you and your ladies alone. I know they know your every move."

"We have been here all along," Meg protested innocently. "I don't even know what this uproar is about. What has happened?"

"Someone has helped Hannah escape and I think it's you."

"What?" Meg hoped to portray shock. "How could I accomplish such a thing?"

"Don't give me that me that tired old routine. I know it works with father, but really, Meg. It's ridiculous."

"I don't know what you're talking about, William."

Suddenly distracted, William saw something out of the corner of his eye. He stomped over to Old Addy and examined her incredulously. "What are you still doing in here?" he gibed, his face rudely close to Adelaide's crinkled cheek.

Still as a statue, the old nursemaid said nothing.

"Should've sent you out to pasture by now," he said disgustedly, looking her up and down, "or the bloody butcher. I asked you a question, you shriveled old crone. What are you still doing in here?" William gritted his teeth, shaking his head in disdain as he walked toward the duke.

Lady Byron walked to Addy's side opposite William and said, "She fulfills a great need in the princess's chambers. As you know, your own mother chose Adelaide to be the princess's nursemaid, but she has always been a storyteller."

"The only thing women need to know is what I tell them, especially in this castle," William flouted and pointed a finger at Addy.

"The Princess Marguerite has her mother's grace and quick

wit and her father's intelligence and compassion," Addy whispered hoarsely. "That's more than I can say for you, you sorry, gormless, grotty madman."

"What did you say?" William crossed the floor quick as a snake, ready to strike.

"Let it go, Will," the duke encouraged, tightening his belt and adjusting his weapons in an implied threat. "If we're going to get to the bottom of the disappearance, we must press ahead with other interviews. Clearly, the princess and her ladies have been here all night."

The duke came closer to Meg, casually inspecting her from head to toe. His eyes roamed the nightgown and rested on the blood near her foot. He raised his hand in consolation to touch her battered shoulder. She told herself she would not flinch. She would not. Instead, he pulled a tiny leaf out of her hair and flicked it to the ground.

"It appears her ladyship has had a long night. Let us leave her in peace," he said. His mouth curved in a knowing smile, eyes glinting with malice.

8
AN INNOCENT BYSTANDER

Meg tried to concentrate, but her eyelids kept drooping. The book she read was as dull as a sermon and every time her mind wandered, she couldn't help but envision the glorious eyes of her warrior. She'd never seen eyes so light blue before, like the color of the sky nearest the mountains. His expression looked so pained the last she saw him, staring at her from the tunnel. How she wished they could've taken the time to become acquainted. Maybe she could've coaxed a smile out of him, relaxing those beautiful eyes. The effort to free Hannah had been worth it. Meg received a secret note from the girl's father thanking her. He had already moved the whole family and hoped William would never discover their whereabouts.

"My lady, the prince demands to see you in the courtyard." One of the pageboys entered her apartment at Lady Byron's invitation.

"Prince John Paul?" Meg asked hopefully. Her brother had been gone from the palace for some time and she missed him. He took long sojourns every so often. These piqued her curiosity. Meg questioned him every time he returned, only to have him tell her that he was building Father's army. He offered no details. It was maddening. How she wished she could get out of the castle for good, travel about the countryside, but Meg knew her place was with her father. Still, when she heard the clatter of horse hooves on the cobblestones, she checked to see if he'd come home.

"No, my lady. Prince William."

"Tell him we will come momentarily," Meg sighed, her disappointment thick enough to cut.

She rose from her chair and closed the book. "William still tries to bait me into a confession about the night Hannah disappeared. What do you think he wants, Lady Byron?"

"I'm afraid one never knows with Prince William." Lady Byron grimaced, her face tight, which was often the case when she spoke of William.

"I suppose it is our duty to favor him with our presence."

Her ladies sat with her under the beautiful vaulted windows at the back of her chamber. They set down the projects they'd been working on, sewing for the poor and the embroidery for altar cloths or reading like herself, and lined up to follow her to the courtyard.

When the guards opened the door and held it for the women to go outside, the bright sun hit Meg hard in the face. She could barely see the spectacle in front of her. Squinting, she raised her hand to shade her eyes. She saw William standing next to her horse, tethered to a post that had been pounded into the ground. Golden Cloud snorted and shimmied his head, trying to escape the tight hold on him by prancing, his hooves clanking on the stones. The groomsmen, squires, and stable lads hung their heads low, hands clasped solemnly in front of them. What on earth? Meg thought, panicked. Did William finally find a way to override her father and send her to the King of Edmira?

"Good day to you, sister," he said buoyantly. He even smiled, although it was awkward, the cheerfulness placed on a face unused to cordiality. It was like watching a feral dog simper and then bare its fangs.

Meg couldn't remember William smiling at her since they were children.

Before he'd decided to hate her.

"Good day," Meg replied, eyeing him warily as she curtsied.

"I wanted you to see for yourself what happens to people who cross me, Meg." William still smiled, but his tone had darkened.

"Despite our dislike for each other, my lord," she added, hoping to placate him. "I have never done anything that would threaten your right to ascend the throne."

He ignored her rebuttal, unsheathed his sword, and held it high. He turned it over in his hand as he examined it, the sun glinting on it brightly. The light bounced straight into her eyes. Meg turned her head and blinked several times before she could return his gaze.

"I've been wondering for a long time what I could do to curb your reckless behavior. The war has made the most unlikely things happen," he said dispassionately, as if he were commiserating with a close friend. "Who could ever imagine a princess learning to fight like a soldier or being schooled in the manner of a great prince? But you do it all, thanks to our father and brother. Because of that, there is nothing I can do to control you, unless I wanted to set a permanent guard on you or lock you in a tower."

Meg gaped. She couldn't believe her ears. Was her own brother really going to lock her in a tower?

"And of course, Father would have to agree," William sighed with frustration. "But the thought bores me. I have no desire to chase you around or to watch you rot." He leveled hard, hateful eyes at her. "I much prefer to hurt you." His voice sounded like gravel at the bottom of a foul pit.

"If you're talking about Hannah," Meg panicked, the words tumbling out of her mouth like an avalanche. "I have no idea who took her. I told you that night that I was not a part of any plan to retrieve her. No one contacted me. If you ask me, I think you should interrogate the castle guards to see why or how someone evaded their patrols. We must ask ourselves, how could someone just slink into the castle unnoticed? As I recall," she said, unable to resist the jab, "Father left that job to you."

"Silence!" he roared, losing his patience. He raised his hand to strike her.

Meg flinched and fell silent. Her hands instinctively rose to protect her head.

It was only a feint. He smirked at her fear.

William walked toward her and pointed his sword under her chin, gently toying with the soft skin on her throat. Meg swallowed hard as she stared into his cruel eyes.

He lowered his sword and got close enough to whisper in her ears as he circled her menacingly. "I have no idea what you did or how you accomplished it, but I know you are responsible for helping Hannah escape. I'm the laughing stock of the city because of you. I can't pretend the girl liked me, even for moment, if she was so willing to leave. I will not be mocked."

"William," Meg began, tears beginning to well. She knew now how he could cut her to the bone. "I beg you. Please don't hurt my horse. He's an innocent animal that has no place in quarrel between brother and sister. I know you're angry with me, but please think this through. I could never have gotten Hannah out of the castle on my own. And ... and," she stuttered and blinked, trying to keep her tears from falling. "Father has taken such great pleasure in finding him for me."

"Nice speech. You've just given me the perfect punishment for an insufferable sister." He stepped close to her and whispered in her ear. "Damn our father to hell!"

William turned from her and thrust his sword into Golden Cloud's neck. Squealing, the horse fell to his knees. His eyes rolled into the back of his head, showing only the whites, as he collapsed to the ground, the broadsword still protruding from his beautiful tawny hide. He tried to lift his head and use momentum to pull himself up off the ground. It was the most pitiful yet dignified effort Meg had ever witnessed. His eyes pleaded with her, wondering why she had allowed this to happen.

With tears streaming down her face, Meg stumbled toward Golden Cloud and fell on her knees. She watched in horror as blood pulsed from the wound. Overwhelmed by his suffering, she fell onto his heaving body, wrapped her arms around him, and sobbed.

"It's a small loss," William said almost genially as he wrenched and twisted the sword out of the animal's body. The poor horse writhed in even more pain. Her head lay on the body of her horse, but she turned toward William when he spoke. He seemed quite unemotional as he used a rag to wipe clean his sword, one that a stable lad held for just this purpose. "You couldn't ride him anyway, at least not out of the city. I know that you've begged father a thousand times to let you ride out on the plain and a thousand times he has said no. And now, it will never happen."

He sheathed his sword and tramped toward her, basking in triumph, a wicked grin emanating across his face. "Every time you take something from me, I will take something away from you." He walked into the castle, as if he'd just come back from another day hunting on the plain.

Meg stood, struggling to regain her balance. Her hands were covered in blood, as was the front of her dress. She stared at the gruesome scene before her as her poor horse still convulsed, moaning pitifully. His blood oozed. With nothing but the vision of her horse's suffering in sight, she became aware that her ladies had gathered around her, their soft hands and voices cocooning her against the grisly scene. She tore her eyes from her horse and noticed palpable sympathy on their faces.

Somehow, Meg found her strength. She stood apart from her ladies, wiped her tears, and called for the head groom.

"My lady?" Hopkins came forward with his head bowed and hat placed respectfully in his hands.

THE ENTANGLED PRINCESS

"Will you do me the honor of tending to my horse? Make it quick, will you?" Meg whispered.

"Of course, my lady," Hopkins answered as they both gazed at the horse, not wanting to focus on the dreadful scene but unable to tear their eyes away. When she turned her attention away from Golden Cloud to face her ladies, Meg noticed that many of them wept quietly.

She walked around to the back of her horse, knelt close, and hugged him. She ran her fingers through his beautiful black mane and rubbed his neck. Through her tears, Meg looked up and nodded at Hopkins. He came forward with a sharpened short sword and slashed the animal through the jugular vein in his throat. The horse moaned in pain once again, but then the animal relaxed. She stayed with him until his spirited soul was gone. Meg wanted to remain strong, but she hid her face in her hands and continued to cry over the body of her dead horse.

Lady Byron came close, her hardworking, gentle hands on Meg's shoulder. She urged the princess to stand. Looking into the distraught faces of the castle staff, Meg swallowed hard and tried to calm her breathing.

"Carry on," Meg said with a nod to those who worked in the stables. Her voice faltered. She struggled to keep her face from contorting in grief. She was determined not to allow William to control her, now or ever. She walked back into the castle, straight and stalwart, with her ladies trailing behind.

The great mystery of the tragic episode is that her father would not punish William for the injustices he perpetrated. The king never had, and she didn't know why. It had been going on his entire life, this foul play on everyone around him. The thought made her burn with revenge. How could she give William what he deserved?

She was tempted to poison his blasted drinks. He drank all day anyway and already had a foot in his grave. What was the harm in hastening that a bit? King against king, cousin against cousin, brother against brother, royal houses all over the continent and beyond had been killing each other for centuries over the throne. John Paul would become heir to the throne. Her brother was the one man who had the right disposition, talent, and respect to lead. In the quiet corners of the castle, Meg heard people say how unfortunate it was that John Paul was born the second son.

Could she kill her own brother?

Meg caught a glimpse of her clothing and clenched handfuls of her bloodied gown, the image of her horse stabbed running though her mind. She closed her eyes, moaning, and staggered. How she hated her brother. As her ladies helped catch her balance, she blanched at the thought, recoiling at her own wickedness. Asterias deserved better than that. All those other countries and their royalty could rot in hell for the evil they worked upon each other. She wasn't about to kill her brother. Ashamed of herself for such evil thoughts, Meg quickly swiped at a tear that threatened to course down her cheek.

9
AWAKENING

Meg stood on the balcony wrapped in a warm shawl overlooking the garden. A sickle moon hung in the black night, luminescent and shaded with violet hues. She lifted her head to the millions of stars above, so many dots of light spread across an inky canvas, spilling their lucent aura one into the others, as if someone waved a wand and spread magic dust across the sky. Ancient Asterians believed the stars harbored ancestors that became gods who guided and gave inspiration. Meg sighed, knowing she needed that now more than ever before. William had put her in the most appalling circumstance. She still had no idea what to do.

"I always liked the pink roses best, I think," her father said as he stepped onto the balcony and walked to the railing where Meg stood. "You've heard this story a thousand times, but before your mother died, she planted these roses near the nursery so that they would climb the castle wall and you would always be able to see them from your balcony."

Meg was moved by the thought of her mother. How could one member of her family love her so completely without even knowing her, and another hate her so much?

"I've always felt so aggrieved that we lost her, Father. I am sorry," Meg said as she buried her head in his shoulder, hugging him. "I never knew her and yet I miss her so much. I know you would've been happier. I think my brothers would've been much-improved versions of themselves. Well, perhaps not John Paul. Most everyone believes him to be perfect."

"You are quite right about that, Meg," he chuckled, which he did not do often. It made Meg smile. "Let us sit, shall we?" He escorted her to the stone bench and sat down. "That's why I've come, my dear girl, to speak with you about your brothers, especially William. I've had words with him. I think when the triumph of evil victory wore off, he was truly sorry for what he'd done, as every drunkard is. That's small compensation for you, I know."

"He's a lush and a lecher," Meg objected, scowling into the garden. "How can you trust him to rule? He does such terrible things when he drinks, and then no one could be more repentant. It's a cycle that will not break, though I know you have tried. It doesn't seem so, but I try to stay away from him."

"I'm well aware of your feelings and take them to heart," the king said wearily. "One day he will conquer his demons and make a good king. In the meantime, I would like you and John Paul to stand down."

"What are you talking about, Father?" she asked, brows clashing in confusion.

"It's no secret that you and John Paul are quite capable and could foment a lovely rebellion against me and my heir apparent."

Astonished, Meg tried to contradict him.

"I'm certain there are nobles enough who would side with you, believing that William is not capable of ruling someday," he said, giving her an anguished sideways glance. "But I hope you will not. There is a reason that I cannot punish him for his deeds, except to make him feel guilty. Nor will I try to take the throne from him. He is the crowned prince and has the law behind him.

"You see, your mother saw him in a dream." Tears crept down his wrinkled cheeks as he grasped Meg's hand. "He stood in the grand cathedral before the crowd with a crown on his head and scepter in his hand. I always believed in your mother's dreams and visions. From what I could tell, they mostly came true. Your brother William will rule one day."

"I've never doubted that he would, Father." Meg squeezed his hand and laid her head on his shoulder. "John Paul and I have never envied the throne. We have known for a long time that we would be the ones propping William up, making him appear a suitable king, if only out of love and respect for you and Mother. It is our dreadful duty in this life and we are reconciled to it."

"There is also the added problem of the enemy," the king continued. "We cannot appear weak or divided before them. They would take advantage if they believed such a condition existed. We must at least show them that we are united in our efforts, if not in our hearts."

"I agree, Father. I could not be more devoted to our cause."

"Your mother also saw John Paul leading armies, and she saw you with the love of your life," the king said, looking down at her with warmth in his eyes and a small semblance of a smile.

"And that is why you won't force me to marry for your benefit, for a great alliance for Asterias?" Meg nodded in understanding and kissed his cheek.

"Never," he said softly, the look in his eyes determined. "I cannot part with my dear girl until I know there is a man worthy of you. I certainly won't send you to the King of Edmira, William's attempt to go behind my back to offer you as the centerpiece of a treaty. Aside from the fact that I would never do that to my beloved daughter, I don't believe that evil king will keep his word. He'd take you for himself and all Asterias. I'm the only one who stands in his way."

"Thank you, Father. I know most do not understand your unwillingness to do so." As Meg sat quietly with her father and stared at the distant stars, there dawned upon her a terrible realization.

She was the kingdom.

The great burden of fighting for Asterias went to her brothers, but her fate was sealed with theirs. Her actions would somehow contribute to the outcome of the war. With all the emotional and spiritual longing in her being, she had to save the kingdom and its people. She felt it deeper and grander than she'd ever felt it before. She would somehow have a greater role, almost as if she'd been anointed to it.

Meg shuddered with anxiety. What could it mean? The law did not allow such a thing. Even if she were eligible, she was three steps away from the throne. She would rather die than walk past the sepulchers of her father and brothers. Meg felt certain that her role of caretaker for the king and feeding the hungry and clothing the poor were the only things she could do in this time of travail. A princess could do little in a time of war, except wait in the throne room and pace a great gulf into the cold stone floor. Yet, the stars whispered into her soul something entirely different.

I know what I must do, Meg thought. She stood and walked to the railing, staring into the black depths of the night. "There's got to be someone or something out there that can help us win. And I'm going to find them," she whispered silently to herself.

10
HALF MEN

"Mercy," Meg whispered in surprise as she crested a hill and saw the Asterian encampment spread out before her. Lady Byron approached from behind, panting from climbing the steep knoll. Neither of them anticipated seeing such a colossal array of soldiery. Hundreds of fires lightened the clutter of armaments, the canopies of tents, and the mass of somber bodies huddled about campfires. They looked like half-men, with the front of their bodies illuminated, their backs obliterated, deadened by the darkness. And half-men they are, she thought, as only those in an army on the verge of defeat can be.

In the dead of night, Meg and Lady Byron sneaked out of the castle and fell into a group of people leaving Tirana. Eavesdropping on several conversations, Meg knew that most of them were headed toward the camp, mainly women with children in tow. Some were men, young and old, injured and healthy, urchins and orphans, and a few whores all hoping to take on a job for a bit of coin or a few scraps of food.

Once the stars whispered to her, Meg decided to get out of the city and see what was really happening. Were the king's commanders honest? Were there lapses in communications, or worse, spies feeding him false information? How could her father, his advisors, and John Paul strategize for the oncoming battle if they were not getting the right information? Meg believed if she left the city and came to the Asterian encampment, then she would find what her father needed: a way to win the war. It might be naïve, but she didn't care. It was worth a try. Her hair fell out of the old woolen shawl that she used in part to disguise herself as a peasant. Meg placed it back on her head and tucked her hair in, wrapping the shawl around her shoulders and across her chest. With the homespun, lace-up dress, apron, and cross-gartered soft leather boots, she hoped no one would recognize her.

The women wrapped their arms around each other's waists and descended the hill, trying to blend in with all the camp followers. Sentries stood posted around the perimeter of the camp, but they paid little attention to the people as they came and went, all of them hunched against the cold of the autumn night. The savory scent of campfires danced on crisp air heavy with the musk of dirt and dead leaves, the pungency of many living close together, and a subtle hint of apples, cider perhaps. Listening to the talk of the soldiers and civilians they encountered, Meg determined the direction of the camp headquarters. She wanted to get as close to Commander Kane as possible, to watch him and his advisers, to see conditions in the camp, and keep a keen eye open for her saving grace. Who would stand out? Who could help her?

Eventually, they came within sight of the huge, well-lit tent of the commander, but they had come too close and a guard gestured for them to leave. Looking past the guard and absorbing all she could about it, Meg realized that she would have to find a way to get into that tent if she were to take away any valuable information. Meg and Lady Byron had to walk a ways, but they found a fire with numerous women and a few small children converging for the night. Settling into the last open space near the flames, they sat down and huddled closely together for warmth as they tried to make themselves as comfortable as possible. Meg relaxed enough to doze on the shoulder of her companion; their journey to the encampment had been long and hard. She was in between sleep and wakefulness when the conversation around her began to take shape.

"No courage!" a woman bemoaned, her face so deeply lined that Meg could not place her age. Thirty? Fifty? The rigors of life in the countryside were tough, and that showed on the faces of everyone. "Nope, not him, the big, old gourd! George Edward Longbourne, King of Asterias, just sits up in yonder castle pining away for his long-lost wife while we rot."

"It's all his fault!" another woman said, this one missing some crucial teeth in the front of her mouth. "Years and years he's been leading us down the primrose path with his honest mistakes, he says to us, and now here they are, as unrighteous an enemy as there ever was, about to ram a spear right down our throats."

"Aye, the knotty-pated, lily-livered blighter don't care a wink for us," a younger woman agreed as her dirty toddler snuggled up to nurse. "He'd as soon see us killed for a crack of wheat, let alone a loaf of bread."

"I'd just as soon gut the innards out of King Colestus of Edmira. Him and his wicked army. They side with the devil for certain, for they have most unnatural powers," an old woman cackled. She had papery, crinkled skin, a hooked nose, and wild silvery hair. Meg was surprised the people around the fire didn't fear her. She seemed like a charmer, maybe even a witch.

As the princess listened to the idle chatter of the women, her mind drifted needing respite from their painful observations that her father had become a failure. She noticed small elements in the scene about her— the filthy clothing on the women, their aged faces, coarse language, and worst of all, the awful stench. It hadn't been overwhelming as she'd walked around camp, but somehow the smell congregated at the fire, the trapped effluvium becoming more potent with the heat.

Meg's breathing became short. She felt queasy. In quick response, she stood up, turned from the fire, and coughed violently. When her breathing calmed down, she took several gulps of cold, crisp air. She felt better but realized that people from fires nearby had noticed her spasm and stared at her. Instinctively, she pulled the shawl on her head to make sure it covered most of her face. Two Asterian soldiers paused to watch her before moving on with their patrol. They were at a fair distance, but when they turned around, Meg thought the tall one swayed his shoulders a bit like ... like ... Impossible, she thought. Even if he were here, they'd never bump into each other. The man with the beautiful blue eyes was a needle in a haystack.

Meg's focus returned to those around the blaze. Lady Byron still sat on the ground staring through the fire, as if it were a hundred miles away. Some men had joined the group and caused the women to flirt. Lewd remarks dominated the conversation, now spiced with giggles and crass laughter. Feeling very uncomfortable, the princess was about to reach down and touch her lady so they might leave when one of the men said something that riveted her attention.

"There's much said about him, but the tales are so fantastical. He can't be a real man."

"Could he be magic?" the old witch-woman leered, rubbing her hands together in dreadful anticipation, as if the specter would suddenly appear.

"He's a fearsome and harrowing fighter," a young foot soldier replied. Meg had not noticed him before, his eyes tense as he recalled the memory. He cleared his throat and added bravely, "I've seen him with my own eyes."

"Let's hear the story then," the witch-woman said.

"On the village green of a tiny hamlet, two of his majesty's knights armed with long halberds chased down a small force of straggling Edmirans. As they hacked at the last of the enemy beneath their horses, an invader knight appeared with a wolf skin slung about his shoulders, galloping into the square. One of the king's knights swung his halberd with great might. The man in the wolf skin easily parried the blow with his shield. The Wolf Knight then thrust his lance through the chest of his opponent with such violence that the iron passed through his chest and out of his back. As the king's man fell, the invader's lance broke off. He seized his enemy's mace on his right side, and in one quick motion, he struck the other of his majesty's knights with a mighty blow that crushed his skull inside his helmet."

"What were you doing there?" one of the other women asked. "You can't have been more than a pup at the time."

"Hiding, of course," the foot soldier replied with a shy smile. "I was just a tyke and the fighting terrified me, but I couldn't help watching it all the same."

"I do believe I've heard of him before." The witch-woman narrowed her eyes at the crowd and gestured dramatically with her hands. "But he's not a man as you say, young sir. He is at least eight feet tall and as strong as five men. He rides with flames in his eyes and can kill with ungodly force. One dare not look the Wolf Knight straight in the eye, for his heart will surely stop. His giant horse, which has no natural enemy and fears nothing, canters at least a foot off the ground and breathes fire and smoke. It has been said that his horse is the offspring of the dragon that hides in the Monstrous Mountains." Cackling as the woman finished her story, Meg noticed that the two soldiers on patrol had stopped to listen to the tales of the Wolf Knight. The taller one folded his arms across his chest, skeptical, as if he couldn't believe a single word. The other watched with interest before he nudged his comrade, and they walked away.

Meg found herself angry at the old woman for lying. These stories of the Wolf Knight paralyzed everyone with fear. She'd studied geography her whole life and knew the kingdom by heart, at least on maps, and she'd never heard of the Monstrous Mountains. What disturbed her the most was their lack of confidence in her father and the Asterian army to turn the tide of war. Defeatism, she thought as she remembered a quote from a book, had wrapped its heavy arms about the kingdom, from the golden crown of its monarch to the dirty feet of its harlots. Now the enemy becomes legendary, maybe even invincible.

11
INFILTRATION

She stayed as close to Lady Bryon as she could to keep her fingers and toes from becoming numb. What had once been a huge bonfire burned down to embers. The people around it had crept closer during the night to stay warm. She stood up, stretched, and rubbed her hands on her arms to get warm. As the eastern sky showed its first signs of change from black to grey, Meg knew she had to find a way to get into the commander's tent. Meg told Lady Byron that she was going to search for an opportunity to get closer to Commander Kane. Her lady had become quiet as a crypt and her eyes grew frightened. She tugged on Meg's clothing to convince her to stay.

"Just stay here. I will be back before long. I promise," Meg said and squeezed her lady's hand.

Presenting herself to the baker's tent, Meg received a surly approval to serve in the commander's tent from a dour, matronly woman. She invited the young princess in for final approval by the head baker.

"It's not as if we don't have enough young pretty things wanting the job, but that's what the commander wants," she reproached.

"Commander Kane and his men will certainly approve of

you!" an old, fat man leered as he rolled dough. Despite all the flour on his hands, he pulled the shawl roughly off her head and laughed loud to crude comments from the other bakers. Unappreciative of the humor at her expense, Meg scowled. She replaced the shawl, lifted a basket full of food, and headed toward Kane's tent.

Inside Commander Kane's white pavilion sat a dozen gruff, loud, starving men around a rough-hewn wooden table. Beyond the dining area Meg could see through sheer curtains the commander's room for sleeping. It held a few books and a small writing desk, as well as another part of the tent that looked like it served for entertaining. Even the castle did not have so many furry animal skins and large pillows in one room. Dotted through its entirety were smaller tables with maps laid out and figurines to show the strategy and movement of the opposing armies. A large map drawn on some sort of animal skin hung where the men sat eating. This fascinated Meg the most.

She and a couple of other young women served small, warm loaves of bread with butter, cheese, cured ham, and poured hot-spiced cider or mulled wine for each man. While juggling her task, Meg couldn't help but steal glances toward the map. She recognized markings on it that demonstrated topography as well as strategy and perhaps a new kind of weapon, but she couldn't be sure. She couldn't study it closer and didn't have enough training in map reading to understand it completely.

"And just what are you gaping at, little lady?" one of the men teased her to the leering shouts and whistles of the others.

Meg caught herself staring stupidly at the man. She didn't mean to give him such a long, fixed look, but she had no idea what to say.

He laughed at her.

"None of these lasses can read, you idiot," another jeered. "Can you, love?" He groped her bottom as he spoke. The surprise on her face and skip in her step to get away from him caused all of them howl.

"I think she likes you, son," one of the older men heckled. "She's blushing like a rosy, red apple. Ripe enough to pluck!"

"If only you could be so lucky, you wanton fool!" she scolded in return.

"Tis not an insult, you sweet little tease!" the young man hollered. He grabbed her by the waist and tried to force her into his lap.

"Enough!" Commander Kane roared, silence settling after his outburst. "Let the woman finish her job," he said more genially as he stuffed bread into his mouth. "I need quiet to finish my speech."

When she came around to his end of the table, she curtsied and thanked him.

Before she could leave, he took her hand, kissed the top of it, and placed it on his heart. "Have we met?"

She shook her head, terrified.

Meg dared not meet his eyes. She used her other hand to pull her shawl a little closer to her face. Had he discovered her true identity? Is that why he kept her from leaving? Her heart jumped wildly in her chest and thumped in her ears. She was ready to spring out of sight as fast as a jackrabbit escaping a snare. They'd never met officially before, although he had been at court a couple of times. Still, she hoped there was enough difference in her appearance that he would not make the connection.

"I thought I recognized you from a lovely trounce I had the other night."

Shocked by his lasciviousness, Meg turned her head and gaped at him.

"Give your name to my secretary on your way out, will you? He will find you for me when I am in ... need."

"Hail, the conquering hero!" one of the men shouted. They all toasted their commander. "To victory in battle and in our beds!"

He kissed her hand once more and let go of it slowly, lingering over the touch. The insincerity of the gesture made her cringe as all the dogs salivated and barked their approval, clanking their pewter mugs on the table.

As Meg rushed out of the pavilion, her stomach lurched, thrown into a violent revulsion for the man. She was well aware of his grand reputation in military circles, and that he had a wife and children. Her comprehension of his sordid ways dropped like an anvil so heavy on her chest that a sharpened sword would bounce off its surface in a wild shower of dangerous sparks. She walked back to the baker's tent, threw the basket hard on the ground, and broke it. The baker noticed. "You come back here and fix it or you'll never work for me again, you little hussy!"

~

Meg and Lady Byron congregated with the masses of people, from footman to knights to officers, even camp followers, near the commander's tent when word spread that he wished to address the army. The scene loomed high above the crowd as tall banners waved gloriously in the morning breeze. After a long drum roll and a blast of trumpets, Kane stepped onto the stage. The people received him with silence. In full armor and a long black cape, he moved to the front of the platform. His thick shock of greying black hair caught the bright sunlight as his head emerged from a shadow.

He grimaced before the crowd and bowed his head for a moment. "I understand your silence, my fellow countrymen. This is a difficult time for us. We are closer to servitude than ever in our history and I must take responsibility for that. It was my false move, my bad decision in our last series of battles that put us in this position. I lost a line of outposts on our borders that I did not think could be compromised."

He hung his head sadly.

"I promise that will not happen again," he said with renewed effort. "We have a grand history of running them out of our country, and they have never been content to leave us alone. We have fought battles on our shores, in our mountains, on our plains, and we have driven them back through their borders dozens of times over generations. Still, they come to take away what does not belong to them! Our history as a people has been forged by blood. It's practically all we know. I don't have to tell you how long this war has gone on. So long that most of us cannot remember when it all began or even why.

"But I do know that my conscience will never allow this land or its people, this people, my countrymen, to be subjugated — not ever! I would rather die. So, I ask you, will you fight for freedom?" he boomed, his baritone echoing across the clearing, delving into the hearts of his men. "After a long life and you've become a frail, old man, would you not give anything in the world to go back to the day when you and your men-at-arms were together, slaying a savage enemy? Would you not relish the moment when you raised your shirt-sleeves and show the scars that you have earned to everyone who asks about that great day? Smile at anyone who utters your revered name? Would you tell your enemy, when the day comes, and it is not far off men, that they may take your lives, but never your freedom?

"And so I ask you again, will you march with me and crush this invader? Will you fight alongside me, my fellow countrymen? We cannot fail now. We will go on to the end. And we will win!" He raised his sword high in the air, the perfect gesture for victory, and strutted on the platform encouraging an enormous blast of emotion from the Asterian army, like trumpets blaring before a charge.

Soldiers leapt with raised swords and pikes, pushing closer to their leader in exultation. Despite attempts to restrain him, Kane jumped off the front of the stand into the middle of the mob. He stretched out his arms and touched as many as he could, as if he were a prophet of old and his touch could work miracles.

Though bitterly disappointed in the commander for the way he'd treated her, Meg couldn't help but appreciate his speech. It was just what the men in the army needed to hear. Fearing that she was too far away to hear more if he spoke again, she grabbed Lady Byron by the arm and pulled her toward the commander, struggling as she did to keep the man in sight. Close enough to see him through an opening of people in front of her, she watched as his chin suddenly dropped to his chest and sprung up quick as a whip, his head and neck like a puppet without a string. In terror, she watched his eyes widen in pain and freeze, the unmoving stare of the dead, as he slumped to the ground. A drop of blood trickled out of his mouth. At that moment, someone shouted that the commander had been stabbed. She could see through the shoving crowd the curved handle of a dagger protruding from beneath his shoulder just above the lip of his chest armor. Then she saw his blood spurting onto his arm with the regularity of his heartbeat as his life quickly drained into the dust.

And the hope of the kingdom with it.

The guards started rounding people up. An attempt to gather witnesses and perhaps discover the assassin, it caused great chaos as everyone bumped into each other frantically trying to escape. Meg wanted to stay and help Commander Kane. Maybe he could be saved, she thought, but Lady Byron pulled her up with such force that she almost lifted Meg off her feet. The lady said nothing as she pushed the princess toward the forest.

12
FLIGHT

The Wolf Knight and his lieutenant continued their rapid flight even after reaching the cover of the trees. Sprinting hard, they constantly looked behind them to make sure they had out-run anyone who might have followed. Panting and placing their hands on their knees to catch their breath, Luke stood and slapped Nicholas on the back.

"Well done, lad. You got him!"

"I didn't," Nicholas answered through labored breaths and shook his head.

"Of course you did! That's why we've come and almost sacrificed life and limb, to get the dirty, rotten scoundrel."

"No, Luke," he replied, more forcefully this time. "It wasn't me who shoved that knife through the commander's chest. Someone else beat me to it. I've still got my dagger." Nicholas gestured to its location on his belt.

"What are you talking about?" Luke walked to the other side of his leader to see the dagger tucked in its sheath. "Did you ever take it out?"

"No. I never got close enough. I didn't anticipate that he would jump into a throng of people and move farther away from me."

"Bloody hell," Luke said in exasperation. He sat on a stump, put his hands on his knees, and glowered. "This was all for nothing. And what we will tell our own commander? Sorry, but we missed our target and almost sacrificed ourselves in the process. He's not going to like that."

"No, he won't," Nicholas said flatly. "But I can justify the mission by focusing on the intelligence we've gained."

"You keep saying that," Luke glared skeptically. "What intelligence?"

"I think I know where the next battle is going to be and what new weapon they've developed."

"And how would you know that?"

"I followed a lass who went from tent to tent asking for work this morning. She found a job serving breakfast to the commander and his men. I saw her staring at something inside the tent and it caught my attention so I dawdled a bit, walked by it a few times."

"You followed a woman? Of course you did, sneaky bastard." Luke pursed his lips like he'd just sucked on a lemon, unsurprised by the revelation. "Who was it?"

"I don't know. Didn't recognize her. She covered her head with a shawl."

"Well, Captain," he said, leaning back on the stump and folding his arms. "How do you suppose we get out of here? The Asterian guards are searching the forest and hauling everyone they can get their hands on for questioning. Even the poor peasants would stab a man through the heart before they find out he means no harm."

"I think we're far enough away for now, but I've got an idea..." Nicholas crouched on the ground, took a map from inside his tunic, and smoothed it out. "But first let me show you what I think the Asterian army is going to do."

"I don't like it." Luke looked over his shoulder at the map. "The Asterian guards are likely here and here," he said, pointing.

"You're playing devil's advocate again, Luke," Nicholas sighed in resignation. "We don't have time for this. This is the best route to our camp from here. You know I'm right."

"The odds are against us on this one, laddie. You know I'm right."

"Great Goddess, you're insufferable sometimes," Nicholas scolded. "You're a gem, really. I don't know another man who'd sacrifice himself to the devil for you, but who would grumble all the way to hell."

"I keep you on your toes," Luke smirked and walked toward a clearing in the forest.

They found the place where they had sequestered their gear, dug up their cache, and cleaned off their belongings. Changing out of their Asterian uniforms, they would need anonymity now. They moved toward the path that would take them back to their horses when the captain heard a sound at the other end of the glen. He grabbed the lieutenant by the arm and dropped into a frozen crouch behind some bushes. Perhaps they had not been so lucky after all.

And then ... he couldn't believe his eyes.

A woman stood and slowly turned toward them. Tall and slender with long honey-colored hair, she looked, even from a distance, quite fair. His eyes strained for a moment to see her better. To his astonishment, Nicholas realized it was the same young woman he had followed to Commander Kane's tent that morning. The clothing was the same. Nicholas stood up, never taking his eyes away from her. After far too much speechless staring, the captain walked toward the woman.

"No, Nicholas!" Luke whispered in a rage. "You cannot go to her. We must get back!"

He could hear his friend kick a rock in frustration behind him.

The woman's hair tumbled down in wavy locks around her face, tendrils lifted and blown about by a gentle breeze. She looked like a wild forest sprite, but magnificently calm and composed. By the time he cut the distance between them in half, Nicholas realized that...

It was her.

The woman who made his heart turn over in his chest, the woman who made breathing nearly impossible, the woman whose eyes made it unthinkable to look away was here.

After the initial shock of seeing her, he wondered how she got here. Did the woman never sit still? First, she flitted through the city, then sneaked around in the castle, then she hid in the forest. And damn it to hell, he thought, utterly embarrassed with himself. He still did not know her name.

Heat rushed to his face. A sheen of sweat appeared on his hands. Trying to talk to her made him more nervous than ever. He couldn't understand it. Nicholas never found it difficult to speak to anyone before in his life, but he couldn't open his mouth when he was with her in the castle, as if a magic spell had somehow stitched his lips together.

This time, he would find his voice and talk to her.

When he came within reach of her, he stared into her eyes, golden green like the frost-nipped leaves all around her. Nicholas shifted his focus and noticed how her hair grew more golden when the sun shone on it, how a few freckles danced across her nose and cheeks, and how her face called out for his touch. He'd never seen skin so flawless. How he yearned to experience her softness. It was as if he looked down the long, spiral tunnel into the heart of eternity. The four dimensions tied a knot in the middle of his chest as he reached out gently and touched her cheek with the back of his fingers. Just then, he noticed that she was trembling.

～

MEG WATCHED THE WARRIOR WALK ACROSS THE GLEN AND recognized him at once. She knew the graceful movement of his shoulders, the way he tilted his head as he strained to see her, his warm smile upon recognizing her. For a fleeting moment, Meg wondered if he knew her true identity. Had he contrived to meet to gain her trust? Perhaps the next time they met, he would kidnap her ... or worse. But she saw something in his eyes.

She hoped she was reading them right.

The moment he raised his hand to touch her was at once terrifying and glorious. As the warrior caressed her face, Meg breathed in and raised her face to receive his affection. As his fingers brushed her cheek, her body had a mind of its own. The muscles in her back stiffened. Her arms rose involuntarily. She desperately wanted to return his touch. At that moment, her universe spun inward, as if to disappear into the deep vortex of the man standing before her. With thick brown hair curling at the nape of his neck and a few days' growth on his face, he was rugged and handsome. His eyes held her. They possessed a quality of gentleness in contrast to the rest of his appearance, foreign to his almost reverent demeanor as he returned her gaze.

"Tell me your name," he whispered.

"My name is..."

"Don't tell him!" Lady Byron begged.

"Meg," she whispered back. She couldn't help but give him a shy smile. "I should've told you sooner. I'm sorry that I didn't. And yours?"

With that, Meg watched Lady Byron put her hands to her head as if her temples throbbed and walked away. She found a nearby rock to sit on. The warrior's companion stayed at the other end of the glen, pacing.

"Nicholas at your service, my lady." He gave her a courtly nod and smiled. Meg noticed a little mischief in the glint of his eyes and the way he curved his lips.

"I'm not a lady!" she recoiled, almost too quickly. "My friend and I had heard the most fascinating tales about Commander Kane and we wandered away from the castle we serve to see him."

"It is most unfortunate."

"I'm sure our master has discovered us gone by now," she said fleetingly, turning toward Lady Byron. "We must get back."

"Stay for a little while," Nicholas pleaded. He took her hand into his, gently tugging her toward him, closer than she had ever been to a man before. The warrior gestured toward a rock that could seat two and guided her to it. "I know that we both must be on our way, but stay just a little longer."

Once they sat down, he kept her hand in his. It felt wonderful. She couldn't imagine never placing her hand in his again.

"What part of the country do you come from, Meg?" he asked, looking intently into her eyes.

"You know where I'm from," she scolded him playfully.

"I didn't ask where you work. I asked where you're from. There is a difference, you know."

Meg considered what to tell him. She couldn't tell him that she was the princess. "I was brought up in the castle, like many others who work there."

"So, you've been raised a proper lady?"

She turned her head sideways and gave him a sly smile. He was teasing.

"Not exactly."

"Why is that?"

"It means that after I got my work done, I've tried to keep up with my brothers my whole life. I hate everything I'm supposed to do inside. That's not proper behavior for a lady."

"I can't blame you there. Women work as hard as men outside, especially if they farm, and then come inside to serve their husbands and children."

"It's grueling to be sure." Meg scrunched her face up in distaste. She saw Lady Byron grimace out of the corner of her eye at her unguarded expression. It wasn't royal behavior. She could tell that Nicholas noticed the exchange and smiled through his whiskers, his eyes squinting with curiosity. "I'd much rather be outside, but you already know that about me. What about you, Nicholas? Where do you come from?"

"From a village in the country, very far from here. I grew up on a small farm and herded sheep. We lived in a crofter's cottage, but my father built it in the most magnificent spot in the world, a meadow surrounded by trees and high, jagged mountains in the distance. The sunsets there are the most glorious I've ever seen. My father taught me to work hard and how to survive, but my mother was protective. I thought she would die when I went into the army."

"My mother died when I born. I don't know what it's like to have a mother worry so much."

"I am sorry for you then." He smoothed the top of her hand with his thumb and interlaced his fingers with hers, which she thought might send her to the moon.

"Me, too," she replied sadly. "I miss her every day, even though I never knew her, but I have my father and brothers."

"They seem to have kept you safe and warm."

"Yes, I suppose they have."

"What will your life be like after the war? Do you ever wonder about it?"

"I'm not sure." She tilted her head toward him and gave him a slight smile. "But I hope that I will be happy and have more freedom to wander without everyone fretting that I will die if I venture away from the castle. As you know, I steal away when I can."

"They are right to worry. War is a dangerous time, especially for a woman like you."

"What do you mean, a woman like me?" Meg bristled, unsure of what he meant.

"Men take what they want in war. Chivalry disappears, and if they can ensnare a beautiful woman, then they will do it."

"I don't think I'm quite like that," she answered with a bashful glance. "My brothers tell me all the time how plain they think I am."

"Oh, do they?" Nicholas chuckled. "I think that must be a brother's way of keeping his sister humble."

"What do you dream of doing after the war, Nicholas?" Meg asked, trying to change the subject. She felt her cheeks getting warm and wanted to deflect his attention. "Will you go home or will you find work in the city?"

"I've been fighting for so long and have channeled my mind only to this pursuit for so many years that I do not know. I've always thought that I would probably die fighting."

Meg leaned against his arm and laid her head on his shoulder as she squeezed his hand. "That's the saddest thing I've ever heard."

He shrugged, looked toward her, and smiled wistfully. "It's a reality a soldier comes to live with."

"That's why you don't know what your life will be like after the war?"

"Perhaps," he said thoughtfully, looking at the trees that surrounded them as he still caressed her hand. "I do know, like you, that I want to be happy. I want to be able to choose how to live my life, rather than have someone above me choose."

"To be free from the army?"

"Yes, my lady."

"Then we agree we both want to be happy." Meg sat straight and smiled brightly at him. "That is a worthy goal."

"I'm happy right now." Nicholas stared deeply into her eyes. After a few moments, he closed his eyes and smiled, shaking his head in embarrassment. "It seems I stare too much, my lady. Forgive me. Thank you for sitting with me."

"I don't want to leave, Nicholas," Meg pouted, laying her head on his shoulder once again.

"We must, but please allow me and my colleague to escort you to safety." He clasped her hand tighter for a just a moment, smiling at her, but then let go.

Meg sat astride his horse and he carried the reins as they walked through the forest. The two men accompanied her and Lady Byron back as close to the city gates as possible, and she couldn't help but adore him already. Even the sight of his back with those broad shoulders, the way he walked, and how his hair moved in the breeze made her smile, like being in his presence was the most normal thing in the world. How the sun caught the golden and reddish strands in his hair was not something she ever would have considered important. In fact, she might've derided any other woman for talking about something so shallow and silly. Now she understood it. Noticing and even loving the smallest detail about him had become the most important thing in the world.

When he placed his hands around her waist to help her down from his horse and brought her close to him again, she felt a quick intake of breath. Her pulse surged. Never in her life did she think that the one place she would want to be was right here.

"May I see you again, my lady?"

"I'm not a lady," she said, blushing. "I've already told you that. I am just a maid in a nobleman's household." In its barest form, completely true, Meg rationalized.

"You are to me."

"I do want to see you again ... very much." She paused when saw the disapproving expression on Lady Byron's face and a heard heavy sigh from Luke. "But I don't know how it can be done. So many terrible things are happening."

"If you can make it here, I will make sure that you are safe as we travel." He brought his hand up to her forehead to move an unruly tendril away from her face. Her breath caught again. "Why not on the night of the next full moon? Right here. I'll be waiting."

"Yes," she said, smiling, as Lady Byron quickly shepherded her away from the soldiers.

∽

"You stupid, befuddled, bewitched lunatic!" Luke seethed as they rode away. "Have you any idea what you've done here? You cannot see her again, Nicholas! It's too dangerous, aside from the obvious fact that this place is too far away."

"Our camp will not be far away for long."

"So you think."

"No, Luke. I know. I've got good information and I believe I've interpreted it properly."

"It doesn't matter where we are encamped. You cannot venture out to see her again."

Nicholas contemplated that possibility, and he couldn't bear it. He could see her smiling down at him from on top of his horse, the dappled sunlight dancing on her golden hair and sparkling in her eyes.

"Look, I don't expect you to understand, but I've wondered my whole life when I would know what woman was right for me. I can't explain what's happened. All the troubles in the world melted away when I searched her eyes and took her hand into mine."

"That is the most absurd excuse to bed a lass that I've ever heard."

"When have I ever bedded a lass?!" he roared at his companion.

Luke flinched a little at the outburst, but gave him a knowing smile.

"Lately," Nicholas amended. "When have I bedded a lass lately?" He had not taken the momentary comfort of women following the army for a very long time. He'd never experienced what anyone would call courting. He was always too preoccupied with planning and winning each battle.

"I've given my entire life to this cause," Nicholas continued, "and as more time goes by, I'm not even sure what that is. And now I find myself wanting to become more acquainted with this extraordinary woman. I thought you, of all men, would understand that. I don't intend to bed her, you callous churl."

"She's a mystery, you fool. Nothing but trouble, dabbling in the unknown," Luke replied easily, trying to placate his commander.

"Aye," Nicholas said as he shot a crooked smile and a look of mischief to his friend, "but a most intoxicating mystery, one I am most willingly obliged to unravel." He sighed. "I don't know, Luke, there's just something about her."

"Don't wax rhapsodic on me now, laddie. Must I point out that you lovebirds are on opposing sides of a great war, one that is about to get much worse?"

"I'll find a way to protect her."

"And then what?"

"If I survive this war, I'll find her. Maybe she'll have me."

"Sweet Mother Earth, give me strength."

∼

MEG RODE HER HORSE IN THE SURF. THE BREEZE CHURNED SMALL, choppy waves on the shore that frothed and slid back out to sea under oncoming swells. Not far from her, giant cliffs jutted vertically into the sea as vibrant green grasses grew to their rocky edges. In some places, long stretches of beach and soft sand lay before her. In other places, the sea was deep and dangerous and toyed with the rocks, roiling, crashing, splashing, and causing mayhem against their silent walls. She turned her face up to the overcast sky, closed her eyes, and breathed in the fresh air mingled with salt from the sea.

Opening her eyes, Meg watched the clouds turn, circle, and rush by. Another horse cantered up beside hers, big and black with a long, flowing mane. She turned and saw Nicholas smiling at her, such warmth in his eyes. With the wind whipping her hair and cloak behind her, Meg spurred Golden Cloud to full speed and turned in the saddle to make sure he followed. Racing behind her, she could see him standing up in his stirrups to avoid the jolting of his horse's movements. A superior horseman, he would soon overtake her lead.

Nicholas pulled his horse in front of hers, which made her own slow down and rear up on its hind legs. Laughing a deep, jovial rumble, he climbed down from his saddle into the surf and walked over to her. He lifted his arms, and she fell into them. Meg wrapped her arms around his neck and stared at his noble profile as he carried her toward the sand. It wasn't long before he dropped to his knees and laid her on the ground. Nicholas lay down beside her, propping one hand under his head with the other arm across her waist. Meg gently pulled him closer to her. She stroked his whiskers. His soft blue eyes had fire and passion in them. She couldn't resist running her fingers through his thick, dark hair. She pressed her lips to his in a slow, soft kiss that could've gone on forever. As the kiss grew more passionate, Nicholas bore down harder with his lips. His hands ravished her hair and face and neck. When he lifted himself on his hands to look more closely at her, she saw tears running down his cheeks.

"I'll not dishonor you, my lady," Nicholas said, though she could tell it pained him to say it.

"There's nothing dishonorable about loving you, Nicholas."

She tightened her arms around his neck and lifted her body to his as she gave him fiery, frantic kisses. He slowly pressed his body on top of hers and she felt his desire...

∽

"You were moaning, my lady. Was it another nightmare?"

She could feel someone nudging her.

"Huh? What did you say?" Meg sat up in bed, confused. She placed a hand over her thumping heart and tried to calm her breathing. Forcing her eyes to focus, she realized that Lady Byron had already opened the curtains around her bed and stood over her, a look of suspicion yet concern crossing her thin, wrinkled face.

"I asked if it was another nightmare," Lady Byron persisted.

"A nightmare? Yes, a nightmare," Meg said through parched lips. She stood up to get a sip of water from a goblet on her bedside table. When she put the cup to her lips, her hands trembled, and she wondered how her secret desires for Nicholas had suffused her mind so thoroughly. It hadn't been that long since she'd seen him, yet she couldn't stop thinking about him.

"What was it about this time?"

"Why are they so real, Lady Byron?" Meg asked, hoping to deflect the question. "The dreams feel like they're actually happening."

"You are sensitive to the things around you. You always have been," Lady Byron said with a shrug of her shoulder. "Old Addy would say that you take after your mother. There was talk about Louisa. She wasn't a prophetess or a seer sayer, but sometimes the things she dreamed came true. Your father would know more about it than I do."

"Lady Byron," Meg said after she'd put her goblet down. "I want you to know that I will not let our people down. I promise. I know you don't understand, can't understand, why I must see him. I can't explain it myself, but I do know I will not betray my king, my country, or my people. Nicholas is a soldier in my father's army."

Meg had thought more and more of why he was in the castle that night. There could be no other answer; he had to prove that the castle guards were an utter failure. After witnessing their incompetence while leading Hannah to the castle and her escape, there could be no other explanation.

"There's no harm in falling for a simple man who's loyal to Asterias, is there? I don't think my father would deny that, especially when the outcome of the war is so uncertain. There may not even be a kingdom to be the princess of when all is said and done."

"You are a princess. He is a soldier, common as hair on a dog," Lady Byron said, irritated. "You can't possibly think that there is any way in the world you can pursue this."

"I will see him again," Meg replied stubbornly.

"How? Do you think you have not been missed?" Lady Byron persisted. "If William figures it out, he will clasp an iron with a chain around your neck and pound the stake in the ground just like he did your horse. It's not like he hasn't threatened before."

"William will not keep me chained up." Meg bristled like a cat caught in a corner. "He blusters and threatens, but if I don't interfere with his business, then he will not clamp down on me. He is far too lazy to worry about what I'm doing. He's shown that propensity for a long time."

"Not if he's listening to the Duke of Breckenridge." Lady Bryon turned her back and walked to the balcony.

"What's that supposed to mean?" Meg answered angrily, stomping in front of Lady Byron so that she would be forced to look at her.

"I mean the man is as cunning as William is cruel. They will use you however they must to accomplish their horrible deeds."

"Then I will play chess with them and I will win." Meg gestured defiantly with a hand and pointed to her chest.

"They are too powerful, my lady." Lady Byron shook her head in disagreement. "When your father dies, William can compel you to do as he pleases. You must know that."

"My father is not going to die," Meg scoffed. "He's far too young to die and it would be the end of my world. It would go tumbling off its axis and send me spiraling with it."

"I am only worried for you, foolish girl," Lady Byron said softly, in resignation.

"Lady Byron!" Meg cried unexpectedly, grabbing her companion and pulling her into a tight embrace. "I know you cannot understand. Of all the men I've met in my life, there is not another who is more genuine, more kind, more doting and chivalrous. And his eyes..." Meg stepped back with a sigh, clasping Lady Byron by her shoulders. "I don't know how to explain it, but I felt at home in his presence. I felt as if all these terrible things in the world ceased to exist. With everyone else in my life, I'm nothing but a pawn on a board."

"You are a princess." Lady Byron repeated in an annoying, patronizing tone. "It is your duty, body and soul, to do the bidding of your king, be it your father or your brother, and to secure the power and prosperity of your country through marriage if necessary."

"My whole being is repulsed by the thought!" Meg whispered savagely. "I will continue to do my duties and do what is right by my father and the kingdom, but I will see this man again. This may be the only time in my life that I will love."

13
DEATH AND CONSEQUENCES

"Word of Commander Kane's assassination has spread like wildfire, but you bring old news, Captain. You acted outside of your orders ... again. What makes this little jaunt of yours not worth punishment?" Commander Burrage growled, glaring at the Wolf Knight over the top of his clasped hands. He sat in his tent near a rough-hewn table and laid his hands on the pommel of his overturned sword, point digging into the earth.

Nicholas spent a few tense moments wondering if his commander would act on his threat, but he was convinced that Burrage would regard the intelligence he supplied too much to keep him from doing his job, which was far beyond that of an ordinary captain. Next to the commander himself, no one in the army knew more than he did or acted on the information with such efficiency.

"Sir, I have intelligence I think you'll be interested in." Nicholas slid the map he had drawn across the table. He and Luke stood at attention in front of the commander. Burrage scanned the contents and leveled a stern gaze at them.

"Is this what I think it is?"

"Yes, sir. I believe so."

"How did you come upon this?"

"That's a story involving a woman you'd probably rather not hear, sir," Luke interjected. He'd said it to lighten the mood, but Burrage scowled him into silence.

"It's true," Nicholas replied. "I saw a maid serving Commander Kane and his men their breakfast, and because of her, I was able to get close enough to his headquarters and copy, the best that I could as I understood it, a map of their next offensive and its location."

"I know this plain." Burrage creased his bushy eyebrows, concentrating, his mouth pursed under a black, bristly beard. "With its ridges and narrow neck to the south. We've marched by it a hundred times. Why would the king choose such a well-known area?"

"Hiding his battle plan and its location in plain sight? I'm not sure, sir, but he has greater numbers. We've always known that, but it seems he has a weapon never used before. I think he's banking on those two factors to win the next engagement, but the army is in shambles. They are mostly a rag-tag team of ne'er-do-wells. Their morale could not be lower, especially since Commander Kane is out of the picture."

"Excellent work on that, by the way, even though it was outside your orders," Burrage chided. He planted his sword more firmly in the ground and let go, held the map up to the light, and squinted. "If I had known what you were up to I would've forbidden it. Too risky, but since the dirty work is done..."

Out of the corner of his eye, Nicholas saw the frustration on Luke's face. He had not yet revealed to his leader that he had not killed the man. "Sir, you must know that I am not responsible for his death. That was one of my intentions when I left here, but I did not accomplish it."

"Who is responsible then?" Burrage asked, puzzled. "Great Goddess!" Realization hit him like a rock. "Someone on the inside. They are falling apart brick by brick!"

"It would seem so," Nicholas answered, tight-lipped. "However, this weapon is a good bit of armament that I find surprising due to their crumbling state."

"What is it?"

"Long bows, sir."

"Ah, yes. Time and money involved there and it is difficult to train that many archers. How did this slip by our spies?"

"I'm not sure how it got by us, sir. I'm guessing these bows shoot much farther than ever before. Plus, the arrows must be thicker and harder. I believe they could penetrate armor, or at least, injure and distract a man enough so that his opponents would have a perfect opportunity to finish him off. Notice how they have the archers protected, placed behind a huge fence of wooden spears. And they are not placed in a single location, but in many areas surrounding the battlefield."

"With that many archers, they could devastate charging knights and foot soldiers. Well, with this new development, we've got work to do. We've got to counter this somehow. I'll leave it to you to present this intelligence to the war council and your interpretation of it tonight, which I think is spot on."

"Thank you, sir."

"Just don't disappoint me," Burrage snapped, switching ferocious glances between Nicholas and Luke. "We need to make this a decisive victory, so we can climb out of the hell hole we've made for ourselves and go home."

Luke opened his mouth to disagree, but the commander stopped him.

"Not one word about occupation forces," Burrage warned, his voice raspy and menacing. "That's someone else's job. Dismissed!"

～

They dueled in a practice arena near the stable and armory. John Paul had taught Meg well. She was so proficient at swordsmanship that she could intercept and stifle his attacks and then thrust and cut for a crippling blow, either to the head, the neck, the shoulder, or the heart. They took turns aiming for the kill after they had parried several blows with their dulled blades.

"John Paul, I have a confession," she blurted through gritted teeth in the middle of defending herself from his on-coming clout above her head. "William's suspicions of me are right."

"What are you talking about?" He spun around in an agile maneuver and angled his sword to strike her legs. "When is William ever right in your estimation?"

"Fair point," Meg conceded as she wedged the flat of her sword to his blade and prevented him from thwacking her legs, "except that I do sneak out of the castle regularly to help feed our people. If William knew, he'd probably ... Well, I'm not sure what he'd do. Malcolm and Lewin Cooksey, their wonderful wives, and an army of people in the city took my proposition to heart. Father allowed some of the reserve grains for use to help feed the city's hungry. They provide the carts to pick it up, take it to gristmills, and then distribute the flour to volunteers to bake. It's turned into something much bigger than I ever imagined. This, of course, gives me new excuses to sneak out. Not like I need them..." she finished, smiling mischievously at him.

"I knew about the enterprises to feed the hungry. They are much needed, but what else have you been up to?" he asked, breathless as he lowered his sword.

"I did help Hannah escape." She backed away from the swordplay and wiped the sweat from her brow.

"I had a feeling you did something. William was beside himself with rage, though he couldn't prove a thing. I'm terribly sorry about your horse, Meg. It's a great loss. If I had been here, it never would've happened."

"I know." Meg smiled sadly. "You are my greatest defender."

"William was sopped in his cups after he'd killed the poor

beast and then bragged to his entourage. I came back to the castle just after the incident and I couldn't get him to leave his room for days. The conscience under the drunkard is there. It just can't function properly with all the spirits drowning it to death."

"I'm aware of his sordid condition and how long he spent in his chamber after the deed was done, but it doesn't help me much when he's in a rage." Meg said it more tersely than she intended and caught herself, ashamed by the outburst. Flushed with embarrassment, Meg turned away from him. She hadn't meant to be rude, not to John Paul.

"Dear sister, don't worry about offending me." He put his hands on her upper arms and turned her to face him once again. He searched her eyes and spoke in an achingly soft and sweet voice. "You have the brunt of labor at home, tending to a father who can only function when he leans on his daughter. So..." He raised his eyebrows comically and changed the subject. "What other heroics have you been up to?"

"Well," Meg began, but she suddenly felt shy about being truthful to John Paul. He might think her foolish for sneaking into the Asterian encampment. Lady Byron had already chastised her a thousand times for her error in judgment. "Lady Bryon and I fell into a crowd migrating out of Tirana. We spent the night huddled around a bonfire with peasants. In the morning, I found work in Commander Kane's tent serving him and his advisors breakfast. I witnessed his murder and ran for cover into the forest. When we felt safe to move, we made our way back to the city gate, which was open, much to my surprise. It was easier than I thought to sneak back into the castle, despite the chaos. No one seemed to know what to do."

"Hmm," he said, as he cocked his head and narrowed his eyes, contemplating. Then he quickly kicked her in the abdomen. She fell backwards and hit the ground in an eruption of dust.

"Hey! That was illegal!" Meg shouted.

"Never let your guard down," he growled back. "And it wasn't illegal. You just weren't expecting it."

He walked around her several times, trying to keep his temper in check. "Why in the name of all the stars would you do such a foolish thing? I know you can protect yourself within the city; I've trained you for that. Our gate guards watch for known ill-seekers, but sneaking out? You could've been captured, tortured, abused, ransomed, any number of foul things. What were you thinking?"

He extended a hand and pulled her up. They walked to some shade and a grassy pad behind the jousting arena.

"Why did you risk this?" John Paul demanded.

"I feel so useless, John Paul. I'm like a marble rattling around in a pot. I had to get out into the midst of the people and see how I could help. Kane was our only hope. I wanted to get a feel for the man, to see how he would lead us away from the brink of disaster. Now, I guess we have no chance. Father can't even decide on a new commander. It still comes to me every now and then that there is someone out there who could turn the tide for us. Although I've failed so far, I will keep looking. I did see a map, and I've been trying to decipher the markings ever since."

"You saw a map? What map?" John Paul asked, agitated.

"It was huge. It looked like it had been drawn on a bearskin or some other very large animal. It included topography and military markings. I think it's a battle plan."

"And Kane had this in full view?"

"Well, no. Not entirely. I served them breakfast, remember?"

"Yes, but it's possible that others could see it through his curtains?"

"Probably, if they were really looking."

"Damn him," he said, and sat on a rock wall. "That means that our plan is no longer a secret. Why would he do that?"

"Why is it no longer a secret?" Meg sat down beside him.

"Because my dear sister, if you can slip in and figure it out, then a spy has done the same thing."

"Spies?" she trilled, alarmed. "The enemy is in our camp?"

"I believe so. In fact, you may have led them to it."

"What? I wouldn't do that for anything."

"Well, you are rather lovely, and it's not like men haven't followed you around before."

"John Paul, I was not followed!"

"How do you know? Can you tell me for a fact that you were not followed? Did you keep track of your surroundings well enough to tell me beyond a doubt that you were not followed?"

"No. I suppose not," Meg sighed, resigned to her error. "So, are the military markings symbols for long bows?"

"I've got to come up with better codes! If my own sister can figure it out, then we are done for!"

"John Paul, you know I would die rather than hurt our cause, and I'm not your average sister. I've been figuring things out for a long time now."

"I have to assume you're the reason the invader may have our battle plan. I must change the plan, at least certain elements of it."

"Where are they training, anyway? And how on earth do we have the money for this? How did you keep this a secret for so long?"

"Too many questions which I will not answer. You're already a danger to yourself for what you've discovered."

"Then I will find out on my own. I will dog you and nip at your heels until you give way."

"Good luck with that, sister." He rose to leave, pulling her with him away from the wall. "It's always a joy to knock you down flat, my lady." He did so again and smiled over her at his triumph.

"Don't sneak to the encampment again. It's too dangerous," John Paul warned. "I will not cover for you another time."

"You didn't cover for me. You didn't even know."

Meg shuddered at the thought of John Paul discovering that

she met Nicholas in secret. There'd be no sneaking out of the castle, easily, ever again.

"You're sure about that?" he said over his shoulder as he walked toward the armory to the other knights who gathered at the practice arena for another match.

14

LOVE IN THE MOONLIGHT

Nicholas stood waiting in the shadows of the forest. The harvest moon shone bright and beautiful. Everything underneath absorbed its unearthly silver glow. As he endured the sweet anticipation of seeing Meg again, he couldn't get over the notion that he was the most selfish bastard in the world. What decent, honorable man would ask a woman to go from the safety of the castle to face the dangers of the countryside? And what kind of foolish girl would agree to it? Meg could take care of herself in the city, but this? It was different.

Ever since the assassination of Commander Kane, the people in the countryside had gone mad. The pressure of enduring the war built up and released with the death of their best commander. It was as if they were a great body of water pressing against an earthen dam and pushed through, the roaring water crushing everything in its path. He received reports from his scouts of heinous, barbarous crimes. No one outside the city gates was safe. Holding his horse's reins, Nicholas refrained from musing too much. He worried about her. Concentrating on the beast's cold breath as it exhaled, he rubbed Zander's snout and cheeks.

Then he heard a quiet step.

He looked up to see two cloaked figures peeking from behind the trunk of a very large tree. One stepped forward and removed the hood of her cloak, revealing a tumble of long, wavy blonde hair. The moon's light bounced a glorious ray from her head across the glen to him. She looked like a fairy. She stepped toward him, but then she turned and gestured to her companion to come out from behind the tree.

When they met in the middle of the glen, he stopped short of grasping her hands. Instead, bowed to her. "My lady," he whispered. "I'm glad you've come."

"Wild horses could not have kept me away," Meg replied breathlessly, stealing a glance toward her companion. "Although, she might have."

"Oh, aye. I have the same problem. I've been getting a good bit of Luke's famous taciturn treatment." He gestured with his head toward his companion.

They shared a huddled laugh between them.

"My companion worries for me," Meg continued, searching his eyes as she talked. "She says that I'm impetuous and that it gets me into trouble."

Nicholas stared into her moonlit eyes, hypnotic golden-green compasses that made him unable to look away. Startling and expressive, they also had an inexplicable combination of fiery passion and sweet tenderness. He could not imagine never looking into them again. "I imagine it would, my lady."

"Believe me, I do try to serve to the best of my ability, but..." Meg paused, searching for words. "I just feel like a prisoner sometimes. And I'm not your lady! I don't understand why you keep calling me that."

"Only because you are to me." He smiled and took her hand, leading her to his horse. "You can ride while we walk to one of the loveliest spots on earth."

"You have no idea how I've dreamed of such a thing."

"You've not seen the rare beauties of this land?"

"I wish!" Meg lamented. "The castle and the city have kept

me captive. I've heard so much about them, but I've never seen them with my own eyes."

"You will tonight." He lifted her onto his horse and watched her settle into the saddle. Luke twisted the reins on his horse and rode deeper into the forest. Nicholas knew he would stay close, guarding, watching to make sure that no danger encroached. But what was he to do with Meg's companion? Nicholas found himself sighing in frustration. Well, she was just going to have to walk.

∽

THE BRIGHT LIGHT FROM THE MOON MADE EVERYTHING IN THE forest sparkle from millions of tiny reflections on a layer of dew. The horse's hooves padded on soft ground. Somewhere nearby, a meandering brook gurgled over pebbles. The heady scent of the pine was intoxicating. Meg inhaled the fresh air, feeling it tingle in her lungs. She had dreamed of this her entire life, of enjoying the forest. Her father would never have allowed such a thing. Of course, she couldn't blame him anymore, not with the countryside in an uproar over the death of Commander Kane.

She watched Nicholas lead his horse with silent but stealthy steps. He seemed taller and stronger than she remembered. Dressed in the same colors as the forest, he wore a long green tunic with brown pants tucked inside of his boots. His dagger and sword were tucked into a thick leather belt knotted at his waist. His cloak caught her attention, so dark green it appeared almost black as night. It could cover him completely, like a magical shield. Nicholas wore no chainmail or metal armor, but rather thick, etched leather armor on his chest and forearms. His clothing seemed made for speed, agility, and camouflage. No one on a battlefield would ever see him coming.

The horse bent his back legs and lengthened his front legs to remain stable as they traveled down a steep hill. Nicholas clucked softly to his horse, led him to a branch, and tethered him. Cloaked in tall pines, the alcove was surrounded and she couldn't see where he had led them. Nicholas walked to the side of the horse, opened his arms, and smiled. Meg slid from the saddle, his gentle touch breaking her fall. Small patches of moonlight slanting through the branches illuminated his handsome face and glinted in his blue eyes. They seemed more animated than she remembered, perhaps due to his expressive eyebrows. She detected a devilish smile under his closely cropped whiskers.

Nicholas took her by the hand and led her to an opening in the trees. She gasped at the beauty of it. A scenic lake stretched before them surrounded by short cliffs. Roots of ancient trees burrowed out of the rock, and vines clung to its fractured walls. Above the cliffs and below, closer to the lake, pines and aged oak towered, some of them so thick and gnarled they looked a thousand years old. The moon shone bright on the lake. Its brilliant reflection moved in gentle ripples from a small cascading waterfall. In the middle of the lake, boulders lay close enough together to create a path. A couple could hardly resist walking across.

"Shall we, then?" He offered his arm to escort her.

She laughed at his gesture, such gentlemanly behavior from a shepherd boy, and put her arm through his. Leaning close to him as they walked to the lake, she wanted to feel the strength and power of his body, memorize his rugged good looks, and absorb everything he knew about the world. How she wished that she'd grown up without the reality of war. Maybe she wouldn't have this overwhelming desire to leave the stone walls of her home behind and live in a cottage with a man whom she already trusted more than anyone. If only life could be so simple.

Meg glanced toward Lady Byron, who sat on a rock near the shore of the lake, glowering. Her jaw moved contemptuously, like she ground pebbles into dust with her teeth. Her ever-present guardian was just going to have to endure the time. Meg was determined not to miss out on a single moment with Nicholas. She followed him into the middle of the lake, stepping on rocks to cross the water. He spread his cloak on a boulder with a smooth, flat spot for them to sit and kept hold of her hand as she sat down. They spent a few moments in silence as they both surveyed the landscape — the lake, the trees, the rocks, the cliffs, the moonlight, the soft grasses, all separate, yet together they created the most stunning mural she'd ever seen. Indeed, she felt as if she were the lovely maiden and Nicholas the handsome knight in a great work of art.

"Thank you for bringing me here," Meg said at last, breaking her reverie. "It is truly the most beautiful place that I have ever seen."

"My pleasure, my lady," he said, smiling warmly, his eyes luminous in the moonlight.

She paused to chide him for calling her that again. "Call me Meg." She reached out to touch him on the arm. When he put his other hand on top of hers, she suddenly felt more alive, her skin somehow more sensitive than ever before. She was distracted. She couldn't look at him yet felt foolish looking away. "Out here, I want to be just Meg and just Nicholas, if that's all right with you."

"These are heavy times, Meg," he replied. "Even for a maid and a shepherd."

He brushed an unruly tendril away from her temple and let the back of his fingers linger on her cheek, like he did the day they met. She could never forget the feel of his hand on her face, how his touch made her heart flutter, and how the passion in his eyes sent her spiraling into ecstasy. No man ever made her feel this way, but no other man sent her existence swirling into his, like two cyclones that gravitated to each other to become one.

"Everything about it scares me to death." She turned toward him and used her hand to feel his beard and run her fingers through his soft hair. "You should hear the stories Old Addy tells."

"Who's Old Addy?"

"Oh ... uh..." Meg fumbled over the words, wondering if talking about Addy would expose her as the princess. Maybe it was selfish, but she didn't want him to know, not yet. Meg knew she couldn't keep it from him forever, but she wanted to be herself around him, to enjoy every moment with him. She didn't have the heart, nor the desire, to add another obstacle to an unlikely relationship. "Old Addy is the nursemaid at the castle and a storyteller. She says this enemy is so vicious and cruel that they will make everyone suffer in the end. Why won't they leave us alone?"

She felt him stiffen a little at her words, but he said nothing.

∽

A RIPPLE OF CHILLY AIR BRUSHED BY MAKING MEG SHIVER. Nicholas pulled his cloak up from the surface of the rock and wrapped it around her, tucking it in to make sure she would stay warm.

"Let us just enjoy each other's company then, shall we?" He leaned back on his elbow, looked at her a bit mischievously and asked, "Have you ever heard the story of the boy who would be king?"

She cocked an eyebrow at him. "Hasn't every child heard that story?"

"I imagine so, but it's still fun to pull it out every now and again and rehearse favorite parts. So Meg," he said, emphasizing her name, "what is your favorite part?"

"Oh, let's see." She sat up a little straighter and pulled the cloak closer to her. "I rather like the queen and her favored knight."

"Why would you like that?" he asked, bemused.

"Forbidden love." She looked at her hands and blushed. "They tried so desperately not to love each other. I think they both loved the king more, but times were so difficult that they fell into each other's arms."

"I guess I can see that, except women always like that part the best." He nudged her playfully and then leaned forward to pick up a rock. He checked its shape, kneeled to position himself, and threw it into the lake. It skipped across the water a dozen times before it sunk below the surface.

"Well, I am a woman." She gave him a wry look. "What's your favorite part?"

"How a boy from humble circumstances became a king." He shrugged and smiled shyly as he sat down.

"Oh, I see." She looked down and smiled, trying to hide her amusement from him.

"I also admire his leadership, how he drew good men to him, and how he made them an important part of his government."

"Hail to the king," she whispered into his ear, her lips just brushing by. He could feel the tenderness of them and the sweetness of her breath. Had she meant to do that? It was bold, but he wasn't about to complain.

"Are you making fun of me?" he asked, a little surprised by the gesture. He gently tugged her toward him.

"Of course," she answered, smiling. It was one of those smiles that added warmth to her eyes, and he realized he couldn't wait to hear her laugh. "Men always like that part the best."

Pulling her closer to him, he put one arm around her shoulders and used the other to feel her soft cheek and run his fingers through her glorious hair. Just the touch of her and the scent of her made him realize how dangerous it was to be in her presence.

"I wish the King of Asterias had that kind of cunning and bravery," she continued. "I wish that he could muster his forces, lead them, and drive these invaders away for good."

"You don't think he can?"

"I only know what I've heard," she shrugged sadly. "It's no secret, Nicholas, that the king is weak. Everyone says that the young heirs will rise and fight for their father."

"Yes, I've heard that, too."

"I just want the world to get back to normal. I've never known anything without war."

THE ENTANGLED PRINCESS

"Neither, have I, my lady. Neither have I."

Meg gave him a seductive side glance, one eye closed a little more than the other with a shy smile. Somehow, just that look fired him up unexpectedly. She lay her head on his shoulder and entwined her arm around his, her fingers caressing the tender skin on the underside of his arm.

He could barely breathe.

Nicholas watched her carefully. Meg stared at the reflection of the moon on the water, but he was convinced that she didn't see it. She was lost in the moment. The sexy innocence of her touch made him wonder how impossible it would be to keep himself in check if he ever were to have her in private. She would drive him to complete distraction without even trying. All she'd have to do is smile, brush her hair away from her face, or say thank you with a sweet kiss on the cheek and he'd be completely enslaved.

He cleared his throat and turned his face away. He felt tremendous heat in his face and hoped she couldn't see him flushing. Thank the Great Mother Earth for whiskers.

"Let me ask you this," Nicholas said, trying to gain control of himself. "Have you heard the story of the woman who launched a thousand ships?"

Meg cupped her chin in her hand, thinking.

"That's one of Addy's favorites. You've heard a lot of stories for a shepherd boy." She narrowed her eyes at him, playfully suspicious.

"I read them, or my mother read them to me until I could read myself. She taught me. Can you read?"

"Old Addy, the nursemaid I told you about, always let all the children in the castle hear her stories. As I got older, I learned from the ladies-in-waiting. They took an interest in me. So, what about the woman in the story?"

"I've often wondered about the true nature of this war. No one seems to understand why we fight. What's the reason for it?"

She cocked her head in an inquisitive way and chewed the

inside of her cheek, listening. "You think the war is about a woman, like in the story?" Her eyes became round and she almost guffawed.

"I don't know. No one knows. All anyone can tell me from leaders down to the rabble is the two sides could not come to terms with an ancient peace treaty. Many battles were fought, but a resounding victory finally came and Asterias should have been left in peace."

"I don't think the cause of the war is why it continues." She folded her hands in her lap and stared across the lake, far away from him. He regretted bringing it up already.

Nicholas knew that the cause of the fighting no longer mattered. So much blood had been shed between the two peoples that they had become the most gruesome kind of kin, their blood mingling together and digested in the bowels of the earth. Generations had passed in these two kingdoms whose citizens knew only continuing warfare and the hatred and blind violence that grow out of it, like the grasses and wild flowers that spring forth more riotously because of the rotting bodies beneath them.

"Here I am sitting with the most beautiful woman I've ever seen in my life, and perhaps one of the brightest, and I couldn't help but make the comparison."

Meg turned back to him and smiled, the corners of her mouth just turned up. "You should be glad to know that I am not the woman who launched a thousand ships, nor have I been kidnapped by an infamous pirate. If we believe the tales, she enjoyed him more than her ancient husband." She cocked her head and raised an eyebrow at him.

She was too innocent to toy with him ... but Great Goddess above. The heat was back.

Meg smiled at him, showing for the first time straight teeth, except for a couple near the front that slightly overlapped the others.

Nicholas forced himself to look away and swallowed hard. She already had a power over him that he had not expected.

He pulled her closer and tucked in the cloak to ensure her warmth but kept his arm around her. She turned to him and stared into his eyes, then at his mouth and back again. When he didn't move — didn't dare — she traced her lips along his cheek to his ear and whispered, "Thank you, Nicholas, for bringing me here."

"Holy Mother," he whispered as his heart thundered in his chest. How would he ever let this woman go?

15
VISIONS

Nicholas rode on horseback, surveying his pastures and sheep, making sure his traps were set, the enclosures secure, ensuring that the animals would be safe through the night. Confident there would be no incidents with wolves poaching his stock, he headed for home. The setting sun sank behind the mountains he knew and loved, casting orange, pink, and purple strata into the sky, tinting puffy clouds.

After he stabled his horse, Nicholas walked through the door of the cottage he'd grown up in and saw his wife preparing dinner. Her back was toward him. He noticed that she'd braided her long hair and wore an apron tied around her waist. Stepping to the cradle, he admired his sleeping child, the baby's downy hair sprouting all over her head. At that moment, Nicholas decided to surprise his wife. He stalked up behind her, wrapped his arms around her waist, and plunged a deep kiss into her neck. Dropping the wooden spoon she used to make lamb stew, she turned into his embrace and kissed him back deeply, passionately. No longer able to resist her, he picked her up and laid her on their feather bed as he knelt beside her. Desperately trying to untie his breeches, she laughed at his fumbling, pushed him onto his back, and straddled him. She gave him the most ravishing look. Her eyes slanted and teasing, her full lips open just a bit, she lifted her skirts...

THE ENTANGLED PRINCESS

∼

NICHOLAS BOLTED UPRIGHT IN BED, HIS HEART RACING. Sweating so much he became cold, he grabbed a thick, wool blanket. He wrapped it around his shoulders and left his tent. The nights had become frosty. He gritted his teeth against the frigid air and stalked about the camp anyway.

What use was there in trying to sleep when Meg constantly invaded his dreams? She'd haunted his nights for a long time, a chimera that he could see, that floated nearby, but whenever he reached out to touch her, she was gone. His subconscious fluttered with beautiful, innocent scenarios of them meeting, smiling shyly at each other, maybe taking a stroll and looking into each other's eyes. Since he'd spent more time with her, the dreams became much more needful, physical, and intense.

It was so dark that all he could see were the dying embers from campfires. Trudging along a segment of the camp boundary, Nicholas found everything in order. He stopped at a large boulder and climbed to the top of it. He stood for a long time glaring at the sliver of moon and all the distant stars, a constant reminder of her. His yearning for her overwhelmed him. The hopelessness of their relationship multiplied his agony. In his scarred heart, she formed a haven of warmth and peace. To forget her had become utterly impossible.

He'd never been with a woman so sweet and innocent, yet so enticing. It made him ... well, wish she were his wife. That would be the only proper way to manage his overwhelming desire for her. He wouldn't do anything unwanted, yet something beyond the physical drew him to her. She had a certain curiosity, an intellect, and a hint of mischievousness that he'd never seen in a woman before. He found himself wanting more.

Overwrought by his thoughts, Nicholas collapsed in a heap of bitter frustration. Readjusting the blanket on his shoulders, he sat on the rock, wrapped his arms around his knees, and bowed his head. He told the Goddess above through his tears that he would rather die than betray his trust to his men, but then the awful horror of it came to rest upon his agonized soul. He would also rather die than be without her. He had fallen in love with a woman from Asterias, his mortal enemy. How could he have been so foolish? At first, he thought the attraction was harmless and would only lead to flirtation. Nothing wrong with talking to a lovely lady. The war, of all things, had flung them onto an intersecting path, and they did not turn away from each other. And he wouldn't turn away from her. It was too late for that.

He wished for a simpler time. If only she'd lived in his village and there was no war...

"I've got some frozen missiles you could hurl at the stars," Luke called from below. "Or perhaps you should howl at the moon. You are the Wolf Knight, after all. Might make you feel better." He climbed the rock and sat down beside Nicholas. "I've watched you suffer from afar, lad, seen you pacing like a restless lion more times than I care to admit."

"I can't get her out of my head or my heart, and I can't abandon my men."

"The simple take on the story."

"I'd hoped you, of all men, would understand."

"I do," Luke whispered hoarsely, his voice wavering. "I was once a lucky man. I know what it's like to be loved by a magnificent woman and to kiss my lovely daughters goodnight. The war stole them from me, but your burden is much greater."

"How can I save her? Every time she leaves the castle, she puts herself at risk, and now I'm one of the reasons she leaves."

"I don't know that you can."

"I won't sacrifice my men. There's no honor in it."

"You've stepped in it, lad," Luke said, his voice bordering on his usual sarcasm.

"After all these years, I don't believe you've ever seen me pine over a woman." Nicholas felt foolish saying such a thing, but he had unintentionally strained his friendship with Luke in the midst of his own suffering.

"I'll stand by you, lad, as long as you're not too bloody foolish."

Nicholas stole a glance toward Luke. He could just make out the hint of a reluctant smile.

∼

Standing on the stone dais in front of her father's throne, Meg wore her best gown, waiting for the festivities to begin. A form-fitting bliaut with a short train made of white silk, the gown was embroidered with gold thread in intricate scrolls around the collar and from her knees to her hemline. A gold belt adorned with delicate rubies hung low on her waist and accentuated pleats that gathered around her. The sleeves puffed at her shoulder. More gold brocade wrapped tightly on her upper arms and led to gold-trimmed, elegant sleeves that fell almost to the floor. Her ladies had meticulously curled her hair and it fell below her waist in long, full waves. She wore her princess's crown, thin and gold, set with single pearls on top, like a garden full of white daffodils placed in a row.

Presently, it was her duty to oversee a knighting ceremony and banquet. Her father, brothers, and all the ministers of war had retreated to a castle in the country to choose a commander and plan a new offensive. There they would make the final plans for the battle that would soon come. Hopefully, a very sound and harsh treaty to extricate the Edmiran army once Asterias triumphed would follow.

She knew that the armies were headed for another great battle, but this one had a sense of finality to it. It was as if both sides knew they were running out of air, the lungs gasping for what little breath was left. Both kingdoms would have difficulty gleaning their resources for the monumental effort it would take to strike the killing blow.

Meg walked to the bottom of the dais and took the ceremonial sword from her uncle, Lord Ellesworth, her mother's oldest brother and her godfather. A pageboy laid the velvet pillow for kneeling at the bottom of the stairs and she began the long process of knighting men. With difficulty, she kept her emotions in check as she thought about all these strong, healthy men going to the battlefield. Most of them were so young, not much older than herself. Her arms shook each time she raised the sword over their heads and shoulders to dub them. Struck by their willingness to serve what seemed like a lost cause, her heart broke.

After the ceremony, Meg stood behind the high table, toasted their accomplishments, and thanked them for their service to king and country to much applause. She sat down to begin her meal when her uncle walked up to her.

"My lady?" Lord Ellesworth beckoned. "May I approach?"

"Come forward, Uncle."

"Would you do me the honor of giving a speech to inspire the men?" he asked, taking the chair next to hers.

"Oh," Meg said, caught off guard. "I hadn't intended ... Well, I didn't think they'd want to hear from me."

She suddenly lamented the absence of her father. He was so good at speaking to his subjects, so good at inspiring their confidence and convincing them to do what he no longer could do for himself. He needed these men to fight for him. Why did he leave it to her to galvanize a new force of knights? Meg remembered watching her father when she was a child, marveling at how much the people adored their king, how they shouted his name, tossed rose petals under his feet, and felt honored to do whatever he asked of them. They were willing because he took care of them. He was a good king. The fates had smiled upon him as a young man and provided a way for him to care for his people, even during a time of war. And they loved him for it.

"In the king's absence and even your brothers," Lord Ellesworth began, "the men need a reason to fight. Here and now, they have no symbol, no banner to give them courage, no light in the darkness, except fighting for freedom. We've all lived with that vague notion for years." He sighed in frustration and looked around the room, tapping his fingers on the table. As Meg watched his profile, she noticed for the first time how his features seemed so familiar. She'd studied portraits of her mother her entire life, but even at his age, Meg could see the resemblance, the same shape and color of the eyes, the high cheekbones, the lilting smile even when he was sad.

"I'm sorry, Uncle, but what do you mean?"

"Forgive me for saying so because I love him as my brother," Lord Ellesworth said, lowering his voice so only she could hear, "but your father has lost the heart for fighting. It happened when your mother died. I understand this perfectly because I also lost your mother, my youngest and dearest sister. William Henry, named after my own father, will rule with an iron fist when he gets the chance. Not necessarily what Asterias needs at the moment. John Paul is known throughout the realm as handsome, brave, valiant, strong, and in military circles for his excellent work in battle planning. There is no question he could lead."

"I think he has you to thank for that," Meg said, smiling wistfully at her uncle. "I was always jealous of the times when you took him under your wing to instruct him."

Lord Ellesworth paused, his face etched with deep lines of sorrow. Meg thought she understood him. The loss of his sister, the king's failures, the eldest heir undeserving of the crown, the war almost lost, all thrown into a mournful stew that was difficult to chew and near impossible to swallow. How had they borne these tragedies?

"I will do as you ask," she said, looking into his doleful eyes. "I owe it to my father, to you, and to these men." She stood and walked to the front of the high table on the dais. "Although, you must know," she said over her shoulder to him, "it terrifies me to death."

He chuckled softly behind her.

"I believe that this will be the final battle." Her voice rung so loud in the great hall that it surprised her. They stopped and stared at their princess in stony silence. No more loud conversation, no more raucous laughter, no more vigorous displays of bravado from the young bodies eager for soldiering. No more musicians playing or jesters juggling. Just an echo of her voice rebounding off the stone walls, back to her.

Upon seeing their reaction, Meg could've melted into the floor. Her brows pressed together, her palms sweating. A lump formed in her throat. She swallowed hard and tried again.

"I know that we have done nothing but fight all of our lives," Meg continued, nervously regarding their fervent response to her. "And we are tired, fatigued to death, but if you can muster your hearts once more, I think this is the one battle that will finally end it.

"I know that you believe that there is little to fight for, that this ceremony and feast are nothing but a fraud to show support for a broken-down king and his ailing kingdom. But I can assure you, it's not true. I have faith in our king and his advisors. Right now, they are working on plans that will surprise and overwhelm our enemy. And we have much to fight for — our very lives and our freedom.

"I beg you to walk the galleries in the castle and see what a history we have. See what your king, my father, and his father before him have accomplished. And many others in support of our cause. We, as a people, have won important battles. We have driven the enemy out of our country many times before, and I believe that we can and will do it again.

"I beg for your loyalty, bravery, and courage. You will decide the outcome of the battle. You will determine whether or not we send this vicious enemy back to hell, right where it belongs." Meg didn't know what else to say, had no idea how to excuse herself and sit down.

Suddenly, her uncle appeared beside her to speak. "When we are in the heat of battle and the trenches of warfare, we feel uneasy and so we look to you, our beautiful princess, to inspire us. You are the one who instills in us the courage to fight. And that's all a soldier needs, to see a pretty face smiling at him and hear sweet words of encouragement whispered in his ear, as he tries to gain the confidence he needs to risk his own life for a greater good."

"You humble me, my lord."

"We will fight for you, won't we, men?" Lord Ellesworth called to the crowd with a pump of his fist as they cheered. "You are the one who helps us remember what we are fighting for when the world around us turns ugly, strewn with dead men and chaos, blackness and smoke."

Meg stood for a long moment, her head down, her hands clasped in front of her, trying to compose her thoughts. "Then I will not let you down," she replied as she looked up to face the crowd, silent once again. "I will be here for you. And when we win, you will be rewarded. I promise that I will be your advocate. I will fight for what you need. You have served this house so well. We owe you nothing less."

"Then let us dance!" Lord Ellesworth gestured with an outstretched hand. Meg placed her hand in his and let him lead her to the dance floor. Other couples gathered around them in anticipation. When the music started and she began to dance, skipping and hopping in time, she wrapped her arm around her uncle's waist and held her other hand high as they twirled together. The exertion made her weak and lightheaded. She hadn't eaten anything but the evening meal. Meg knew she would soon faint and tried to signal Lady Byron. Too late.

Sound faded and then came darkness. As light entered her consciousness, so did the muted white world of winter. Lovely, thick flakes of snow fell all around her. She sat astride a beautiful white charger. Dressed to royal perfection, she wore a long, deep-purple cloak trimmed with ermine that covered her completely. It fell below the flank of her horse. Long locks of her hair escaped the ties and fluttered softly in front of her. She looked down to see her gloved hands holding the reins and clutching her horse's long mane as it slowly cantered forward.

"Are you all right, my lady?" Lord Ellesworth asked urgently. He held her from falling to the ground as she slumped against his chest. As she came to, Meg tried to understand the meaning of the vision. In her entire life observing her father and hearing stories about faraway kingdoms, she'd never heard of such a thing. A princess sitting on a horse on a snowy plain. Doing what? She would wonder about the meaning of it for a long time.

"May I walk you to your chamber, my lady?" her uncle asked kindly. "You may still need a shoulder to lean on."

"Yes," Meg answered before Lady Byron could speak. "Thank you, my Lord Ellesworth."

16
STILL FALLING

Early afternoon sun lengthened the shadows near the lake by the time Nicholas arrived. Pleased at not having seen any troops within a league or so, he still worried that Meg would not be there. What if she decided that she never wanted to see him again? Or worse, what if harm had come her way? He'd never forgive himself. Reaching the edge of the cliffs that surrounded the lake, he slipped from his horse and led the animal down the steep path to a gathering of tall pine. He tied the sturdy brute to a branch and walked through the trees.

And there she was.

Meg's beauty assaulted his senses, just as if a hardy breeze swept past him and carried with it fresh air, fragrance, with delicate particles from the earth penetrating his skin. She sat on the ground in the shade behind a large rock, her cloak spread beneath her. Looking off into the distance, she did not notice him until he said hello. She turned her head and her eyes lit up, glorious light green pools that mirrored the lake nearby. He walked toward her, his jaw slack, his heart pounding. Meg made no attempt to rise to her feet, but she straightened her back and smiled.

"I was worried about you," she said, her brows drawn together with concern.

"Were you now?" he sassed back, gingerly sitting beside her. "I'm always worried about you. I should not ask a lady to meet me in the woods with everything that's going on out there."

"They're getting closer, aren't they, Nicholas?" Meg whispered with a hint of fear.

"I'm afraid they are." Nicholas couldn't help touching her cheek again to brush her hair away from her face. "But it's my job to know where they are. I will keep you out of harm's way. I promise."

"Where is your companion?" Meg scanned the area, trying to find Luke.

"Probably the same place as yours." Nicholas smiled at her mischievously. "Nearby, but not here."

Meg laughed. It was a quiet little giggle that showed him her teeth in a broad, beautiful smile.

Pushing his cloak backward and unhooking the scabbard of his sword to get more comfortable, Nicholas winced as he lay down beside her. The pain from an arrow grazing his hip began to bite.

"What happened to you?" She cocked her head and scanned his torso, her eyes narrowing with concern.

"Oh, it's not much. Just an arrow."

"You were shot with an arrow?" She was incredulous.

"It's just a scratch."

"You were shot with an arrow today and still came to see me?"

"Not shot, almost shot," Nicholas clarified. "We've had a few scuffles lately," he answered, shrugging his shoulders. "Wild horses could not have kept me away."

While Meg's mouth curled into a slight grin, the fire in her eyes told him she wanted to slap him. Nicholas smiled to himself, knowing that he could tease her. He detected precociousness in her and couldn't wait for her to sass back. They lay down on their cloaks side-by-side and looked up at the sky. Through arching, graceful branches, they watched odd-shaped leaves turning a brilliant red, some falling to the ground. As he adjusted his body for comfort, his elbow fell onto her hip, his hand lingering on her thigh. He should've removed it, but it felt ... right.

"Tell me more about the places you've been with the army." Meg turned on her side and propped her head on a hand while she drew circles on his arm.

"All over, Meg. I wouldn't know where to start," he replied tiredly, the pain in his hip growing uncomfortable.

"Please, Nicholas." She affected a shrewd pout and looked at him with big, round eyes. "You have no idea how jealous I am that you've traveled all over and I've rarely even been out of the city. Meeting you in secret is the greatest adventure of my life."

"Does that work with all the men in your life?"

"I don't know what you're talking about." She avoided eye contact and looked down to dust and straighten her long skirt, playing the innocent.

"That sweet little thing you just did with your eyes? Who could ever refuse?"

Meg met his gaze and then swatted his injured hip. Nicholas practically jumped out of his skin with the shock of sudden pain, but he was having too much fun flirting to care. He leaned over and pinned her to the ground, arms over her head.

"Well, since you've been so deprived..." he said through gritted teeth as his hip throbbed.

"I'm so sorry, Nicholas." She tried hard not to smile, suppressing a giggle. "I forgot which hip got hurt. It's just that you were teasing me, so I had to punish you."

"So, that's how it works. I see now." He rolled onto his back once more and let his hands fall to his chest. "I have a better idea."

∽

"But you're hurt," Meg protested when she realized Nicholas wanted to show her how to sword fight.

"It's nothing but a mosquito bite. I'll live." Nicholas gestured toward his hip. "It's not fighting with a sword that I want to teach you, although it is quite fun." He cocked a playful brow in her direction. "Just a few fast moves to get you away from a bad man if, heaven forbid, anything like that should happen. I feel guilty enough asking you to travel in a dangerous countryside to meet me."

"All right," Meg agreed hesitantly.

"Come here, then. Let me show you a couple of things," Nicholas said, standing behind her. "If you can get in position to turn your back on your attacker, you can use the butt of your sword to surprise and disarm him by knocking the wind out of him. See how that works?" He guided her body through the moves, his warm hands magnetic. She could feel the tingling, the pull of her body toward his. "You may also be able to strike him in the knees and when he bends over, kick him in the face and break his nose. He'll drop his sword when that happens."

"What do I do then?"

"Run like the devil, sweetheart."

They stood in such close proximity to each other that Meg felt awkward. How she just wanted to fall into his arms. Nicholas must've felt it, too. He cleared his throat and changed the subject.

"Can you get your hands on a cloak like mine? The cloak you have is fine for the city, but in the country I think you would do better with something larger, and green. Make it dark green."

"I suppose so. Why?"

"Because you need to go unnoticed," he explained as he took her hand and pulled her toward him. "It will not only shield you from the elements, but it will keep you hidden in dark allies or in the forest. Blend into the shadows. An adversary could walk right by and never see you if you know how to disappear. Be firm, be strong, and never panic," he emphasized, pointing his finger at her. "He could be a hand's width away from your face and not see you. If you don't move, don't even breathe, you'll be safe."

"Is it really that dangerous out here?" Meg furrowed her brows in concentration. Of course, she knew the dangers in leaving the castle. John Paul had taught her well.

"If you don't attract attention, you'll be fine." He placed his hand on the back of her neck and pulled her face toward his. For a splendid moment, she thought he was going to kiss her, but he kissed her forehead instead.

Disappointed and unwilling to let the moment go just yet, Meg raised a sardonic brow and issued a challenge. "What about a killing shot? Could you teach me that?" She loved being in his arms as he taught her how to escape and wanted just one more excuse to be close to him.

"You bet," he grinned, looking down into her face. "But first I need to see if you can wield a sword."

"Wait, what?" Meg stammered, her stomach clenching into a tight knot and her mouth became dry. She instantly regretted asking him. How could she have been so stupid? She already knew how to wield a sword, somewhat, thanks to her brother.

No need to worry.

Meg parried his blows like a clumsy fool. Even if she'd given her whole effort into fighting him, it would not have mattered. Nicholas was toying with her. He didn't put his full speed or strength into the effort. Still, she was amazed at the resounding power behind the sword. He must be an absolute demon on the battlefield, she thought, never taking her eyes off his slashing sword. When Meg clashed her sword to avoid a killing blow to the head, it occurred to her how much fun it would be to watch Nicholas and John Paul practice in an arena. She'd never seen two swordsmen equally matched fight to exhaustion.

"What are you smiling about?" Nicholas asked, lowering his sword.

"It's nothing, really." Meg couldn't help it. Her smile reached ridiculous proportions, stretching across her face.

"I've made it my life's goal to see that you smile. I have selfish reasons for that, so I'd like to know what it is that makes you smile."

"You and my brother seem equally matched in sword fighting. I was thinking how interesting it would be to see you two practice."

"I see," Nicholas smiled and circled her. "It seems you've learned a bit from watching him."

"I don't know about that," Meg scoffed, thinking of her training with John Paul. "He mostly just torments me."

"Ah, well. That's what brothers are for." He cocked his head, giving her a crooked smile. "Are you ready for more?" He wiped sweat from his brow and readied his stance.

"How can one ever be ready for a wolf lunging for the throat?" She widened her eyes, raised her brows, and gave him a thin-lipped, sarcastic smile.

Nicholas gave her a double-take and then stood quite still, as if she'd said something that surprised him. His expression was unreadable as he stood staring at her.

"Fair point." He said it quietly and nodded his head, somehow assessing her, and then took a fighter's stance.

Swordplay with John Paul was like dancing — slower, precise, even artful. Swordplay with Nicholas was like getting charged by a bull, powerful, relentless, unpredictable.

"This makes no sense, Nicholas," Meg said, tossing her sword to the ground. "Why make me do this? I'll never win."

"You'll never win an engagement with a man," he replied matter-of-factly. "You're not strong enough, but you're skilled enough to get away and that's what I wanted to see. You're actually very good for a..."

"Don't say it," Meg said, quite cross. She scowled at him, folding her arms across her chest.

"All right," Nicholas said, suppressing a smile. "I was going to say for someone who hasn't been extensively trained. You didn't give me the chance." He turned from her and hid his short sword in the crevice of a tree.

"Why are you doing that?" Meg asked, watching him curiously. "I can't be that helpless, can I?"

"You're not helpless at all," Nicholas said as he walked up to her. He put his hands on her waist and looked into her eyes. "It's one of the things I love about you. Let's just call this an extra safeguard. I would never forgive myself if something happened to you." He picked up the other short sword, stood in fighting position, and waggled his eyebrows comically. "Let me show you how to make a man fall on his back so you can stab him straight through the heart."

"Ah, you know the path to my heart," Meg smiled, patting her hand playfully over her heart, and walked toward him. Of course, she secretly hoped she'd get one more chance to be in his embrace.

For an autumn day, the sun shone quite warm, but the shade of the ripening oaks brought an occasional chill. The evening settled on them prematurely as the shadows stretched and bent across the silent lake. The plaintive song of a bird would now and then course through the trees toward them, but they had passed into another world.

"Nicholas?"

"Hmm?" he answered as she roused him from a gentle doze.

"I'm sorry to say it, but I think it's time to leave."

"Just a little longer," he pleaded and pulled her hand onto his chest. He kissed the palm of her hand and caressed her wrist. He laid his lips to her tender skin and began a slow journey up her arm.

She sighed breathlessly. "What are you doing to me?"

"Begging you not to leave."

"How can I leave?"

"You are the most enchanting woman I've ever met. I wish I could court you properly, so you know just how devastated I am by one look of those green eyes."

She sat up and smiled at him, her eyes warm and loving. "Of all the men I know, I've never been so drawn to a man in all my life. Were it not for the war, I might consider ... I don't know ... doing something rash."

Nicholas closed his eyes and sighed. "And I'd guess there have been plenty of men in your life."

She gave him a knowing look, lay down beside him, and placed her head on the heavy muscle below his shoulder. As she snuggled closer to him, he closed his eyes again and blessed her with a sigh. He stroked her arm that crossed his chest, her delicate hand resting on his collarbone. His mind sailed above the trees, floating above ground. He could feel nothing but her.

Meg shifted her body closer to his and kissed his cheek, sensuously, and far better than any woman ever had. He couldn't remember a woman who seemed to need the soft touches and warm embraces as she did.

Nicholas rolled onto his side and looked at her lips. With his finger, he stroked them gently, wondering if he should kiss her. He wanted to devour her, but he could think of a thousand reasons why he should not. The relationship had no future, even though he prayed that fate would somehow deliver a miracle. He loved her too much to taste her lips perhaps never to do so again.

Suddenly, he heard something and strained his ears in the direction of his horse. The animal was restless. Together they peeked from behind the rock to see a knight on horseback walking on the other side of the lake. It was far, but Nicholas recognized that bald head anywhere.

Prince William's friend.

Meg gasped, covered her mouth with her hand, and retreated to her cloak.

"Do you know him?" Nicholas whispered urgently, watching to make sure the knight climbed out of the depression and back into the forest.

"Not at all." Meg shook her head and frowned.

"Then why are you so surprised to see him?"

"I've seen him before ... at ... at the castle," she stammered.

"Did he follow you here?"

Her eyes grew large, shocked at his question. "Why would he?"

"What's his name?" Nicholas's spies had not yet returned with this vital bit of intelligence.

Meg stood up, a look of panic dawning on her face. She paced a short path, turning abruptly every few steps while she gnawed on her thumbnail.

"I must go, I think, Nicholas." Meg packed up the few things she'd brought. She tried to tie her cloak, but her fingers would not cooperate and she became instantly frustrated.

"May I help you?" he asked, a little amused. He placed both hands on her shoulders and fiddled with the tie, hoping to calm her down.

"No! I must go," she stomped impatiently.

"Not with him out there, you're not," Nicholas said more forcefully. He placed a hand under her chin and lifted her face to his. "I can see the man has got you a bit rattled. Are you well?"

"Yes, yes, I'm fine," Meg insisted. "It's just ... I don't know. I thought that I was smart enough to be safe. Maybe my master has missed me! Maybe that's why he's out here!" She sighed in sudden realization and melted into his arms.

Nicholas held her tight. "Just stay with me for a while and I'll make sure you get back safely. I promise."

They spent perhaps another half an hour lying in each other's arms, he doing his best to comfort her as she trembled. They said little. Their breathing and gentle touching of hands and arms said everything. She turned away from him, her back to his belly. He wrapped his arms snugly around her waist. He couldn't resist touching her lovely hair. What glory, he thought. Will I ever get over her? Can I go on without her? She turned onto her back, her head toward him, and stared into his eyes. He looked down at her and felt more emotion surge through his soul than he had ever imagined possible. Reaching down, he placed his palm on her cheek, bent over, and kissed her on the temple.

It had haunted him with its translucent fairness ever since he had seen the breeze blow it back during their encounter in the forest. Nicholas could scarcely believe that he had his lips pressed to it. But the time had come. Meg pulled away from him, stood up, and pulled her cloak around her shoulders against the gathering chill of the evening. She faced him with a sad smile and walked into his embrace once more. When she turned away from him, she breathed deeply as she stood tall, summoning her courage, and walked ahead of him out of their retreat and into the dark woods.

17
REVELATIONS

"I can't believe the king is dead," Nicholas whispered to Luke. "Everyone in Edmira must be reeling from the shock." Commander Burrage had gathered his high-ranking officers to deliver the news. They'd finished another long day of training on a nearby plain where it was overcast and cold, but dusty. Laden with sweat and grime, Nicholas couldn't wait to get his hands on a cup of mead and some warm stew. Nicholas and Luke sat in the rear of the congregation slumped on a log, hands on their knees, heads together as they spoke.

"Rumors among the officers say that old King Colestus just dropped dead," Luke replied, sitting up straight to stretch his back. "He was older but seemed to be in good health. One can't help but wonder if one of his seven sons tainted his wine with the bitter dust of some herb to push him out of this world a bit faster."

"The eldest son, Caius, has already been crowned, but I wonder if he has the support of his brothers? There are whispers of an illness..." Nicholas frowned, rubbing his hands tiredly over his face.

"You mean his ruthlessness?" Luke slapped his knees in mock realization. "Now in that regard, he has a grand reputation. None can impale better than Caius. Or was that his father, Colestus? I can't keep track of them all."

"There's that," Nicholas agreed, "but word has filtered to us that Caius goes through long periods of silence, as if he were in a trance, and then experiences violent fits of rage. There seems to be little time when he is rational. Great Mother Earth, Luke, there will be nothing left to fight for."

"Oh, hold on there, laddie," Luke warned. "Nothing has changed for us." He put a fatherly hand on Nicholas's shoulder and looked at him. "That's the real reason for this meeting."

"Well, that's not quite true." Nicholas sat back and folded his arms across his chest. "It changes everything at the top, especially if the sons are fighting for the throne. For us, the grunts who do their dirty work, it changes nothing. When Commander Burrage announced the meeting, I hoped it would be to tell us that they had come to an accord with Asterias." He sighed, acknowledging his naivety.

"Oh, no, laddie. You're dreaming. Our orders are the same as always, no matter who's in charge. They want their land back and rightly so."

"Rightly so?" Nicholas scowled and then whispered furiously. "I have no idea what we are fighting for anymore, Luke. Until recently, I thought that we had a just cause. I thought Asterias was a rebellious and runaway province that thumbed its nose at its ruler and dared the king and army to try and take it back. Now I see a country that has earned the right to be left alone. They obtained it through victory in battle many years ago, but we have not been content to leave them alone."

"You and your rules..." Luke sighed. "You always have some dreamy notion about what is unacceptable, this distressing sense of fair play in battle. I'm not sure it exists, Nicholas."

"Perhaps not, but if we don't have rules, then we're bloody animals. Asterias has too much bounty for the kings of Edmira to ignore. They cannot stop wanting it, even though it has not been theirs for hundreds of years. All I can see is fighting among our leaders, brothers willing to kill for power, and an unclear objective except just to kill and conquer. I don't know anymore."

"Those are treasonous words, man," Luke whispered, nervously looking ahead of them to make sure none of the other men heard. "Best not go spreading that about."

"Don't worry, my friend," Nicholas smiled and clapped Luke on the back. "I'm not the idiot you think."

"One more thing you should know before we crowd the mess tent for supper," Commander Burrage called from the front of the men, trying to recapture their attention. "King Colestus proposed marriage to the Princess Marguerite before he died."

"And Caius, if he's the hound we've heard he is," Luke whispered out of the side of his mouth, "will put out feelers to see if another proposal would be so ardently rejected. Do you think the women back home are sows or some awful thing?"

"Sows?" Nicholas tried not to laugh.

"I don't recall the women being that homely. I can't imagine why Caius can't find some handsome duchess," Luke said, circumspect. "Of course, it's been a very long time since I've looked at women with interest. And you, well, you're looking at the most beautiful one I've seen in a while."

Nicholas cleared his throat and felt heat rising in his cheeks.

"It's a development that we will need to keep an eye on," Commander Burrage continued. "King Caius may make a similar offer to the Asterian government, and if he does, then that changes everything for us."

"Caius has no sons and will need to sire an heir quickly if he's to keep his throne from the dirty hands of his younger brothers, assuming they are in league against him," Nicholas expounded. "We've all heard the stories about the princess, that her beauty can bring a man to his knees just by gazing into her glorious face." He paused, looking at Luke, who looked ready to burst with laughter, and shrugged. "That's what the men say, but she's been indulged by her father. She's not going to marry an enemy king. She has no reason to, especially if she knows her own father won't use her to meet his ends as ruler."

"Smart woman," Luke admitted, watching the reactions of the other captains. Some held their heads together in quiet conversation as Burrage talked with one of his aids. "Maybe we underestimated old King Colestus. Perhaps he really did want to end the war. A marriage to unite the countries and an heir produced from the union would do that."

"If he succeeded in doing that, it would be a pretense at best. It has been developing for some time, but I think the mission of the Edmiran kings is only to conquer," Nicholas said, shaking his head. "A newborn son wouldn't live a long life, not with seven already vying for the crown. If they're not beyond killing their own father, they would have no qualms about killing an interloping young prince and a foreign princess after that. The Asterian king would know that."

"I think you're right. Let them deal with their foolish politics," Luke said, standing up and twisting at the waist to loosen his back as Commander Burrage dismissed them. "I'm famished. Let's get some grub."

~

As Nicholas and Luke walked back toward their tents in the afterglow of a silver sunset, they noticed a man on horseback leaving camp. Nicholas squinted and stared, watching him go.

"Do you know him?" Luke asked.

"There's something familiar about him," Nicholas said, dread weighing on his shoulders. "Cursed cloaks with hoods. I can't see a thing, but I'll bet my wages that man is bald."

"Says the man who uses a cloak to savage perfection," Luke chortled.

"You didn't by chance see him at the lake, did you?" Nicholas asked, ignoring the joke.

"I saw a knight wander through and then find a place to change from his showy armor to the more obscure clothing of a mercenary," Luke said, "but I didn't think it wise to engage him. He didn't seem intent on harm. Besides, I was too busy cleaning my nails, so I wouldn't have to watch you canoodle with the lass. It's a tortuous affair for me, watching you. I try to keep my distance."

"We don't canoodle," Nicholas grimaced at Luke's wry humor. "I taught her to fight the other day."

"I saw. Not bad for a lass."

"How did I not know that this...?" Nicholas struggled over the words, raking a hand roughly through his hair. "This errant knight, whoever he is, is a ruddy spy."

"I think you've been a bit preoccupied." Luke said, shrugging and quirking a sardonic smile.

Nicholas stormed to Commander Burrage's tent, barged in, and found that he was already in conference with his aides. "Sir, I must speak with you now," he demanded, pacing in front of him.

"Not now, Captain," the commander replied diffidently as he studied letters at his desk. He did not even raise his head to acknowledge Nicholas. "As you can see, I am busy."

"Sir, it's urgent. It's regarding the man I've just seen leaving our headquarters."

The commander sighed. He dismissed his aides, leaned back in his chair, and surveyed the young captain for a few moments. "His name is Brantley, the Duke of Breckenridge," Burrage said, "and he brings news of a change in the kingdom's battle plan and a promise to deliver the princess to King Caius."

"How is that possible when the King of Asterias himself will not offer his daughter as part of a treaty? Even if this knight could deliver, what will he get from us in return?"

"His own province in the south when Asterias becomes ours again," the commander said tiredly as he gathered his papers into a pile. "Personally, I think he plans to steal the princess for himself."

"Her again." Nicholas moaned and sat down.

"She's more of a player in this than we anticipated. Many of the Asterian troops carry her banner. They fight for her. The king is weak and the kingdom is falling, but the heirs remain defiant. There will be no surrender. They will fight to the bitter end. This is not good news, Captain, now that they have something to fight for."

"What news does he bring?" Nicholas asked, now a little more calmly. "How have they altered their plans?"

"The younger prince has hidden away a large force of archers in the country."

"We already know he plans to use archers."

"He must've suspected Edmiran spies in his midst." The commander paused and gave Nicholas a look of disdain, insinuating that Breckenridge already knew the spy. The idea was ludicrous. While Nicholas had seen the man with Prince William and at the lake, he was certain that the bald son-of-a-bitch had never laid eyes on him. "He changed the location of the battle," Burrage continued, "the position of the archers, and other important aspects. Breckenridge gave us the new intelligence."

"Sir, I urge you, do not consider seriously a single thing this man says." Nicholas stood and paced, gesturing with his hands. "He was with Prince William the night I attempted to assassinate him. I heard them talk. Breckenridge has already promised the prince armies and armadas for autonomous rule, which to my knowledge, he has not delivered. The prince has already promised him his sister if the alliance with Caius fails. He's playing both sides of the war to his advantage. He will get what he wants regardless of the outcome. You cannot possibly trust him."

"I don't trust him," Burrage replied, irritated, "but I can't ignore him, either. Not if he can help me win."

18
SUSPICIONS

"And just what are you about, young lady?" came the brusque, rumbling voice of the castle's head cook and Lewin's father, Malcolm Cooksey. A few years older than the king, having served him since his coronation, Cooksey was a short, stout man, but brawny. No one would ever mistake him for a doughy baker. He had the thickest forearms Meg had ever seen, along with greying copper hair, freckled skin, and a bushy mustache.

Like a child caught with her hand in the cookie jar, Meg startled at his voice. Embarrassed, she turned around, wiped crumbs from her mouth, and assumed her most charming smile.

"Aside from sneaking one of Tilly's pastries, I've come because I want everything to be perfect for my father's return."

"As you wish, my lady," Cooksey replied, shrugging unenthusiastically as he cut slabs of meat on the butcher block. "Even though it pains me to watch your pig-of-a-brother return along with him and enjoy himself on the coattails of the king. William deserves the gallows for the way he treats you."

"I'm concerned about my father right now," Meg said, deflecting Cooksey's criticism, hoping that none of kitchen staff overheard and were sympathetic to William. She didn't think they were. He'd been unkind or cruel to just about every servant in the castle, but still, one never knew for certain of their loyalties. She stood beside him at the table and whispered so only he could hear. "Let us not give anyone a reason to tell my brother your true feelings, please, Cooksey." She looked at him with wide, pleading eyes. "I need you."

He wriggled his mustache a little and then winked at her.

"I guess there's a reason I can't refuse the child, eh, Tilly?" he said to his wife, who gave him a knowing smirk as she pulled more confections out of the oven. "Ah, little Meggie, I've been watching you outwit him your whole life and I've enjoyed every minute of it."

"Tell me the menu again." Meg sat on a barrel cross-legged near the butcher block.

"Well, let's see," Cooksey began. "I sent the young prince's advance guard of archers far into the hills for game. I'll get the butchers to kill us some pigs and chickens, and we'll roast 'em. It won't be a fancy feast, but it will fill hungry bellies and it'll taste good, or I'll go to my grave swearing that I was born to the wrong profession."

Meg couldn't help but roll her eyes at him. He was brilliant in the kitchen.

"I have no doubt that it will be good. I just want to prove to my father that I am responsible enough while they are gone to provide a decent meal upon their return. Besides, I want to listen to everything they have to say."

"There it is. The real motive."

She raised a single eyebrow and gave him a crooked grin. "Indeed."

◈

HER STOMACH CLENCHED INTO A KNOT WHEN MEG REALIZED she would be sitting next to the Duke of Breckenridge at the high table with William on his other side. It was the ideal spot to eavesdrop, but he made her skin crawl. She would rather have watched and listened to him from a distance. The men were seated around large wooden tables in the great hall with an abundance of attendants on staff.

Though a humble feast by royal standards, it was tasty and filling, and everyone there knew they were lucky to get a good meal at all. Things would get meager the closer they got to the next onslaught, as most of the supplies would go to the army. John Paul's archers had saved the day. They brought back delicious deer, elk, and even a boar from their hunt, which Cooksey roasted to perfection in pits outside the kitchen. With the addition of multiple vegetable dishes and Tilly's soft rolls and pastries, Meg could not have hoped for more. The soldiers kept toasting their princess and thanking her for the food.

"Your Majesty." Lord Cronmiller stood to address the king, raising his hand for a toast. A tall angular man with sallow skin, an aquiline nose, and bags under his eyes, he wore the traditional black robes and round felt hat of a minister. Meg noticed that he fingered the large links of the necklace hanging about his shoulders and down the front of his chest, an ornament that demonstrated to everyone how much authority was vested in him. "I want you to know I'm quite satisfied with these plans," he continued. "With William Henry as the new commander-in-chief, John Paul as an adjutant and chief commander of the archers, and all their aides and advisors, we've superior leadership and a most outstanding battle plan, thanks to your sons. How can we lose? Here, here!"

Meg almost choked on her wine. Trembling, she put her goblet down on the table, but it nearly toppled. Did she hear that properly? William was the new commander? How could her father have done it? Nauseated and sweating, Meg almost put her hands to her ears when the men erupted in a loud cacophony of cheering. She felt like she was in the middle of a vast, swirling vortex of men that could sweep anything along with them to the battlefield.

Meg caught sight of Lord Cronmiller drifting from noble to noble, shaking hands and patting shoulders as he went, when he stopped to speak with the Duke of Breckenridge. As they watched the antics of the men, the minister appeared quite happy and at ease as he rocked from his heels to his toes, hands behind his back with a satisfied grin. The duke darted his beady little eyes around the room, as he always did. If Cronmiller suspected Breckenridge of foul plotting, he didn't show it.

She could think of nothing but the duke after she'd seen him at the lake. What business did he have in Edmiran territory? Breckenridge was neither stealthy nor subtle. Meg had a hard time imagining him going anywhere and not being recognized as a knight from the Asterian realm, the name of his homeland emblazoned on his breastplate and shield. How could anyone not know this man? Then she realized that if she could disguise herself so easily, so could he. It wouldn't be hard to cache his belongings and hide under a cloak. How could she be so convinced of Breckenridge's treachery and her brother be so oblivious to it? William must have his reasons to trust him. One thing she comprehended fully about her brother was that he was not a traitor to his country. He wanted the kingdom and the crown for himself.

"Have you heard talk of their great warrior, the Wolf Knight?" Breckenridge said to William. He sat down next to her brother, picked up his goblet, and took a long swig, his eyes in constant surveillance of the crowd. Meg realized that he wasn't as amused by the men as he was keenly aware of the action behind the scenes, discreet conversations at the tables, in the corners, behind the pillars.

"Nothing specific," William replied, signaling a servant for his third plate of venison. "Is he their savior then? Every army has a legendary warrior who will win the battle for them at the last moment."

"He could be their man," Breckenridge replied, circumspect. "Sources tell me he is an extraordinary fighter, an imposing figure of a man, dark and deadly with piercing blue eyes. He is fearless with no hesitation on the battlefield, and he has no equal in strength for wielding his weapons and unseating an opponent. The whores tell me they'd give up their earnings for a year to roll in the hay with him, but to no avail. Not lately, anyway." He drank from his goblet and swallowed hard, chuckling.

"A chaste warrior," William laughed. "How sweet."

"Well, he won't be worn down on the day of the battle. That much is true."

"And who is our man? Who do our soldiers revere?"

"Withstanding present company," Breckenridge said with an artful, cloying nod to William, "I'd say it's John Paul. No one compares to his organizational and training skills. He has done you a great service by championing that force of archers. He is an exceptional horseman and swordsman, and the women swoon in his presence, but I don't know if he has the stamina to outlast everyone on the battlefield. If the battle were to be decided by two lone fighters, John Paul and their Wolf Knight, there is no question in my mind who would win."

"So, we've got to kill the Wolf Knight ... before the battle."

"Yes, I think that would be best."

Meg chewed her food slowly as she contemplated what they had said. From William's perspective, it made perfect sense. Of course, he'd try to kill a formidable warrior who stood in the way of victory for Asterias. He considered himself a soldier and believed he had skill, but his opponents always let him win. Meg could tell during the matches, and the rumors filtered to her before long. If Breckenridge spied against Asterias and wanted to Edmira to win, then why would he support such an idea? Why wouldn't he suggest, cleverly as always, perhaps that wasn't the best idea after all? Maybe he just wanted to see two legendary warriors fight to the death and decide the battle? Maybe he could control the outcome if it came down to two men. And what would he get from King Caius if he pulled it off? If he were spying for Caius, then Caius would know how to use Breckenridge's services without making any promises, unlike William. He wouldn't get anything from the Edmiran king, so what was the man's motive? She felt the bottom of her stomach drop into gut-wrenching nausea. She would have to talk to William about this.

∽

"WHAT ARE YOU DOING HERE?" WILLIAM ASKED GROGGILY when he saw Meg sitting at the table next to the fireplace in his apartment. He had just gotten out of bed and looked more rumpled than ever. Disheveled and unshaven with nothing on except his nightshirt and a luxurious robe, he scraped calloused heels along the stone floor as he walked toward her.

Meg smiled sweetly and gestured to the table that she set with leftover rolls from dinner and warm milk.

William's chamber was much like the king's, only smaller and darker. While the king didn't find solace in lavish surroundings, his son most certainly did. The same extravagant chairs, cushions, carpets and tapestries made his room much like the antechamber near the great hall. He would never suffer discomfort if he could help it. William fell into the other chair and laid his head on the table. He covered it with his hands and moaned, the mussed up remains of his constant over-indulgence.

"Meg, what are you doing here?" he repeated insistently.

"It is my job as your sister and princess of the realm to present harmony between us for your future subjects."

"Oh, no, you don't." William waved a finger at her in warning. "The last thing I need right now is a conversation with the woman who stole the loyalty of my troops."

Surprised, Meg gaped at him.

"The men," he said, leveling a hard stare at her. "They march with your banner, not mine. I cannot inspire my own men to fight for me, their commander and future king."

"William, I am just as surprised by that as you. I will speak to our uncle Lord Ellesworth. He has encouraged them to carry the banner."

"You're up to no good, as usual," he said. "Now, tell me what you want or get out."

"Fine," Meg snapped, straightening up in her chair. She swallowed hard before proceeding, still wondering if it was a good idea to bring it up, but she had to know. "I wonder if your friend the duke is a spy."

William rested his head on his arms. He lay there silently, not moving for some time, which she thought rather odd. Meg expected a volcanic reaction.

He shuddered and laughed, pounding his fist on the table. "Let me get this straight." He sat up and looked at her. His brows shot together comically, a smug smile on his lips. "You think the Duke of Breckenridge is a spy for Edmira?" His rude guffaws were so uproarious that Meg thought they would claim the attention of his valet and his attendants. In fact, she thought he might fall out of his chair.

"What proof do you have, dear sister?" He sneered and grabbed some bread, shoving it into his mouth.

Meg's back was as straight as a flagpole. With her arms folded and pressed against her chest, her lips a taut line, she glared at her brother. "I have none, except my intuition."

She could not mention that she saw the duke at the lake, a location she knew was now in Edmiran territory.

"Women's intuition? You expect me to believe your suspicions based on some crazy notion that got stuck in your pretty little head?"

"I've been leery of him ever since he came. I see him sneaking around in dark corners of the castle, talking to people in huddled whispers, people I'm not sure we can trust."

"Stop. You're embarrassing yourself."

"William, please hear me out," Meg cried in frustration. "I've seen him sneaking out of the castle several times, and who knows where he goes? He follows me around as if I'm a child he has to keep in line."

"We both do, and not without warrant!" he yelled. Laughing one moment, angry the next. She always had to balance her act when she was with him. She felt like the lone trainer in an arena with a silly little whip in her hand, trying to keep a ferocious lion at bay.

"And he acts like he lives here. I know he expects to rule the southern reaches of the kingdom, your future kingdom, on his own. I think he has too much to gain by being disloyal to you."

He said nothing as he filled a cup from the pitcher and took a sip.

"You brought milk to a man?" William roared and threw the goblet into the fireplace.

Flinching, Meg backed away from him. He stood up and grabbed her by the throat. When he backed her against the wall, he pressed her hard into it.

"You listen to me, you conniving, meddling little wench!" His saliva sprayed into her face. She winced. William grabbed Meg by the hair and pulled her head painfully farther back. "The Duke of Breckenridge works for me. Do you understand? When you see him do any number of things, like leave the castle on horseback, which is not unusual for a knight, you remember that he does so for me. He is my intelligence officer, so naturally he makes contact with the enemy. They think he is giving them information, but instead, he steals it from them for me."

"But how do you know he will not betray you?" Meg asked, struggling for breath and trying not to cry.

"I just know!" William bellowed into her face, a vile tempest blasting so close that she closed her eyes and tried to turn her face away from him.

"Remove your hands from my sister's throat, or this will not be the first time a younger prince has killed an older one. And trust me, it won't be over the throne."

It was John Paul, his whispered voice grinding low and

threatening like a storm unleashing its first warning signs of hail. When Meg opened her eyes, she could see John Paul's thunderous face looming behind William, his great broadsword pointing at William's shoulder. Still in William's clutches, Meg thanked the stars for Lady Byron, who must've run to see if John Paul had returned from training his archers. Foolish, foolish girl. She should've known William would never listen to anything she had say, no matter how important.

"The favored, fair-haired prince has returned at last," William sneered, his voice barbed with contempt.

"Let her go," John Paul said impatiently.

William pushed her away. She crumpled to the floor, hyperventilating as she clutched her throat. Meg stood and edged her way around the room, her back against the wall as she inched toward the door.

"You're not worth it," he uttered despicably. He turned toward John Paul, who backed away but kept his fighting stance. "When did you get back from gallivanting around the countryside, younger brother? How dare you barge into my chambers and tell me what to do?"

"This bit of news comes from father, William, so you had better listen and obey what he says." John Paul enunciated and lowered his sword as he walked closer to William. "You two will stay away from each other. If you happen to be in the same place at the same time for formal duties, you will abide by royal etiquette. We need to provide at least some semblance of harmony in our family. And you, William," he said, pointing his sword at him with slit eyes, "will have to deal with me if you ever lay hands on my sister again."

"Fine by me," William grumbled, switching his gaze between Meg and John Paul. "I will do what father asks only because I know I must, but I don't ever want to see you again, unless the duke requires it." He glared at Meg. "He admires you for some reason. You should lower your standards for romantic love, dear sister. He'd be the happiest man alive if you would just smile at him."

"This is about the Duke of Breckenridge?" John Paul asked, astonished.

"He gives me unwanted attention," Meg whispered.

"Better yet," William added, almost as an afterthought. "If throwing the hound off the scent is what you desire, let him have a trounce and he'll forget about you entirely. Men are like that, you know," he said, eyes glinting with malice.

"Watch your filthy mouth!" John Paul snarled in warning. He dropped his sword and charged William, slamming him against the wall, dagger flashing.

"Meg thinks he's a spy," William smirked, still in John Paul's grip, clearly bemused.

"Well, is he?" John Paul asked, pushing William harder against the wall, dagger at his throat. "Someone has been feeding intelligence to our enemy. I've had to change strategy twice already and I still hear back that it is possible that the enemy has yet another grasp of my battle plans. You'd better make sure it isn't Breckenridge." John Paul shoved William disgustedly and let go, sheathing his dagger.

"Just take her and get out." William gestured with his head, hands defiantly on his hips.

John Paul put his arm around Meg's shoulders and guided her out of William's chamber into the corridor. "Now, Meg, you're going to tell me exactly what you know about the Duke of Breckenridge."

19

DISCOVERY

"This is it," Nicholas said, shading his eyes against a bright afternoon sun. He sat astride his horse on a ridge overlooking an ancient village to the north and a deeply wooded area to the south. In between them lay a plain, very broad at one end and quite narrow at the other. The distance was perhaps two square leagues, although it was difficult to be exact. The more Nicholas studied the topography of the area, the more convinced he became. The lay of the land worked too well in favor of the Asterians and what he thought they planned to use against the Edmiran army.

Despite the possible discovery of the battlefield, all he could see in his mind's eye was the visage of a lovely young woman. He couldn't wait to see Meg again, but it would be to tell her goodbye. Keen and smart, she kept her eyes open and could outrun just about anyone, but as things grew tense in the countryside, he didn't want to take unnecessary chances.

"Bloody brilliant is what that is," Luke said, looking from one end of the plain to the other. His restless horse stomped nervously.

"I know what you mean. Their young prince has contemplated advantage of terrain and he has a great battle plan, but we can make this work in our favor."

"I'd love to hear how you think this terrain and our plan will give us the high ground, laddie. Because, frankly, I don't see it."

"That would be why you're second-in-command." Nicholas gave him a mischievous sidelong glance as he used charcoal to sketch a map of the battlefield.

Luke feigned a grimace and patted his fidgety horse.

"Do you see how the plain narrows at the west end there?" Nicholas pointed with charcoal still in his hand. "I believe that's where Asterias will align their men-at-arms with the archers on each side of them."

"There's no room to fight down there, man. Look at it. It's like a funnel that could syphon men and horses into their little death trap."

"We could spread the battle from the plain, up the hills and onto the ridges, and the forest if need be. That makes the most sense to me, Luke. I will advise the commander that our cavalry should charge first to see if they can destroy the spiked wooden walls protecting the archers, then spread out and flank."

"In theory."

"Things change in a heartbeat in the thick of battle." Nicholas held up the map as he drew to compare it to the landscape, trying to make an exact copy.

"Oh, aye. Need I remind you of the understatement, laddie?"

"I think it's possible. Despite their strategic battlefield advantage, we have thousands more heavily mounted and armed knights who could strike a fatal blow at the beginning of the battle. I must protect as many of them as I can. In addition to the cavalry charge, I would station our crossbowmen in the hills and forest on adjacent sides of the plain. They will remain hidden until ordered forth and sneak up behind them when no one expects it. No one will ever see them until they engage in the fight. We'll attack on both flanks, and then our foot soldiers will attack the center and move in for the final kill."

"You've left out one important thing there, lad." Luke's voice was laced with worry as his horse snorted and shook its head. "The most crucial element they've got, but we don't."

"Longbows. I've lost a good deal of sleep over that." Nicholas took a deep breath and sighed. "We haven't had the time, nor has King Caius sent us the men or the coin we need to raise a force of archers, but I've been talking to our smithies. One of them has learned a new bit of craft to combat that element. We'll see..."

"Their talk of compounds and alloys makes my head spin. And I can barely heft my leg over my horse's arse. I keep telling you I'm too old for this foolishness we call soldiering, but you keep insisting I fight. I must question your sanity, sir," Luke chuckled, shaking his head in mirth as they turned their horses around to descend from the top of the hill.

When they reached the shelter of the forest, Nicholas always felt a sense of relief. The trees swayed in the breeze at the very top, so high above him he had to crane his neck to see. Their trunks creaked with the movement. It gave him a sense of constancy and even a little peace. The trees would sway no matter what was happening in the world.

In a blur of motion, a figure in the trees jumped down on Nicholas, knocking him violently to the ground. After a brief scuffle, the attacker separated from him and drew his dagger. Nicholas stood like a wrestler in a fighting pit, anticipating the next move. They circled each other. More assassins appeared from behind trees, boulders, and bushes in the forest, forming a large circle around him.

Nicholas looked over his left shoulder and then his right. Luke had been taken hostage. Two men restrained him, one with a knife at his throat. Nicholas swore an oath under his breath, wondering how he would fight at least ten men. He clenched his jaw, wrinkled his brows, and glowered at every single adversary, blue eyes blazing. He drew his sword and positioned himself to fight.

"Well, well. It looks like we've caught a Wolf Knight in our net," an older man said, clearly their leader. Walking forward, he clapped his hands slowly in a scornful way. Tall and formidable, the man had a wide face, protruding chin, and wrinkled forehead with close-cropped blond hair and beard spattered with gray. He wore no metal armor but sported expensive leather finery. He was wealthy and perhaps a knight, but no sigils or banners were present. Not as rich, well-kept, or clean, the rest of the men looked like mercenaries.

"What makes you so sure?" Nicholas clashed his brows together in confusion. "I imagine the Wolf Knight has far more important tasks at hand, like sharpening his broadsword to hack off ugly heads like yours."

"Let's just say the man who hired us guessed that the Wolf Knight was high up the chain of Edmiran command. He could be the one surveying the field, bolstering the outposts, and doing all of Commander Burrage's dirty work," the leader explained, a vile grin spreading across his face. "I think we've bagged our quarry."

"The Wolf Knight is the stuff of legends," Nicholas argued, feigning ignorance. "He comes and goes. The men think he's a blessing from their gods when they are losing a fight, a specter to rally the troops. You know nothing."

"We will skin you alive, wolf," one of the men growled. Tall and brutish, he stepped closer to the captain, rubbing his knuckles against his palm.

Unimpressed by the gesture, Nicholas spoke nonchalantly and cocked his head toward the knight. "I know who you work for, and you can tell your master that when I finish cleaning the rubbish out of this lovely piece of forest, I'm coming after him."

"After I cut him down, I'm going to rifle through his saddle bags and find his famous white wolf pelt," another man said, smirking. He studied Nicholas from head to toe, gauging how a fight between them would go. He was gangly, but wiry and strong. Nicholas had no doubt that he could fight. "I'd wear it across my shoulders, wouldn't you?" He nudged a comrade with an elbow and smiled absurdly. "What a trophy that would be, wearing the Wolf Knight's legendary pelt."

"Now, now gentlemen," the leader said, gently scolding as if he really wanted his men to stop taunting. "This will be a fair fight. Isn't that right?" He got close to Nicholas and nicked his cheek with the tip of his sword. "Drop your sword or I'll give the order to have my men slit his throat." He whispered through gritted teeth, gesturing with his head toward Luke.

Nicholas stood still despite the stinging pain and dropped his sword. He gave his adversary a stony smile, his eyes unwavering as he stared into fathomless pits, swirling with the misery of others. "You don't want to do this," he said, his voice barely a whisper. "I've put more men in the grave..."

"Have you ever met a man more cocksure than this?" the leader laughed as he bounced his glance from man to man, pointing at Nicholas.

He was too late to intimidate his prisoner. After a small nod toward Luke, Nicholas turned swiftly from the knight and punched him in the face with the back of his battle-hardened knuckles. As the leader staggered to his knees, Luke elbowed the man holding him in the stomach. He backed him into the trunk of a tree and pummeled him savagely in the face and stomach. The other man guarding Luke rushed him from behind. Luke grabbed the dagger that had fallen and plunged it into his neck. Luke drew his sword and ran toward the fray.

Two other men rushed toward Nicholas from opposite sides with their swords raised. In a lightning fast move, Nicholas used his right leg to strike the man behind him in the stomach, and just as quickly leaped to kick the other coming straight at him. Another soldier leaped onto his back, trying to strangle him with a rope. Nicholas flipped the man over his back to the ground. Grasping his fallen sword, he stabbed him through the heart. Luke cursed and slashed with his sword, men grunting from exertion and pain, until Luke fought with him back to back.

One fighter came at Nicholas with legs in the air, flying almost horizontally. He tried to pound both of his feet into Nicholas's chest. Nicholas slashed at his legs mid-air. The man skidded to the ground, saw that his legs were almost cut in half, and screamed at the rest of the men to kill Nicholas. Another rushed toward Nicholas, roaring. He held his sword high, positioned for a killing blow to the head. Nicholas deflected the thrusts, clanging his sword and parrying the strikes. He socked the man in the stomach. The man fell like a ragdoll, flopping backward onto other fighters. The man rallied and charged again. Nicholas leaped back to avoid the swipe at his torso. Clenching his knuckles, he swung an uppercut under the man's lower jaw and heard a sickening crunch of bones. His jaw askew, the man fell, moaning as he hit the ground.

Luke fought two soldiers at once, but he was on the defensive. Nicholas took on a man who tried to kick him in the face. He grabbed the man's knee and twisted, broke it, and sent the man crashing to the ground. He turned around just in time to see Luke stab a man through the heart. Another attacker armed with a pike flew head-long at Nicholas. He grabbed the pike and socked him ruthlessly in the stomach. As the man doubled over, Nicholas threw the pike, cleaving in two the skull of another mercenary who aimed a dagger at him.

Their leader, the last man standing, attacked Nicholas with a spear. Nicholas defended himself with his sword, but the man had perfect leverage. He could inflict damage from a distance. When the leader thrust toward his heart, Nicholas swerved sideways. He turned his back toward his adversary, bent low, and kicked the man in the face. The leader lost his grip on the spear. Nicholas stole it. He used the weapon to stab him in the ribs and clip the back of the legs. When the man fell, Nicholas hesitated.

"I always knew you were a coward," the man spewed. "Don't have the courage to kill a man in cold blood. Is that it?"

"It's hardly cold blood, old man. I know Breckenridge is a spy," he yelled hoarsely at the leader. He grabbed him by the collar, lifting his torso off the ground. "If he wants the Edmiran army to win, then why kill me? Why kill any Edmiran leader?"

"To level the playing field, you oaf. Why else?" The knight cackled a bit of blood backed up in his throat. He leered, showing bloodstained teeth.

Frustrated, Nicholas let him fall to the ground. The man writhed in pain. This makes no sense, Nicholas thought. Breckenridge has too much to lose in betraying his country.

"Don't walk away. Fight me! Kill me!" he said, trying to stand up.

"Sorry to deprive you the honor of killing the Wolf Knight," Nicholas answered with a mocking grin, "but you're about to die." He turned his back on the man and tossed the spear to Luke, who caught it one-handed.

"I'll search the bodies and see if I can find anything that ties Breckenridge to this gruesome scene. You check their satchels and saddlebags. We'll send in a crew to clean up and bring the animals to camp."

"Aye, Captain."

Nicholas kneeled and searched a man's pockets. The mercenary, clearly not dead, grabbed him by the tunic with a vice-like grip. Lacking leverage and momentum, Nicholas struggled. He was caught in a spider's iron web and could not escape.

The mercenary shoved a dagger into the side of the Wolf Knight.

Luke heard the scuffle and ran to his captain. He slit the throat of the attacking mercenary and pulled the dagger out of his torso. Nicholas let out a tortured grunt and fell onto his back, breathing hard and sweating, as he covered his wound with his hand to slow the flow of blood.

"What a fool I am," Nicholas whispered as he lifted his hand to look at the wound. More blood rushed from the gash.

"Don't do that!" Luke yelled. "Push on that hard with your hand until I can get something to stanch the flow." He bolted to his horse. After frantically searching the saddlebags, he came skidding on his knees back to Nicholas. "You should've worn your breastplate today, you stupid, stubborn ass."

"How bad is it?" Nicholas huffed through the pain.

"I won't be able to tell until I get these clothes off you and the bleeding slows." Luke used his dagger to slit through the tunic and pulled the fabric away from the wound. "You're not going to like this one little bit," he warned as he poured a concoction of distilled wine on the wound.

The pain was sudden and sharp. Nicholas groaned through gritted teeth and tried to pull away.

"Okay, laddie. The hard part is done. Push pressure on that cloth for a while," Luke soothed. "Let me get some clean rags to wrap around your body." He walked back to the horses and untied the saddlebags.

"Luke," Nicholas gasped. "Do you remember the protocols? In case..."

"You're not going to die, Nicholas. You're the luckiest bloke I know, remember?" He shot him a mischievous grin as he wrapped cloth around his torso.

"I've got to go to her, Luke, after I get situated. It's going to hurt like the devil, but I've got to do it," he whispered through panting breaths.

"Oh, no. No! You're too badly injured. We've got to get you back to camp."

"She could be in trouble. I've got to make sure she's safe."

"Was this little outing an excuse to see the lass?" Luke asked, outraged.

"It was both. Help me, please. I'm going to her," Nicholas said with a strained voice as he tried to sit up.

"Don't try to sit up yet, Nicholas." Luke pushed his saddlebags under his neck so he could rest more comfortably.

"You can go back to camp if you want," Nicholas continued. "I wasn't going to see her again, but I thought I should tell her myself that we shouldn't meet anymore. It's too dangerous. If someone can do this to me, what would they do to her?"

He couldn't bear the thought of someone hurting her. He'd hack them to pieces, even in his present condition, but he needed to look deep into those beautiful eyes one more time. He had to feel her body against his own. He had to run his fingers through her hair. He'd give anything to feel the touch of her lips on his. Nicholas knew the memory would get him through the grisly work to come. It was risky, especially with a deep gash to his side. He'd been wounded so many times he couldn't count them anymore. There was a chance he wouldn't make it back.

"I won't leave you," Luke mumbled under his breath.

"You're going to have to stitch me up, man."

"When the bleeding has stopped, I'll stitch it and put a poultice on it."

"I'd appreciate it if you would collect some of that bark and boil it down. It will help with the pain."

20

CORNERED

Every step Meg took with Lady Byron made her realize that they should've been stalking in the cover of the trees, bushes, and rocks instead of walking down a quiet lane. The forest still displayed its fall splendor in the cold. Between towering oaks and maples grew younger trees with dark branches and bright gold leaves arcing over the lane. Patches of grass grew here and there, scattered between rusty leaves that had already fallen. With dappled sunlight shimmering through the leaves, Meg daydreamed of walking hand in hand with Nicholas through the golden tunnel.

Two horsemen shook her out of the vision, careening around a corner and galloping toward them with frightening speed. The two women barely had time to jump out of the way, only to watch them race ahead and disappear down a hill. Trying to quell their racing hearts and gasping for breath, Meg realized she could no longer hear the horses' hooves and ran to the edge of the lane to see if the men had taken the switchback to the road below. They were nowhere to be seen.

Frustrated, she gnawed on her thumb and paced, trying to think. They were a tattered couple of peasants riding expensive horses equipped with fancy gear, which meant they were thieves.

Who knew what other crimes they were capable of? Meg didn't want to find out. She froze in her tracks when she saw the heads of their horses rise above her line of sight, then the men themselves. In a snippet of conversation, Meg heard one of the men say, "After we've had some fun, we'll use her for ransom." It was as if someone had pushed her in front of a target for archery practice and slapped the bull's-eye on her forehead.

"Run!" Meg screamed at Lady Byron and pushed her up the hill as she darted across the road and ran downhill.

The horsemen twisted their mounts and raced to the switchback that led to the road below. Running breathlessly, Meg tripped near a large pine tree and almost hit her head on a rock. Looking around in a haze of panic, wondering where she could hide, she realized she had stumbled into the den of a deer. She crawled inside the shelter of low-hanging branches and hid herself behind the trunk and sat, her knees bent to her chest. Meg tucked her hair under her hood and covered most of her face as she wrapped her new dark green cloak around her, a trick she'd learned from Nicholas. Blend in. Learn not to be seen. From her vantage higher up the hillside, Meg peeked from behind the trunk and watched the men canter back and forth along the road below, waiting for her to emerge.

"Did you get a look at the young one with long hair and bright eyes?" a man with a high-pitched, raspy voice called to his crony. Tall and excruciatingly thin, his legs were far too long for the stirrups on the horse.

"She's a ripe one, all right. I'd kiss those sumptuous lips right off her face, I would," his partner said, leering. Younger and smaller, he seemed to have a hard time controlling his horse.

"I'd do a hell of a lot more if I could get my hands on her."

"Did you hear that, woman? Come down out of the trees and we'll have ourselves a wee little party."

"Here, pretty little lady," the older one shouted. He dismounted his horse. Tethering it to a tree, he began walking up the hill. "Come out, come out, where ever you are."

The crony dismounted, too, and took a different route up the hill. He kept clapping his hands and jumping behind trees and bushes, Meg guessed, to startle her. He must've thought she had climbed a tree because he kept looking up. He easily pulled himself onto a large branch and crouched down, looking around him. As they got closer, she covered her face and adjusted the cloak to cover her whole body, hoping they would look at the lump in the den and think she was a small, mossy boulder.

"We're going to find you, little lady. No use hiding," teased the tall one who walked up the hill toward the pine tree. He was getting closer, spreading the branches of bushes and checking behind rocks. Meg's heart thundered in her ears as he shuffled around the pine tree she sheltered in, his feet crackling dead leaves and twigs. He snapped his fingers and clapped his hands rhythmically as he circled. When he got farther away, he must've picked up a branch because he hit everything he walked by, a boulder, the trunk of a tree. Every strike sounded like the dull thud of a brick pounding a wall and falling to the ground. "Where is she?" His scream pierced the silence of the forest.

His screech almost made her jump. But she wouldn't do it. She would not bolt like nervous prey. Meg wouldn't breathe if it meant staying out of his clutches.

"Well, I'll be..." the tall one said, scratching his head. He had hiked all the way to the road where they first blasted past her. "Clever little wench. I don't see her any anywhere. Do you?"

"No. No sign of her." The crony jumped off the branch and landed lightly on his feet. "We should get going anyway. The rest of the gang will wonder what happened to us."

Meg allowed herself a sigh of relief, but waited several minutes before she walked back up the hill to find Lady Bryon.

Hoping that Lady Byron would not appear on the lane again, Meg hid behind a huge rock and listened for the telltale sign of creatures in the forest — the snap of a twig. It finally came and Meg sneaked up behind her lady, grabbed her, and muffled her mouth so she could not scream. Meg gestured for her to be quiet, her eyes pleading.

"Let us go back to the castle," Lady Bryon whispered frantically. "Please?"

"We'll be fine if we hide ourselves," Meg insisted.

"My lady, I beg of you. As the next battle looms closer, the commoners will become brazen. They have nothing to lose if they get thrown in a cell for a crime. They think they're going to die anyway."

"Lady Byron, get a hold of yourself!" Meg shook her lady by the shoulders and looked steadfastly into her eyes. "I'm sorry to endanger you, which I've now done more times than I care to count. You've been exceedingly loyal to me, much more than I deserve."

Lady Byron wiped a tear and nodded grimly.

"I know you disagree, but I have to see him one more time, to tell him that we cannot journey into the forest anymore. It has become too dangerous for us both. Do you understand?"

"Yes," Lady Byron said, but the look in her eyes remained fearful.

Meg took her by the hand and they began their journey to the lake high above the lane in the depths of the forest.

∼

"There you are, pretty little lady."

Meg shuddered at hearing that high-pitched, raspy voice again.

"We've been looking for you," the crony leered, hands on his hips, his eyes pilfering her body from head to toe.

Meg stood and pushed Lady Byron away from her, signaling for her to stay out of the way.

"That's fine. We don't want her, anyway," the tall one said, gesturing at Lady Byron as if she were a pile of rubbish.

"We want you." The crony raised his eyebrows in twisted, rakish delight.

"Never seen the likes of you before." The tall one walked behind her and fingered her hair.

Meg closed her eyes and swallowed hard, trying to remain calm, trying to figure out what to do. Where was Nicholas? Surely, he could slice through these two miscreants in one swipe of his broad shoulders and muscled forearms.

"What are you doing out here?" The tall one raised his brow in question. He ran his tongue along his teeth and licked his lips delectably. "You must be from some rich manor. Didn't your master tell you it's dangerous in the woods? That bandits and brigands and wicked men like us would take advantage of a lovely piece of meat like you?"

Just as he tried to grab her from behind, Meg leaned into his body and kicked the younger man in front of her with such force that he fell backwards and knocked the wind out of him. Out of the corner of her eye, she saw Lady Byron come up behind him and hit him on the head with a rock and run away. Her movement caught her captor off-guard and gave her enough time to draw her dagger.

"So, you want to play rough," he rasped at her, his voice failing. "Well, that's fine with me."

"I promise you," Meg whispered fiercely, her voice ragged. "If you touch me, I will kill you."

"I think you need a good hard knock in the teeth before you'll cooperate," he said with a fiendish grin. He smacked her so hard across the face that she fell to the ground. Meg jumped up and charged him. She tried to stab him but her dagger had dropped on the ground when she fell. He threw her back down and smirked triumphantly over her. This time she found her dagger. She wiped a trickle of blood from her mouth, stood up, and charged again.

He laughed when he saw her coming, but his expression changed from amusement to shock. Thick blood covered his hand as he checked his wound and stared stupidly at her as he fell to the ground.

"You'll pay for that," his crony bellowed, finally able to stand. "He's my brother."

He ran forward with his own knife out and swiped at her several times, but Meg dodged and parried his blows easily. "I won't kill you if you promise to leave me alone," she hollered as she tried to catch her breath.

"You won't kill me?" he responded sarcastically. "You're going to die for what you did to him. He's the only family I have left."

"Then you should've left me alone!" she yelled back, hoping she could reason with him. She didn't want to kill him.

He roared and ran toward her, his eyes blazing with hatred and hot tears. Suddenly, Meg remembered the short sword Nicholas had hidden in the nook of a nearby tree. She grabbed it from the crevice, made a backward turn, and slashed him on the chest. It caught him by surprise and made him stumble backwards. He screamed and charged her again. She ducked and let him pass, but then she maneuvered and hit the back of his legs. His legs fell out from under him. He grabbed her by the collar of her cloak and pulled her with him to the ground, Meg unable to control the sword. She rolled away and stood, tears welling as she surveyed the scene.

She hadn't to, but she'd stabbed the boy through the heart.

Meg approached him carefully, watching as his body contorted with pain.

"You should've stopped," she whispered, utterly sad.

He tried to respond, but he gurgled, his mouth full of blood.

Meg pulled the sword out and watched the life go out of him, his blood draining into the forest floor.

Staring at the sword in her hand with revulsion, Meg dropped it, and let it fall to the ground. Then she fell to her knees and wept over the slain boy.

Nicholas could not believe his eyes. He and Luke heard commotion nearby and hurried to see what was happening. They watched from atop the cliffs that surrounded the lake as his beloved Meg fought off two young men and did a damn fine job of it. Before he could dismount and come to her aide, she'd already killed them both. Now she was sobbing. Her companion stood with her back against a great boulder gaping at the bloodshed, panicked and out-of-sorts. He spurred his horse to a path that led to the lake, leaving Luke to take watch. He dismounted and practically fell to the ground from the jolt of pain it caused, but he ran to her.

"Meg! Meg, are you all right?" Nicholas kneeled beside her and the mangled lad. He put his hand on her back to soothe her.

She jumped out of his grasp and crawled backward, her eyes glazed and unfocused, her breathing rapid and shallow.

He put his hands up in surrender.

"It's me, Meg. Nicholas." He slowly opened his cloak and laid his dagger and sword between them, within her reach. "I love you. Will you come to me?" He opened his arms to her.

"Oh, Nicholas!" Meg wailed. "I didn't want to do this." She held her head in hands, sobbing. Her shoulders shook with grief.

He stepped toward her, pulled her up from the ground, and she fell into his arms. Meg clung to him and trembled in his embrace. He looked down into her face, so lovely yet creased with such sorrow. He wanted to be soft and smooth with her, to prove that he could be a gentleman if he ever had the chance to show her physical affection, but he couldn't contain himself. He was in such agony himself and so much in love that he took her lips to his and devoured her. He was passionate and rough, taking her head in his hands. He kissed her face, her eyes, her cheeks. He tasted her tears.

Meg seemed to heal a little with every kiss. His touch alone intensified her grip on him, as if the comfort of his embrace offered the balm she so desperately needed. She tightened her arms around his waist, her arms traveling up his back and resting around his neck, pulling him closer, the ardency of her gaze telling him that she needed more of his tender kisses.

He wrapped his arm across her shoulder and guided her to a rock close to the cliff and sat down. With his back against the wall, he cradled her, wiped her tears, and wrapped his cloak around her as if she were a small child. He cuddled and caressed her, ran his fingers through her hair, and wished that he never had to let her go.

~

"What happened to you?" Meg asked, alarmed when she found the blood-soaked rags on the side of his torso.

He winced as she touched the area. "I was attacked by bandits, just like you, only you fared much better." He gave her a feeble, pained smile.

"Oh, Nicholas. I am so sorry." She hugged him and kissed his cheek.

"How did this happen, Meg? Do you feel well enough to tell me?"

"I was careless, Nicholas. We were walking in a lane and these men," she said disgustedly, "raced by on stolen horses. They decided to come back to kidnap me."

"How did you get away?"

"I pushed my companion up the hill and screamed at her to run. I ran downhill, hid in the den of a deer, and used camouflage."

"And they couldn't find you?"

"I did what you said, to hide and blend in, but they found me here instead."

"I saw the whole thing, Meg," he said in a measured tone, his expression wary. "And I'm not sure what to think of it."

She froze in his embrace, a little fearful at his comment.

"What do you mean?"

"I mean that you have received training, well above rough-housing with me and your brothers, as you've told me."

She didn't deny it. She couldn't. Not anymore. She sagged a little at the relief of it.

"My brother trained me, the one who is skilled like you," Meg began, trying to keep her emotions in check. "He wanted me to be able to protect myself if need ever arose. And it has." She gestured toward the men lying on the forest floor as tears welled in her eyes. "Nicholas..." She sighed. "It is clear to me, and has been since I saw you in the castle that night, that you are more than a mere soldier in the army. We have not been completely honest with each other. My question is, what are we to do about it?"

Nicholas was silent for a moment as he cocked his head and contemplated her. He lifted her chin toward his face, searching her eyes. "I guess meeting in secret has been a bit reckless." He gave her a crooked smile but then furrowed his brows in seriousness. "My gut tells me that we cannot see each other anymore. It has become too dangerous for both of us. But my heart tells me," he said, his voice soft with emotion, "that I can never let you go." He whispered fiercely. "I'll never love another woman ... ever ... as much as I love you."

He gave her a loving smile as he brushed a willful tendril away from her face.

"I've known since the day we found each other in the forest, the day you finally spoke to me." She smiled through her tears. "That there was not another man for me. I am hopelessly in love with you, Nicholas," Meg said, half laughing, half crying. "You are everything I thought a good man could be, but you are a mystery, and I want to spend the rest of my life searching the pages of this closed book." She gave him a small smile and placed her hand over his heart.

He shuddered and looked at her with great desire. How she loved it when he showed his feelings for her. No man had ever deigned to do it.

"Can't we just get through this battle and see what happens?" Meg leaned away from him and quirked a brow. "Maybe we will find a way to be together."

She wanted to believe that with all her soul, but she knew deep down that her life was too complicated. Who knew what would happen after the battle? Perhaps there was a chance. She found all of her hopes, for Nicholas and for her kingdom, balancing on a wire not knowing which way they would fall. Couldn't she somehow have both?

He laughed, a low rumble in her ear that reminded her of distant thunder. It made her want to kiss him all over again.

"I was just telling Luke that the other day. If I survive, I will find you."

"You must survive!" She grabbed him by his cloak and shook him a little too vigorously. He recoiled from the pain.

"Oh, my lady. You know better than that," he said, smoothing her hair. "The most wicked men in the world cannot keep me away from you."

She smiled at the words, and then he kissed her ever so softly.

∽

NICHOLAS CLAMBERED DOWN FROM THE ROCK. THE PAIN HAD grown so excruciating that his whole body trembled as soon as he placed his feet on the ground. Meg stood under his arm to steady him and helped him walk toward his horse. Luke brought the animal forward so he would not have to walk as far. Nicholas looked at his tall warhorse, from its hooves embedded in the soft grass to its back where the saddle lay, as if it were a steep mountain. Climbing to the top would be tortuous affair. More importantly, once he put a foot in the stirrup and stretched his leg across his mount, he would not see Meg for many months, maybe even years. She was the woman of his dreams, the woman who'd stolen his heart and stirred his desires. Leaving felt like a black hole in the center of his being.

Unable to face the prospect of enduring such misery just yet, he turned to Meg. Grabbing her by the shoulders, he pulled her roughly toward him in the tightest embrace. The movement caused him to blanch with white-hot pain, but at least for that moment, she was close to him, her head to his heart. When she lifted her face to look at him, tears streamed down her cheeks. He cupped her face and used his thumbs to wipe the tears.

"Please, Meg. Don't cry."

"I can't help it," she shuddered. "My heart is already weeping. You are my love. How can I live knowing I may never see you again?"

"We must both be brave," he consoled. His emotions overwhelmed him and he shouted, "Live, damn it! Do you hear me? Live! Get through this and I will find you. I promise I will find you."

With her glorious green eyes staring at him through her tears, she stood taller in his embrace. She took a deep breath and nodded her assent. Meg kissed him on the cheek and pushed some hair behind his ear as she stared longingly into his eyes.

"Take care of him, will you?" Meg turned her gaze toward Luke.

"I will do my best," Luke said, sadness inundating his eyes.

Meg turned and walked toward her companion. Nicholas did his best to mount his horse without swearing to the Goddess Above.

"I'll escort them to the border, laddie," Luke said, reading his thoughts perfectly. "I'll catch up with you." He pulled his horse by the reins toward the women and gestured for them to mount. "It's not like you'll be riding fast," he grinned, just a little.

Nicholas nodded and tried to return the smile, but he just couldn't. He nudged his horse away from the lake. When he looked over his shoulder one last time, hoping for a wave goodbye or a flash of her beautiful smile, she was gone. Grief overwhelmed him. The promises they'd made didn't feel empty, yet they filled him with an aching hollowness. Could they really find each other? Would it be possible in the chaos after a battle? His soul already bled for something he wasn't sure he would ever have. Yet, Nicholas knew no matter what, he'd fight to hell and back just for a chance to look for her. A thick fog had crept in and settled on the forest with a deep wet chill. He shuddered with a coldness that penetrated his bones. He had no idea how he got back to camp, for he was unable to see through the mist of his sorrow.

21

MISTAKEN IDENTITY

John Paul's archers and countless companies of the Asterian army had assembled at the castle and just outside the city wall. He planned to march his men out in a few days if the weather permitted. They would convene with the main force of the king's army on the distant plain and journey to the battlefield together. At John Paul's request, Meg took charge of readying cloth supplies for the army. She and her ladies-in-waiting directed where the stock should go. They recruited women who were quick with a needle and thread for sewing bandages, blankets, and clothing for the army. Everyone worked at impossible speed. She'd even seen a few ladies nod off with needles still in their hands. Meg ran from the courtyard and into the long halls of the castle to make sure the project functioned. She kept running because she'd rather move than sit and struggle awkwardly with a needle and thread.

Meg almost passed by a window with a view of her brother and Breckenridge dawdling. She shouldn't have, but she paused to watch them for a moment. This burst of activity doesn't faze them at all, she seethed. The duke, always clear-eyed and steady on his feet, had William on his heels. He backed him into a corner and swatted him on the rump with a wooden sword. Will stumbled over his feet a few times, laughing as if he'd just gotten thrown out of a tavern. He saw her staring at them through the window and comically toasted her. The duke gave her an absurdly low bow. She heaved a disgusted sigh and kept running.

In the courtyard and outside the castle gates, men yelled for more animals, carts, and wagons to transport the goods along with the army. Hundreds of horses and mules would pull the loads for food and supplies, tents, tools, construction materials, armor, and weapons. With plenty of sheep, cattle, and pigs meandering along the way for food, and chickens and other foul in crates, no one would be hungry for a while. In addition to the thousands of men and horses the nobles brought with them, there would be the camp followers.

A long line of townspeople had formed. Villagers, soldiers, and squires waited to be paid for their wares or to pledge allegiance to their lords. Meg scanned the line for women, hoping to find more who could sew quickly, but stopped dead in her tracks.

Was it Nicholas? Had he survived his terrible wound? Was he really here?

She walked toward the man who had turned away from her. He was as tall and broad enough across the back, had the same color hair, but the clothes weren't quite the right and neither was the horse. Meg realized this too late. She couldn't just turn around and act like she had no business with them. The other men around him became silent, knelt on one knee, and bowed their heads before her. The man with the horse had no idea what happened until he turned around, embarrassed.

"My lady, forgive me." He held on to the reins of his horse as he knelt.

"It is my mistake. Please arise, all of you. I thought you were someone else." Meg smiled a little forlornly at the man who caught her attention.

He may have looked similar to Nicholas from a distance, but up close, he had suffered more in battle, at least on his face. Scars ravaged the side of his mouth and twisted pitifully toward his ear. A deep gash sliced the other cheek, crusted with blood and pus. It needed the lance to release the infection. As Meg studied the man, his wounds looked worse upon closer inspection. He had pulled the long hair from the top of his head to hide the hideous wounds from his missing ear and side of his scalp.

"Do I offend you, my lady?"

"No. Pray forgive me." Meg lowered her gaze. "I have not seen the scars of battle so closely. You are to be commended for your sacrifice to our kingdom."

"It is my honor to serve for our freedom. I've little else," the soldier said wistfully, looking at the ground. "I'm needed here and can't return home, even though it needs defending. The enemy is tromping through our best fields and burning them on their way to battle. Everyone is in hiding."

"Where do come from?"

"The bustling township of Honeyvale, where our wheat grows on the golden plateaus, perhaps thirty leagues south."

"I know that name. Doesn't it provide our best stock of wheat?"

"Indeed, it does." His eyes crinkled into a smile. "The whole village turns out with scythes during the harvest. Bakers from Tirana are some of our best customers."

"I'm well aware of how much our bakers in town prefer your wheat," Meg replied, nodding. "Pardon me, sir, but I must find my brother. You've offered new intelligence. I'm sure he already knows, but I really must make sure."

RUSHING ACROSS THE COURTYARD TO FIND JOHN PAUL, SHE saw her banner in the distance, the one her uncle made for his men to carry into battle. On a sky-blue background, an angel dressed in a glowing white gown was clearly a depiction of her. A halo crowned her head, blonde curls clung to her waist, the palms of her hands raised to the sky. The angel's head bowed and her eyes closed as a dove perched on one of her hands with an olive branch clasped in its beak.

"Peace," she whispered miserably. "How can they think I will bring peace?"

As Meg wiped a couple of unexpected tears from her eyes, she suddenly became light-headed. She wondered how long it had been since she'd eaten. Everything began to spin. Men yelling in the yard, animals braying, the horrible wound on the soldier's face, William's ridiculous toast to her, the duke's smug smile, women pulling their needles through fabric so fast that she couldn't keep track of their hands.

Meg swayed and looked for something to hold on to. She held out her hands to break her fall. Blackness swirled in her field of vision, overtaking her.

"Oh, no."

As Meg surged to consciousness, she realized a man carried her, yelling for someone to help. It was the wounded soldier.

"Put the princess down now!" Malcolm Cooksey ordered gruffly.

"She fainted!" the soldier said between panicked breaths. "I didn't know what else to do."

"You did the right thing, lad," Cooksey said with a little more warmth in his voice as he approached them. "Now put her down on this barrel and go fetch some food out of the kitchen for you and your comrades as a thank you for tending to the princess."

From a distance, William clamored at the top of his lungs and stomped across the yard toward them. "What the hell happened now?" he blustered, demanding as always.

"Nothing. I'm fine, thanks to this good man," Meg assured him.

William scowled at the wounded soldier from tip to toe, appraising him, and glared at the gathering crowd. "Pray, tell," he inquired falsely sweet. "Just what did he do? Why did you need help?"

"She fainted, my lord. I saw her fall to the ground and so I picked her up and ran to find someone who could help."

"And you thought the cook would be the one to tend to the princess? The highest lady in land."

The wounded soldier opened his mouth to respond but thought better of it. Flushed with embarrassment, he looked at his feet, ignoring the murmuring crowd.

"My lord, I am well," Meg insisted. "What this man deserves is our thanks and a good meal. Cooksey was just arranging that."

"And is the cook our commander and future king?" William sneered, acting affronted, playing to the crowd.

"William, please. Not now," Meg begged tiredly.

"I will determine what reward this man should be given," he snarled, his spittle landing on her cheek.

Disgusted, Meg stood up from the barrel and curtsied low. With her knees on the ground, she hoped the submissive gesture would calm him. "Yes, my lord."

But William would not stop.

"I am appalled that any one of you allowed the princess to fall." He stalked in front of everyone who had gathered. "She is your lady, the one with the loveliest visage in the land, the one whose beautiful face will come to mind when you charge and lay down your life for your king."

"William, please," Meg implored. "Let this alone."

"What is wrong with you?" William came close and whispered in her ear. "You faint a great deal. Do you carry a bastard in your belly, because…"

Meg slapped him in the face so hard that the force of it made him turn his head.

The silence of the crowd was deafening. William returned his gaze to her. A trickle of blood oozed from a crack on his lip. He wiped it away, never taking his eyes from her. He took her by the arms and shook her.

"You will not ever lay your hands on the king again!"

"You're not the king! Or have you forgotten about Father?"

"Everyone's forgotten about him!" William raged. "All he ever does is pine for Mother, whether he's sitting on the throne or in conference with his aides. He's worthless. Someone's got to step into the royal shoes and act like a king."

"You're acting like a king, all right, standing out here in public inviting your subjects to see just what kind of king you will be." Meg outstretched her arms and turned in a circle, the faces in the crowd truly dismayed.

He raised his hand to hit her, but the wounded soldier stepped between the feuding siblings and took the blow intended for the princess. William struck him with the butt of his dagger and sent him reeling. When the soldier gained his balance, all could see that William hit the festered wound on his cheek, and it bled. He charged William. The Duke of Breckenridge stepped in front of Will just in time, casually positioned his sword, and plunged it into the heart of the poor man. Some of the women in the crowd screamed. Meg heard a few men shouting in outrage, but complete stillness settled as the soldier fell to his knees. He looked at the duke in shock and tried to stop the bleeding with his hands. The duke raised his foot to the soldier's chest and used the force to extricate his sword. The soldier fell to the ground, writhing in pain.

"Mercy. Please, mercy."

"How dare you?" Meg railed at William and the duke, her fists curled in fury. The anger of the crowd rose with her own. "How could you stab an innocent man?"

They ignored her as they huddled in whispered conversation. The duke cleaned his sword as they stole glances to the fallen soldier. They did not even have the grace to look ashamed. William had worn the same expression since he was a kid. When he broke the rules and comprehended that there were no real consequences, he learned to walk away from his misdeeds as their father swept away the mud from every foul-covered step. Now he wore it with blood on his hands.

Meg dropped to the ground beside the wounded man, crying as she comforted him.

"I am sorry." Her tears fell on his chest. "I will always think of you as a friend, someone who cared enough to protect a lady. That is the essence of a true knight, and I am grateful."

The poor soldier shuddered in pain. His eyes fluttered as he choked on the blood in his throat.

"Be still." Meg held his hand tight in hers and pressed it to her heart. "You must think of home and soon you will be there, walking through golden wheat fields on a fine day."

The duke sheathed his sword and pulled Meg up from the ground. He positioned the corpse with his foot for a final look at the ghastly expression on the soldier's face. Grabbing Meg by the arm, he forced her away from the crowd. She struggled and pounded him with her fists. She even called him a few choice names, but he would not let her go. When they were out of earshot of everyone, he reprimanded her.

"This is the last time you will embarrass your brother in public. Is that clear?"

Meg opened her mouth to respond, but the ridiculousness of his accusation was stunning. "I don't know what you're talking about."

"Oh, yes, you do. I think you faint on purpose to gain sympathy from our supporters who would follow William. Because of you, there is divisiveness. The men should follow their commander without question."

"He hates me and cannot control his temper. That's what everyone sees. As for the fainting spells, they are real. I don't know why they happen, and I am not with child! If you think that I'm trying to steal the throne from William, you are more insane than I thought. Someone would have to kill my father and both of my brothers. I can assure you, that is never going to happen as long as I can help it."

"Good. I'm glad to hear you say it."

"Say what?"

"That you're a virgin. I wouldn't have it any other way."

"You disgust me."

"Why? Because I can't wait to bed the most beautiful woman in the land?"

She tried to push past him. He pulled her close enough again for him to whisper in her ear.

"Just remember that you owe me a great deal for my silence the night you stole Hannah out of the castle. You know that I can influence William to do with you whatever I wish."

"You know nothing about that night and I owe you nothing," Meg seethed, struggling against grip. "As for William, he's not king yet, and he will not cross my father or my brother. He desires the crown too much."

"Your great protector, John Paul, is hardly ever here, and I believe your father will not live long."

"Traitor!" Meg tried to push by him again. "I will not hear these murderous words against my father."

"You're the prize in this great war," Breckenridge continued, his eyes slit, his mouth curved like a scimitar. "Did you not know? William will promise you to King Caius if he can. Depending on the outcome, the enemy king may have the pleasure of you in his bed. If our fortunes turn for the worst, I'll just take what's leftover and you'll be at the top of the heap. You can count on it."

"I'll die first," she hissed and shook out of his grip. She stomped through the confused, uneasy crowd to Cooksey and planted herself behind him. No one would dare pass the robust cook to try and speak to her.

John Paul arrived on the scene to survey the damage. He looked at William with palpable disgust. Meg could tell that Cooksey would have loved to crack William's head with one of his huge iron pans. Instead, he stood with his burly arms folded defiantly across his chest, his face a mask of complete loathing.

"Your father, the king, bids you all come to his chambers."

Lord Cronmiller had appeared, silent fury in his expression. "Now!"

William lined up first, then John Paul, and then Meg. It had always been this way. The people of the highest rank went first. John Paul took a step forward and positioned himself beside William. He glared at his brother, eyes roaming from the blood on William's boots to his red, glassy eyes, his mouth a straight line of contempt.

"Small wonder they carry her banner," he said.

22
AN ANGRY FATHER

Lord Cronmiller led William, John Paul, and Meg into the king's private apartment and directed them to stand in a line before their father, each of them silent and wary. He paced in front of the fireplace with a willful blaze that threatened to nip at his royal robe. Wringing his hands, he stopped and stared furiously at his children until he found his words.

"I have known for some years now that you, William, my oldest son and heir to this kingdom, hate my beloved daughter."

William opened his mouth to object. His father silenced him with a glare of blood and thunder, daggers shooting past long, wiry brows.

"Do not think that you can pull the wool over my eyes." He glowered at William as he paced with his hands behind his back. "I know that you think little of me, that all I ever do is sit in here and long for your mother. Much of that happens, but I am not blind to what goes on in my kingdom, let alone what goes on in my house!" He stopped in front of William and shouted, jowls quivering. "And I am grievously disappointed that you show this hatred to your own sister in public. How many times must I ask that you not abuse her? I am well aware of how much it happens."

"Father, it's not as it appears," William said, phony penitence seeping into his eyes amidst the spawning of a lie. Meg and John Paul couldn't help but turn their heads toward their brother, astounded, mouths agape.

"The murder of an innocent soldier is not as it appears?" the king asked incredulously. "Especially when what led to it is the intended assault of my own daughter? Do you really think I don't have my own sources telling me everything, William?" The king stopped in front of his oldest son again, shaking his head in disgust. "You damage our chances of winning this war by demonstrating to everyone how little you think of Marguerite. Right now, our people believe that if you brutalize her in public, then you are quite capable of doing much worse to her in private. That makes you a monster, not a commander. This is not leadership, Will. It's stupidity, it's foolishness, it's crass and cruel. It will backfire if it hasn't already. I should've stopped this belligerent treatment of my little girl ages ago, but I had hoped that you both would outgrow your mutual dislike for each other."

Meg felt her breath catch in her throat. She didn't think she'd done anything wrong, at least not in the courtyard. Her eyes burned with resentment.

"Don't deny it, Meg," the king warned, pointing a finger at her and glaring. "I've watched you both for too long." Silence engulfed the room as the king stopped pacing and exchanged glances with Lord Cronmiller. "I'm not sure that you are ready to lead an army, William."

"No, no, no, you don't want to do that." Still drunk, William lumbered toward his father but stumbled, twisting his ankle. He recovered and acted like he really meant to bow before the king. "Let me prove myself to you," he said somberly.

"Oh, sure," the king sighed, observing the absurd behavior of his son. "You can knock another knight off his horse, and you use a sword well enough, but can you lead? What our fighting men think of you is paramount right now. What they've seen and what will spread throughout the ranks is the story of a brother who tried to hit his sister when a valiant young soldier, already dreadfully wounded, stepped up to take the blow for her. Your temper, your anger and hatred, your immaturity, and your laziness have put us all at risk.

"I am an old man. I have been fighting the same war my entire life. It is not news that I am worn out and that I pray for a miracle every day. However, I believe this battle will decide it all. I think we can win. I feel it in my gut and down to my bones. There is something about the strategy, the geography of the battlefield, the archers, our superior numbers that encourage me more about this particular battle than I have felt in a long time. I think the stars must be telling me that we have a chance. But we do not have a chance if the men in our army don't trust you, William."

He shifted his attention to Meg and pointed an accusatory finger at her. "And you, stay away from him!"

She wanted to argue. She wanted to say she tried hard every day, but it would do no good. She gave her father a small nod and tried to blink her tears away.

"John Paul."

He stood straighter and met his father eye to eye.

"Yes, Father."

"Make sure those archers of yours are worth the money I paid for them. We must win this one, son. It means everything."

"Yes, my Lord Father. I am well aware of your thinking on this."

"I am as well, my Lord Father," William said, still kneeling, clownishly imitating his brother's example.

"Then act like it, damn you!" he roared at William. "Play the role, son. You were born to lead. You have the fighting ability. It's time to develop the skills that every good king must have, that of a leader and peacemaker. And I expect you to start with your sister!" He took a deep breath. "Leave me in peace, my children, before I lose my patience again."

Meg's heart thumped in her chest as they filed quietly out of the king's chamber. Unable to believe that William had it in him to apologize, she thought he might act on their father's orders in his own way. Perhaps a glance that held no hostility or sad shrug of his shoulders. Instead, William curled the side of his mouth up and huffed a single breath of delight, his eyes dancing with vitriol and triumph. He fastened his cape tighter around his shoulder, straightened his tunic, and marched away.

"I should've walked out of the yard as soon as he arrived," Meg said, watching William strut down the hall.

"From what I've heard," John Paul replied, "you were the only one who behaved responsibly through the entire abominable episode, and William walks away from the murder of a soldier. It's despicable."

"He didn't shove his sword through that poor man's heart."

"No, but he would have if the duke hadn't done it for him. It's a complete farce. No one believes that Will can lead an army, the wine-ridden sot, and it's happening right before we march out. I could strangle him."

"I don't think you can rely on him, John Paul. You know as well as I do that Father will not deprive him of command." She thought of when her father revealed to her why he allowed William to get away with so much. "You will have to lead, you and your advisors. I think you've always known that, haven't you?"

"Yes, I suppose so, but it doesn't make it any easier."

"No, of course not." Meg said sympathetically. She walked to him, putting her arm through his. "I would ask something of you before you go."

"What is it, sister?" The malice gone from his voice, he looked down toward her, eyes softening.

"I'm looking for someone in the army and I hoped you'd be

able to find him and give me word before you lead our forces out."

"Really?" His brows clashed in confusion while his mouth crimped with suspicion. "How do you know anyone in the army besides the men who report to Father? Is this who you've been sneaking out to see?"

"Just as you sneak out to see a certain lady in town?" She raised a playful brow.

"Great skies, Meg. Does nothing get by you?" he asked, flustered. "I have taken the greatest care not to be noticed."

"Well, my ladies notice when you're not around." She tried to quell a smile. "I hope she's interesting and a challenge. Most women can't keep your attention."

"Oh, she's a challenge. I adore her, but I can't court her. At least, not yet. If we lose the war ... but I can't think like that," he said, shaking his head sadly. "Her connections are not quite high enough, if you take my meaning." He frowned and put his hand on top of hers. "Never mind. I've already told you too much. And I don't want to know the details of your..."

"His name is Nicholas. I think he's an officer. I've heard his companion call him captain, but I've also seen him dressed as a foot soldier. He seems like a knight and rides a warhorse, but he doesn't wear or carry any recognizable sigils. He's tall, broad across the back, very strong looking with long dark hair and beard, but his eyes are ... soft."

"Soft?" John Paul said, amused. "I'm supposed to find a man out of thousands based on a girl's mad-about description of his eyes?"

"He's badly injured," Meg said hastily, as if adding that last bit of information would make it easy to find him. "The last time I saw him, he had been stabbed in the side of his abdomen. I don't even know if he's alive." Meg closed her eyes and bit her lip, holding back the tears. Watching Nicholas mount his horse to leave looked like one of the painful things she'd ever seen a man do.

"I'm sorry to hear it, especially if he means something to you. My mind is already whirring about how you know this chap." John Paul put his arm around her shoulder.

"I'll tell you the story someday. There are no details about which to be ashamed, if that's what you're worried about."

"No," he laughed. "I'm not worried about that. You're nothing if not dutiful. Maybe a little too anxious to be dutiful." He gave her a crooked smile. "He doesn't sound like anyone I know, but I will check. I will send aides to make the rounds for you, dear sister. In fact, I will also send them with the signal to move out. If the weather is suitable, and it looks like it will be, we will leave in the morning. It's up to you to keep things running here at home. Your first and foremost responsibility is to keep our father from going insane. He will be very anxious until he hears word of the battle and how it went."

"I think we will all feel like we are hanging from tenterhooks until you all return home to us safe and sound."

"Then you know what to do," he said seriously. Turning her toward him, he searched her eyes. "You know how to keep the household running. You know the protocols if things don't go our way."

"Yes, yes. I know it all," Meg sighed. "I'd rather be going with you."

"No, you wouldn't," John Paul said flatly. "You wouldn't say that if you knew what war is really like."

He ruffled her hair, like a big brother annoying his little sister, kissed her on the top of her head, and left her alone, very alone, in the great hall.

23

DELIRIUM

Nicholas woke to find Meg right above him, iridescent and wispy. Her soft golden hair dangled from her shoulders and fell onto his chest, her sweet breath spreading across his face. The sun shone behind her. It cast her face in shadow, except for her eyes, which seemed lit from behind, so intense and dark green. He could've mistaken them for night in the forest, emeralds sparkling from moonlight. Ever so slowly, she kissed him all over his face. In between kisses, she looked so deeply into his eyes that it seemed she was pouring her heart into his, making them one. He raised his arms to wrap around her, to take those soft lips to his, but as soon as he touched her, she dissolved into a thin film of glittery dust and blew away, carried by a breeze into the meadow.

He let out a guttural cry that singed his throat and rang in his ears. Luke came near and looked down at him, his face lined with worry.

"Where is she, Luke?" Nicholas asked gruffly, trying to lift himself. He had no strength and fell back onto the crude litter that carried him. The Edmiran army was snaking its way through the deep forest to its final location before the next battle. "I don't think I can get through this without her." He panted hard and wiped the sweat from his brow.

"You've not got a choice in that, laddie," Luke replied,

sympathy in his eyes as he knelt to check the wound in Nicholas's abdomen.

"Don't touch me, Luke!" He whispered fiercely. "I feel like you're flaying me alive every time."

"Well, I can't let it rot and fester, either. Lie still! You're just making it worse, the more you move around."

"Please, Luke," Nicholas rasped, grabbing his lieutenant by the collar. "Just kill me. I've never felt this much pain before."

"Don't talk like that. I won't hear of it." Luke said it with affection, but the look of uneasiness on Luke's face told him otherwise.

Luke stood to confer with a group of young soldiers, who then scattered at Luke's barking command, "Just find the accursed snake!"

"Luke." Nicholas tried to speak, though his mouth was dry and his voice was hoarse.

"Yes, Nicholas. What is it?"

"I'm burning up."

"You're burning up all right, with a fever, you stupid, lovesick pup."

"I can't live without her."

"I think you've mentioned that a few hundred times in your delirium, my friend. Now, open up."

Luke tried to make him sip a nasty concoction, a thick syrup for the pain, but he pushed Luke's hand away. The medicine splattered on the ground.

"You've got no choice in this, Nicholas. You will swallow this on your own accord or I will force it down your gullet by holding your nose and pouring it down the back of your throat, drop by drop, if I must. I'll even gather our strongest knights with their hundred stone war horses to sit on your chest to keep you from thrashing about."

"I'd like to see you try."

"Don't tempt me." Luke handed him the spoon. "There's a good lad."

Nicholas gagged and tossed the spoon away. His throat still stung from the medicine when he laid down his head and finally relaxed.

Standing idly in a meadow with his face turned up to the sky, his eyes closed, Nicholas felt the sun's warmth sink into his skin. A gentle breeze whisked by and caressed his whiskers, as if a soft hand rubbed his cheek and lifted the hair from his neck. When he opened his eyes, he thought he must be in an enchanted meadow. He'd never seen such lovely tufts of narcissus, or sweet little bluebells, or vines heaving with blooms wrapped around the trunks of trees, their mellow perfume floating in the air. As Nicholas looked behind him, he was in the middle of miles and miles of daffodils in full bloom. Their heads nodded, gracing the rolling hills of the meadow and basking in the sunshine.

When he glanced ahead toward the forested area, Nicholas saw a woman walk behind a tree. He followed. She kept far enough ahead so that it was impossible to know her identity for certain. The train of her gown flowed over the greenest grass. It seemed as if flowers sprouted out of the earth with her every step. Still, he couldn't catch up to her and could not get her attention.

Finally, Meg turned around and smiled at him when he called her name. She walked faster, skipping and dancing around the trunk of each tree as the path curved, slowing to flash a playful smile. She stopped and blew kisses at him, giggling as she frolicked in a small copse of wood, the same one they'd met in. Different and more oddly beautiful than he remembered, the sun shone so bright he could see every golden particle from the forest stirring in the air. When he caught up to her, they each smiled shyly, not quite sure what to do.

But then she ran to him and flung her arms around his neck. She pressed her lips to his in hungered passion. The kiss lasted forever, a sweet deep probing. His body inflamed at the closeness of her. He took a handful of hair into his hand and pressed the other into the small of her back to pull her closer still. He looked down into her face, marveling at the translucence of her skin and her delicate structure. Her lips parted, swollen from desire, her eyes barely open. Her sweet breath mingled with his, tempting him further. He'd waited so long for her, suffered over her, and needed her so much. He knew that now. He knew he couldn't live without her.

As he lifted her up, she wrapped her legs around his torso as she continued her fevered kisses, savaging his mouth and neck. He kissed her back passionately, matching her ardent desire. As he looked down on the flawless skin of her neck, he couldn't help but plunge his lips into it. She moaned in ecstasy, stretched her neck toward him, and moved closer for more. He nipped that soft flesh and moved his lips across her collarbone to her shoulder. When his teeth bit into her dress, he got impatient and ripped the collar of her dress apart. It loosened, but he stopped.

When he stole a glance back to her eyes, he recognized the fiery affection in them, how unafraid she was of giving herself to him. He kissed her on her lips, her cheeks, her neck, as he backed her up to the trunk of a tree.

He wanted this glorious woman to himself, to be married, to spend the rest of his life making sure she was safe and warm, and finding a million different ways to make her smile in his embrace. It felt like they'd kissed for days (which didn't break his heart) before they tumbled into the grass together, laughing, and finally resting. She laid her head on his shoulder and spread her arm across his chest. He wrapped his arm under her, stroked the soft skin on her back under the loosened bodice, and rubbed her silken hair between his fingers.

"Nicholas?" She said his name as lovingly as he'd ever heard it.

"Mmm?" He felt so drowsy and happy that he could hardly reply.

"You must be strong. You must be made well."

He turned his face toward hers. He stared into the deep well of her eyes and recognized the seriousness in them.

"Of course, I am well and strong."

She shook her head, unconvinced

"You must go back and fight, Nicholas. You must take command. It's the only way."

"I don't know what you mean, Meg, my darling. What are you talking about?"

Strangely, he felt himself moving, like he was being pulled away from her. When he opened his eyes to find her, he saw her still lying on the grass with her arms stretched out to him, crying. Tears streamed down her face. She was shouting at him, but he couldn't hear her voice.

Nicholas shook his head, trying to make sense of what was happening. When he found the strength to move his arms, he threw off the layers of heavy furs and rolled. He fell onto frozen ground.

"Whoa! Lieutenant, he's awake! He hit the ground!"

Nicholas stood but felt wobbly, as if the world were spinning around him and his body wanted to spin with it. He resisted. He saw Luke striding toward him, still grimacing as if his eyebrows were stitched together by some cranky old woman.

"Just what do you think you're doing? You can't just roll out of the litter. You've been feverish for days and the wound has not yet healed."

"Luke," Nicholas said quietly. He lifted the bandage from his abdomen. "I'm fine. Look, it's healed."

Luke fell to his knees to get a closer look at the injury. He used his fingers to lift the bandage and poultice, probing other parts of his body to check for signs of injury or infection.

"I've never seen anything like it, laddie," Luke said as he stood and looked him in the eyes.

"You've always said I'm the luckiest bloke you ever knew." Nicholas cocked his head and gave him a crooked smile.

"There was poison on that dagger, Nicholas. Someone was very serious about killing you."

"Assassins are always serious about killing, Luke," he replied grimly. "I know it seems like she was the only thing I thought about when I was trying not to die, but I did understand somewhere in my delirium that I had to fight for my life."

"Well, laddie. I'm glad to hear it because I've heard nothing but her name for days and a few other things I wished had remained private."

Heat rose in his cheeks. Searching with his hands for pockets that were not there, he looked down to avoid eye contact, his dreams of her still quite vivid.

"Did you bag your rabbit?" Luke asked with a devilish glint in his eye.

"What? Oh ... none of your business," Nicholas said, embarrassed. He ran his hand roughly through his hair.

"Good. Now maybe we can get some work done since you're not suffering from wooziness by walking around and bantering with me. Commander Burrage will be pleased," Luke continued affably. "He's been here checking on you every day, wondering who else could educate the men on strategy. Don't think there's another mind in this man's army that can illustrate movement of troops better than you. I cannot believe my eyes," he whispered in amazement. "I did not think you would be capable of such a recovery for at least another week, but here you are, strong and healthy as a horse."

"Luke, let me ask you something," Nicholas said, placing a hand on Luke's shoulder. "How was I healed? What saved me? Do you know?"

"I'm not sure, but you started to show signs of improvement as soon as we found a certain adder hiding out for the winter in the hollow of a log."

"You used snake venom on me?"

"And a few other plants I've learned over the years that seem to have magical healing qualities. White Willow for pain, Solomon's Seal for healing of the flesh, and a dash of Nightshade."

"If I didn't know you better, I'd swear you were trying to kill me," Nicholas shook his head in disbelief. "I can't believe you used toxic plants on me."

"Laddie, my mother swore by them, and just a little bit of venom, mind you. Goodman and some of our other boy soldiers know what adders look like and they found it."

"You'll think me crazy for saying so, but I think Meg had something to do with it. She forced me to leave her ... in the dream. She said something about taking command, but that doesn't make sense," Nicholas finished a bit sheepishly.

"If you're saying she healed you, I'm going to thump you on the head with the butt of my dagger. I nearly lost my mind tending to you."

"Thank you for that, by the way, for being a doting little hen. But no, that's not what I'm saying at all. I just think..." He paused, suddenly quite emotional. "I think she gave me strength."

"To leave her?"

"To fight for her."

"Oh, Divine Mother. Give me strength," Luke sighed, irritated. "Can you not see that she's a danger to you? She puts you in harm's way and she keeps you distracted, the far greater sin in my mind. I thought you'd wake up knowing that though you want her, badly," he quirked an eyebrow at him, "that you must put her behind you. The war, the battles we fight, have nothing to do with her."

"They have everything to do with her!" Nicholas roared. "I've told you before Luke," he said more calmly. "If I live through the next engagement, I will find her, and I think ... No! I know for certain that she will have me."

"And just what will you do with her?" Luke asked caustically. "Drag her along with us from battle to battle?"

"No, Luke. After this, I'm done. I will fight no more."

"It's not that simple, Nicholas! What if we don't win? What if we are not able to broker our own terms? You can't just walk away. King Caius will offer rewards to anyone who finds you and try you for treason. I don't think I could bear to see you on the scaffold, lad." He paused, his emotions catching in his throat. "You're throwing everything away, everything you've fought for, all for a strumpet." He turned and stomped off, cursing at everyone to get out of his way.

24

AN OATH

Luke looked dejected and sullen when Nicholas found him in the mess tent eating alone. Nicholas sat next to him and began eating. After dipping several chunks of hard bread in a thin broth with a few vegetables, he wiped his hands on the back of his sleeve and stared at his friend.

"I owe you for saving my life, Luke, and I've been too stupid to thank you for it. I'm sorry."

For once, it seemed, Luke had no words. He did not acknowledge Nicholas at all, except to reach in front of him to grab another small loaf of bread to dip in his soup.

"You must know that this battle will go badly for us both if we are not communicating. And I don't mean the horns, flags, or couriers we use on the field." Nicholas paused for a moment to ponder the right words. He needed Luke to look straight through the narrow tunnel of physical and mental preparation for war. Every soldier needed blinders by this time before a battle. Admittedly, he knew he was a hypocrite and swore to sharpen his focus. All the bone-jarring training, all the mind-numbing strategizing, all came to a climax here. Finally, the right words came to him. "We must be brothers-in-arms, Luke."

"We once were brothers-in-arms," Luke spat. He turned his back on Nicholas and moved to another table to finish his meal.

Stung by the humiliation, Nicholas ignored the stares that burned into the back of his head. He kept his eyes down and tried to finish his dinner. It was no use. He had no appetite. He and Luke had always been of the same mind, had always been able to overcome their differences. He couldn't remember a time when they didn't. He stood up, walked to the middle of the room, and flung his bowl and goblet into the brassiere. He watched the sparks fly as they consumed his wooden utensils. He shot Luke an antagonistic glare and barged past the cook, who didn't dare reprimand him for ruining good serving ware.

Nicholas left the tent and stomped around the perimeter of camp, his anger and annoyance becoming more frigid in his heart with each intake of frosty air. So clumsy and noisy in his angry march, he alerted several night watchmen who almost stabbed him with their swords through his frozen heart.

Every one of the guards who mistook him for the enemy, Nicholas beat in the face and ribs with his hardened knuckles. He threw them aside and barged on, enraged and ruthless. The men on watch stepped aside and let their leader pass. He blundered on the glacial earth, kicking chunks of ice, and launched frozen missiles at the full moon.

Had it been an entire month since he'd seen his lady? Had he been ill for that long? How many days had he been unconscious?

He tugged at his heart and felt as if he could pull it out. It thumped raggedly, like it was already sitting on the surface of his chest. Staggering to the nearest tree, he plunged his sword into the ground before him, held out his hand for balance, and fell to his knees as he stared at the moon with tears in his eyes. Breathing fast and shallow as a winter stream, he prayed.

"Forgive me," he breathed, the frosty air making his vapor rise. "I've not been myself. I've not been disciplined or in control, and because of that I've hurt others. On the eve of what could be the most important moment of my life, of all our lives,

I beg forgiveness. I know I must put Meg behind me. That's what Luke has been saying all along. As hard as that is for me, I know I cannot be with her, perhaps ever. I beg you give me the ability to forget her, to make her a memory. I must do what I have asked others to do as we prepare for battle."

"Nicholas," Luke called, standing somewhere behind him. "I'll not have you brutalizing the men."

"Words are not enough," Nicholas's voice rasped. "But know that I am sorry."

"You've apologized before."

"I didn't know I was wrong before!" he yelled back, his anger rising.

"When will you learn that you put us all at risk if you even think about this woman? You can't even imagine her whispering sweet nothings in your ear. Now stand up and fight!"

"I will not fight you, Luke. I'm resigned. I know what I have to do." Leaning on his sword to stand up, Nicholas turned around. Several hundred of his men had shown up to witness this enmity between their leaders.

Before he knew it, Luke charged him with a mighty roar and tackled him to the ground. They tumbled together a few turns until Nicholas gained control, scrambled away from Luke, and raised his sword as a cautionary measure.

"Luke, I tell you. I will not fight."

"You have no choice!" Luke bellowed and charged again, this time with his sword raised for blows.

Nicholas parried the blows and matched Luke's ferocity. He thought he had the upper hand until Luke pushed him into a tree, slamming his head and ribs into the rough, hard trunk, rattling his concentration. Just as he regained his focus, Luke charged him again. He was playing dirty and using all the tricks Nicholas had taught him over the years.

As soon as Luke came within arm's length, Nicholas grabbed him by the scruff of his neck and threw him to the ground. Enraged, Luke ran toward him again. Nicholas was ready. As soon as they made contact, each man threw bitter punches to the face and body. Nicholas gained momentum and butted him with his head so fiercely that Luke fell backwards to the ground. Dazed, Luke rose and swung his sword. Nicholas engaged quickly, roughly. It became clear to him that one of them was going to have to give up or hurt the other well enough to stop the fight. Otherwise, they'd kill each other. To end the engagement, Nicholas slashed Luke's arm. When Luke looked down at his arm in astonishment, Nicholas kicked him hard in the stomach and he fell, humiliatingly, to the ground.

Nicholas stood over him, panting hard into the frigid night's air. He plunged his sword into the ground and offered a hand to his friend to pull him up from the frozen earth.

Luke hesitated as he glanced at the hand and then at Nicholas. "Oh, why not?"

Nicholas tugged hard. When his friend stood up, they wrapped their arms around each other and wept like little boys who had just gotten the belt by their fathers.

"I'm sorry, Nicholas," Luke whispered in his ear as he tried to suppress his emotion. "I don't know what came over me."

"I've not been myself either, Luke, and I'm sorry. I tried to apologize."

"Oh, aye. You tried all right. I've never heard such a rancid collection of half-baked apologies in my life. I didn't mean what I said about Meg. She's a fine lass. I was worried about a much bigger problem."

"Luke, the men are..."

"Gathered before you, laddie."

"What is happening?" Nicholas asked, wide-eyed as he turned in a circle to find the men in his companies surrounding him.

"They need their captain back, an awakening, so to speak," Luke said, grinning. "Nothing like a bucket of ice cold river water to bring a man to his senses."

"More like trying to beat some sense into me," Nicholas said with a sideways glance to his lieutenant.

"I'd like to meet the man who could."

"Captain?" Goodman asked.

"Yes, Goodman. What's going on here?"

"The men and I wanted to show our loyalty in some way, so when we discovered that you'd been troubled by certain events..." The boy stopped, swallowed hard, and licked his lips as if he were suddenly parched. "And then endured all that grueling pain while your wound healed, we decided that the best thing we could do was to give you our oaths."

"You've already made your oaths to king and country," Nicholas argued. "There's no need for anything else. I've got complete confidence in you and the men."

"It's not to king and country. It's to you, sir."

"I'm not sure I understand your meaning."

"With everything you've suffered, we figured," Goodman said, gesturing to the men around him, "we could show our support the best way we knew how and that was to make a special promise."

Nicholas gave Luke a suspicious glare and took a deep breath. How he hoped this did not have anything to do with his reprehensible behavior. He shook his head with regret as he saw some of the men he'd pummeled earlier kneeling in the frozen ground.

"Captain, we, all of us, promise to follow you into battle, our bodies and souls, yours for the commanding."

"Young Goodman," Nicholas repeated, getting a little exasperated.

"And we promise to keep your lady safe if she turns up."

No words could match the rawness of his emotions. How clumsy of him to let it be known that he'd been meeting a woman in secret, the very thing that could put them all at risk. And yet, here they were, acknowledging his weakness, offering to help him keep her safe.

"We want to win, Captain, and we thought this might be the one thing we could do to buoy you up. If you're in the right mind to win, we will win. It's that simple."

Row by long row, they all knelt before him, like a huge wave crashing upon the shore, moving from front to back. The motion of the men, like the sea on a beach, took its precious time meandering back. He hadn't realized he had charge of so many men, so many young men arriving from their king almost daily.

"I don't deserve it," Nicholas whispered, fighting back his emotions and nodding his head. "Thank you."

25

A CALL TO ARMS

Commander Burrage would make the call to arms today. Nicholas could feel it down to the chill in his bones. He hated the thought of it, but he knew the man too well. It started raining in the middle of the night and hadn't stopped for hours. Tossing and turning in his heap of furs, Nicholas listened to the pitter-patter on the top of his tent all night. Surprised and somewhat grateful that it wasn't cold enough to snow, he still lamented this new development. Weather was always a factor in the outcome of a battle.

Deciding that he may as well be ready for this ominous day, Nicholas dressed in his usual manner, but added more woolen layers to combat the cold. His leather armor and breastplate were specially made so that he could put them on himself. He required no squire. He was not as well protected as the armored and mounted knights, but the army relied more on his mobility, speed, and the ability to be lethal at just the right moment. After tightening his belts and sheathing his sword and daggers, he wrapped his huge, forest green cloak and wolf skin about his shoulders. He fastened the front and pulled the hood over his head to keep out the wet and the cold.

Tucking a loaf of bread for Luke inside his cloak, Nicholas

stepped out of his tent; he would have ideas on how to combat the elements. The camp had not yet come to life. He stalked about, trying not to step in puddles or burned-out campfires. Most of the men had been issued tents, so at least they were dry. When he found Luke's tent, he paused for a moment before he entered, hearing Luke curse under his breath. Usually amused by his friend's antics, he felt a pang of sadness. Would he ever hear Luke crack a joke again?

"Blasted things! Why is it I can't sleep and decide to get dressed before that gaggle of squires is up and looking for something to do? Blessed little lads would lick my boots clean if I asked them to. This armor will be the death of me!"

Luke must've thrown it to the ground, for he heard quite a comical thumping.

"Luke," Nicholas whispered outside the tent. "I can attend to you if need be."

"Absolutely not! How do you get this apparatus on by yourself?" Luke questioned gruffly. He swung open the flap of his tent. "What are you doing up at this hour?"

"Commander Burrage has been hinting for nigh on a week. I've got a feeling today's the day."

"Come in, laddie. I've got a horrible feeling, too. I don't know why he took so long. Both armies have been stationed here just waiting. I think he wanted to make sure you were fully healed. Most of the men wouldn't want to fight without you. You are their protection and their inspiration. They want to see their Wolf Knight riding high on his steed, the soft fur of that glorious pelt billowing, sword raised high in victory. Ugh!" Luke bent over, holding his hands to his stomach. "I feel like eels are wiggling in my gut trying to get out. Why march today in all this rain and muck?"

"I think the Asterians must be ready. I can hear them celebrating over the few miles that separate us. They must believe that they will win, so what is the point in procrastinating?"

"I guess they feel like wrestling in the mud. I think I'm

getting too old for this, Nicholas. I'd rather be under my furs spooning a woman."

Nicolas chuckled, shaking his head. "Wouldn't we all? I've got something for you, Luke," he said, revealing the loaf of bread he'd hidden under his cloak. "It's not quite a woman, but Poppy thought you'd enjoy it. She's the one who keeps staring at you when we're in the mess tent."

"Oh, laddie. Why'd you go and do that? Turn me into a bowl of mush, why don't you? You've been listening to me whine for too long, I think. Should we eat it now?"

"No, after the battle. We'll sit down at a proper table and eat it together," Nicholas answered emphatically, patting Luke on the shoulder. He sobered when he remembered why he needed to find Luke. "How do you think this rain will affect us? Do we need to make any changes?"

"Well, it's going to be harder to fight in the mud. It will slow soldiers down, but not just ours. Everyone will be affected. The rain will be a detriment to both sides."

"My thoughts precisely. It keeps the odds even."

"I think we need more than the ability to keep the odds even on this one, especially with their greater numbers. I hate to be the lamb going to slaughter."

"If anyone knows, it is me. Pray, my friend."

∽

COMMANDER BURRAGE AND HIS ARMY STOOD AT ATTENTION IN the rain for hours. It was well past noon. He assumed the Asterian army would be lined up, waiting for the Edmirans before they'd arrived at the battlefield, but they were nowhere to be seen. Nicholas felt certain that they were waiting out the storm in the comfort of their warm tents and filling their bellies with a fine meal. They would be ready for battle and the men in his army would not.

When the rain stopped and the clouds lifted to just above

the ridges, there they were, in position. As he studied their formations, Nicholas realized that there would be no movement. They expected the Edmiran army to charge first.

"There it is, lad, the hellfire of arrows ready to launch, just like I told you the first day I saw this place," Luke said, staring at the enemy in the distance.

"I've got eyes, Luke," Nicholas replied, exasperated. "I've done my best to prepare our men for what I knew would come. We've got a good strategy and our smithies have been real heroes. They've worked night and day to produce armor that can withstand those broadpoint arrows."

"I understand there's a wee bit of a problem with that." Luke cleared his throat and gave his captain a sympathetic sideways glance. "I'm sorry to hear the knights won't wear them."

"I can only do so much lecturing. They're fools. They don't know it yet, but they'll die."

"You can lead a horse to water, as the old saying goes."

Nicholas noticed the horses on the Edmiran front line. They seemed anxious, stomping the ground, puffing and snorting, shaking their heads. Their riders had a hard time keeping them under control.

"Luke, take charge of our men," Nicholas shouted over his shoulder. He kicked his horse with his heels and raced to the front line. It was not the time to charge. He needed to confer with Commander Burrage. All the water from the ridges and the upper plain appeared to be draining into the battlefield area. He felt that they needed to give it some time. Let the water run its course. Maybe even give it a few hours to dry. The enemy wasn't making the first move, probably for that very reason, so why should they?

The commander was deep in conversation with many of the knights when he arrived, their horses circled, huddling, so they could all hear.

"Commander Burrage!" Nicholas called. "Don't send them yet. It's too wet."

"Begging your pardon, Wolf Knight," sneered a knight from the king's court, a giant of a man. His black, enameled armor matched his diabolical, obsidian eyes. Nicholas had never liked him, always disagreed with him, and tried to ignore him. "It's the perfect time. Charging through a little mud just adds some color to the adventure, a story for the grandkids. They won't expect us to tramp through the field to engage them. They think we will wait it out just like they are. Cowards."

"Oh, I see," Nicholas smirked with disdain. "Now it's cowardly to wait until the proper moment when we would benefit most from the circumstances? Pardon me for saying so, commander. Don't do it. There's no rush, no hurry. Our enemy understands that just fine."

"We're tired of waiting," another knight complained. He wore blue-tinted armor with flowers scrolled on his breastplate. "If we don't go now, when will we?"

"The horses are chomping at the bit," chimed in another, his armor deep green like the forest, tall pines etched on his breastplate. "The boys behind us are soaked to the bone and beginning to freeze. It's now or never."

"If we retreat to get food and water," yet another knight explained, this one wearing golden armor, the sun's rays shining down on an ancestral castle. "Which could take a couple of days, they could start fighting while we are unawares."

"I don't believe they would do that," Nicholas replied. "They face the same obstacles we do regarding the weather and its effects. They will wait to charge until the battlefield suits them."

"That could take a week and never if the sun don't shine," the black knight groused.

"This field will be muddy regardless of our choice." Commander Burrage said something — finally.

"Now or never. I agree." Black knight wouldn't keep his mouth shut.

"I'm not asking for that much time," Nicholas argued. "Give me a few hours to reconnoiter their formations and movements.

Perhaps I could get some of our little urchins inside their camp. They might hear something of their strategy."

Nicholas could see the commander looked tossed.

"I don't care what this wolf killer does. I'm going now!" the black knight roared, turned in his saddle to face the men, raised his sword, and charged.

"Not yet, you fool!" Burrage yelled, but it was too late. He pulled his sword from its scabbard and raised it to get the men's attention. They took it for a signal to charge.

The entire army roared and followed Commander Burrage and the black knight, stampeding. Nicholas was left behind, a boulder in the middle of an immense river, the water rushing by with the speed and ferocity of great, white rapids.

26

MUD AND BLOOD

Nicholas charged to the bottom of the nearest ridge, observing the battle from the outskirts. He watched in horror as the Asterian archers unleashed their arrows, time after time, and pierced the armor of the best and strongest knights in the Edmiran army. Some men fell from their horses and tried slogging through the mud to engage in the battle. Others fell and never stood up again due to their heavy armor, their helmets facing the ground, drowned in mud. Many fell and were stuck in the mud only to be murdered. The cavalry and foot soldiers behind the knights fared better, the broadhead arrow points less effective on the new armor. More of them fought, but it was slow going. They could barely pull their feet out of the mud, let alone face a combatant with any sort of agility or speed. Worse still, they were fighting over corpses.

It was as if the soldiers were chained to hell from below, the evil one himself keeping a voyeur's eye on the happenings above his world, controlling their movements and laughing at their misfortunes.

Spurring his horse to the top of the ridge, Nicholas needed to see if Luke had set his companies into action to subdue the archers. To his great relief, there they were, sneaking up the opposite side of the ridge. Hundreds and hundreds of his men would soon wreak havoc on them and change the tide of this abominable battle.

Nicholas tethered his horse, strapped his cloak to the animal, and fell in line with them, Luke beside him as always. As they quietly dispatched the first sentries, Nicholas realized that a few farther up the hill had seen the attacks. They ran to sound the alarm. He sprinted after them, hoping to subdue the enemy soldiers for a few more minutes so more of his men could reach the top. He'd have greater numbers to meet the threat on the other side. It was to no avail. They were greeted with hundreds of footmen placed to protect the archers. Nicholas raised his sword and cut down the first to attack him.

Veiled in the haze of battle, he roared, charged, tackled, kicked, clanked, clashed, fought, stabbed, killed.

A mud-covered demon heading straight to purgatory.

No one would've known him, except by the wolf skin trailing down his back. Attacking the archers from behind was a surprise move, and it impeded the Asterian longbow force. Others of his men stayed close to the woods, unleashing their crossbows on the enemy. Some of the Asterian soldiers realized what was happening. They brought the fight out of the narrow funnel and into the woods. Spreading it out, just as Nicholas hoped.

Now, it was just man-to-man combat. Nicholas needed another strategic play to end this abysmal battle. If he could only get to the foot soldiers in the middle of the fray, he could use some of them to sneak up behind enemy forces, beyond the barricades, and outside the narrow end of the plain. The Edmiran army had the potential to surround the Asterians completely.

Just as he was about to slog his way into the middle of the mayhem and make the command, an enemy warrior stood in his way.

"Wolf Knight."

"And you?"

"John Paul Longbourne."

"Ah, the young prince. The mastermind behind the slaughter of my cavalry."

"And you brought my archers to their knees. Brilliant strategy."

"So, we're even?" Nicholas feigned sarcasm.

"Hardly." John Paul smirked. "I had a feeling you and I would meet today."

"Why is that?"

"Apparently, you're the man to beat."

"So I've heard."

Nicholas sloshed toward John Paul with his sword poised, cautiously sizing him up. He was as tall as himself, but not as bulky. Nicholas assumed that what this warrior lacked in brute strength, he made up for in finesse. They raised their swords in the air, clanked them, and held them together as they circled each other, testing each other's strength. Nicholas backed away, grinning, eager for action. He took a fighting stance and gestured for John Paul to attack. The prince ran toward him with his sword raised and jumped high into the air as he bashed it into Nicholas's shield, each thrusting and parrying.

Tired of the easy dancing, and because he still needed to instruct the foot soldiers, Nicholas battered John Paul more forcefully with his shield, hitting him square on the shoulder, neck, and then the face. He took the blows better than Nicholas expected. John Paul did not weaken or give way. Nicholas used the butt of his sword and smashed his wrist with it. When John Paul dropped his sword and grunted from the pain, Nicholas turned and elbowed him so hard in the gut that he fell into the mud. First collapsing to his knees, John Paul rolled onto his shoulder while cradling his injured hand.

Thinking that the young prince was done for, Nicholas rushed toward the center of the field to communicate with the footmen. He was convinced that he could create a third flank and surround his enemy.

THE ENTANGLED PRINCESS

Nicholas heard a roar from behind. He turned around as John Paul charged him and leveled a full-bodied blow to his stomach. They splashed to the ground. John Paul stood up and poised himself for more fighting. Nicholas remained on the ground, pulled back by the powerful suction of the mud. He couldn't move. Nicholas grabbed his sword and readied himself for battle. Surprisingly, he parried John Paul's strikes from the ground until the man used the same move on him and smashed his wrist with the butt of his sword. With no weapon in his hands, Nicholas raised his hands in the air and surrendered. The prince stepped back and waited for him to stand up.

When Nicholas wrenched himself from the grip of the ground, John Paul pointed his sword at his heart. He grinned like a mad man, his face crinkling maniacally, caked with mud and gore. "Didn't think I could take you, did you, Wolf Knight?" John Paul asked, still smiling, enthusiasm for his victory becoming more apparent. "I could see it in your face when we met on the field."

"Let's put it this way: I didn't think you'd win with ease," Nicholas replied grimly. "But you've won. I'll give you that."

"Yes, I have," John Paul said ebulliently. "Your surrender will make negotiating with Edmira an easy task, which I did not expect. Now, if you wouldn't mind, place your hands behind your back." He finished, royal manners perfectly intact.

With his surrender, Asterias would win the battle and perhaps the war. While Nicholas waited for one of John Paul's aides to tie his hands behind his back, he closed his eyes as if in prayer. Moments of his life flashed before him — his mother's tender-hearted eyes, his father's great whiskered face, and Meg.

"Oh, Meg," he whispered to himself. "I thought I could see the path to take. I love you."

"Nicholas!" Luke screamed.

Luke rushed by on his horse, bumping into John Paul and disarming him. They pounded each other brutally, but to win, Nicholas needed another sword. In his peripheral vision,

Nicholas spied a sword in the hands of one of his fallen comrades. He led the fistfight toward the corpse until he was close enough to grab the sword. Pulling it up by the sharp end, he flipped it into the air, and caught it by its hilt. He pointed it at John Paul. Nicholas recognized defeat in John Paul's eyes and was disheartened, though not surprised, when he drew his dagger. They exchanged a few laborious swipes until Nicholas remembered a fighting move he'd seen Meg use to great effect. He turned and gashed the back of John Paul's legs. They dashed out from under him and he fell, entombed in the mud. Nicholas laid a foot on his torso and pointed his sword at John Paul's heart.

"We're done here," he said, his voice gravelly and fraught with exhaustion.

~

THE FIRST THING NICHOLAS NOTICED WHEN HE LOOKED UP was that the sun had gone down. Men from his army crowded around him. Nicholas heard them whisper about the battle, about the fight between him and the young prince, and how most of the knights from Edmira had died or been seriously wounded. Commander Burrage miraculously survived. In the front line of the initial charge, no one had expected him to.

"You've got to kill him, sir," Goodman urged. "It will give us the upper hand in negotiations. They will know that we have no mercy."

"No, Goodman," Nicholas replied. "I will not kill him in cold blood. The true role of a victor is to know when to extend mercy. He will be ransomed. Our enemy will be much more willing to discuss terms of surrender once they know we have their future king."

"My brother is the future king. You won't get much in the way of ransom for me," John Paul coughed, struggling to get up out of the mud.

Nicholas allowed the prince to stand while all the young squires pointed their swords at him. He was delighted. Although they were in tatters with scrapes and bruises, even a few good gashes, they survived. The scrappy little imps, Nicholas thought happily as the haze of battle lifted.

"Oh, I doubt that, little princeling," Luke chimed in as he approached, looking like he'd been dragged by the devil himself through the underworld, spouting his usual sarcasm. As he drew closer, Nicholas embraced him and thumped him hard on the back, relieved to see him alive. "It was a draw until our Wolf Knight kicked your skinny arse across the battlefield. We'll get a good price for your pretty face, all right." Luke made sure to stop in front of John Paul, tap a pointy finger in the center of his chest, and look around the circle to all. He smiled broadly. "We won this one, boys!"

Amid their cheering, Nicholas barked at his men. "Attention! This is John Paul Longbourne, warrior prince, expert strategist, and great leader to his countrymen. He is a prisoner of war and deserves every courtesy of that office. I expect you to guard him carefully, for he is a worthy foe. Take him to the barricades and tie him up there with the other prisoners. I will be there soon."

27

TO MURDER A PRINCE

"I tried to gather the remaining foot soldiers and lead them to the enemy's rear guard at the west end of the plain beyond the barricades," Nicholas reported to Commander Burrage. "We may have been able to secure that area, but things developed differently."

"It seems the battle just petered out," Burrage replied. "I've never seen that before."

"It has been a tiresome rout fighting in the mud, sir, but perhaps they left when we captured their prince."

"We caught Prince William?" Burrage's mouth fell open in surprise.

"No, the younger one, Prince John Paul. I never saw the older prince."

"That's because he was standing on the northern ridge astride his big, fancy warhorse with the long, wavy mane in his shining armor looking pale and frightened beneath his dozens of banners," Luke growled, his feelings for the prince's actions quite clear. "I don't think he ever fought."

"Well, let's go have a talk with their young prince, shall we?" the commander said almost affably, sloshing his way through the mud.

Separated from the rest of the prisoners, John Paul's hands were tied up high to the barricade. His head hung low. His chin rested on his chest. Nicholas didn't think the prince had been seriously wounded in battle or that he'd suffered any harm while in custody, yet he seemed exhausted.

"Cut the man down," Burrage commanded.

"Sir?" Nicholas didn't believe John Paul was as docile as he looked.

"I know what I'm doing, Captain."

As soon as the guards cut his hands from the ropes, John Paul stumbled a little in the mud, but he managed not to fall. They quickly retied his hands behind his back.

As the guards brought John Paul forward to face the commander, they forced him to his knees. There he was, heir to a kingdom, and he looked it, too, despite his appearance. John Paul had that regal bearing. Nicholas recognized it right down to his mud-caked boots, and great intelligence he couldn't help but admire. The hellishness of this battle had been his doing. Nicholas could do nothing but respond to what he thought might happen, always on the defensive, a strategy he preferred not to engage in. The men in the Asterian army fought for him, not his brother. Even though John Paul was filthy, ragged, and beaten, Nicholas detected the hint of a smile, as if his kneeling in the mud before an invading commander was somehow ironic. Yes, he was still a dangerous prisoner.

"My men tell me that you are the son of King George Edward Longbourne of Asterias, the Prince John Paul."

John Paul faced his enemy with a polite smile, but he didn't answer. This was not a game he would play.

"But not the rightful heir," Burrage continued. He paced around his prisoner with his hands behind his back. "Only the second son. *Tsk. Tsk.* Well, don't feel too badly. We have that happening in our kingdom, too. And it doesn't seem to matter who the oldest is, just who has the best poison. It's no secret that Caius killed his wretched father. Kings will be kings."

Burrage stepped back to laugh at his own joke. A few of the guards chuckled with him. Nicholas and Luke stood at attention nearby, uncomfortable with the route the commander had taken.

"You should try it, lad," Burrage cajoled. "Now, that would be a way to outlast your brother and rule the kingdom. Of course, you don't have a kingdom anymore because we are going to take it."

John Paul raised an eyebrow and shrugged. Nicholas knew this type of fighting man. He would not be goaded into rage and give them an excuse to kill him on the spot.

"Where was your brother? Did anyone encounter him on the battlefield?" Burrage yelled, trying his best to provoke John Paul. "I'm told he's a decent fighter and cruel. How could he have missed his chance? What a perfect place to put his evil ways to work. Then it occurred to me that he's not the real enemy here. You are. I'm told these devastating archers and barricades built as high as castle walls and the location of this field are all your ideas. And here you are on the field making sure everything goes just the way you planned. You really should think about killing your brother. You are the natural leader. But you're not good enough for my Wolf Knight. You've got the brains and the fighting ability, but you lack the size. That's what you need to beat this man in battle. So, here you are. What to do, what to do…" Burrage muttered menacingly as he finished circling his prisoner, enjoying the victory dance.

"Sir? If I may?" Nicholas asked.

"What now, Captain?" Burrage said, impatient and annoyed.

"We've talked about this at length before. I believe he should be ransomed."

"Ransom a prince? He should rot in a dungeon in his own filth!"

"Send him back conditionally, of course," Nicholas continued urgently. "We can use the gold and dictate terms of surrender. We can end this, sir. We show good faith by sending him back to them unharmed, our enemy knowing that we want this war to end as much as they do."

It was not what Burrage wanted to hear, but Nicholas felt the need to persuade him. He and so many others came out of this with their lives. They could bank on a future if he could get this man to retreat, just a little.

It only made him mad.

"What about that, lad?" The commander stood behind John Paul and yanked his hair back hard so that he had no choice but to look up. "Does the enemy want this war to end?" he asked, his mouth rudely close to John Paul's ear.

"That depends," John Paul said pleasantly.

"On what?" Burrage growled, still pulling on the prince's hair.

"Commander Burrage, we have been attacked at our rear!" The black knight appeared, roaring in anger as he and a few foot soldiers ran up to deliver the news. "They are slaughtering our men as we speak. He has another attack force!" The black knight pointed accusingly.

Nicholas stole a glance toward John Paul. The small smile he wore had grown to a full-blown grin. It was his plan all along to outflank them in the rear if he lost on the battlefield. Yes, a dangerous prisoner indeed.

"You think it's funny, do you?" the black knight snarled, marching toward the prince.

Nicholas saw the flash of a dagger. The black knight angled his knife to slit the prince's throat. John Paul had somehow freed his hands and fought heroically, cutting his fingers as he defended himself. Nicholas charged the black knight for fear the prince would be killed and tackled both men to the ground in a spectacular display of foul, muddy water. The black knight emerged from the debris, sputtering obscenities. Nicholas stood at once looking for the prince. He saw him behind Commander Burrage, face down in the mud.

"Why did you do this?" Nicholas roared as he kneeled over the body of John Paul and turned him over, searching for wounds. "Don't you want this to end? Killing a royal in cold blood won't do! Asterias has every right to retaliate to this egregious blunder."

Commander Burrage stood between Nicholas and the black knight, as if he must protect the enraged knight from his furious captain. He looked haughty and annoyed for being challenged by an inferior officer. Nicholas heard a grunt of pain. When he looked up, the black knight slumped against Burrage's back. His head lay heavily on the commander's shoulder while his hand slid down his arm. Burrage's face wrinkled into a mask of hideous and unmistakable torture. The end of a spear had burst through his belly. His eyes widened and blood trickled from his mouth. Both men, gruesomely attached, fell sideways and died in a muddy grave, inhaling their own rotten innards into their struggling lungs.

War-weary and accustomed to such cruel violence, Nicholas was still shocked by the ghastly scene in front of him. Turning from it, he looked into the face of the prince who struggled to speak. He knelt beside him.

"Don't try to talk," Nicholas whispered urgently.

"You soldiers!" Luke barked. "Goodman, you're in charge. Save the prince's life."

As Nicholas watched Luke point out where to take John Paul, it gave him the power to focus. He understood what he needed to do. When Luke turned back to him, they nodded to each other. Together they chased Commander Burrage's assassins.

28

MISFORTUNES OF WAR

"It was a draw, sire. I can think of no other way to describe it. I was on the ridge observing..."

Observing, Meg scoffed silently as she stared down at her folded arms and then straightened the pleats of her gown.

"You weren't fighting, William?" their father queried, his fuzzy brows lifting the sagginess above his eyes.

"I led the attack on the rear guard, sire. I sent the assassins to kill their commander."

"So, you did not engage in battle? Unlike your brother, whose heroic actions..." The king paused, his throat strangled with emotion.

"And look where those heroic actions have led him," William countered angrily.

"At least he was out there fighting for his kingdom! He planned this attack. That's more than I can say for you, my son, my heir." The king burst with resentment, his ragged eyes simmering as he glanced at every face around the council table.

"All we know right now," William continued, "is that John Paul was wounded badly enough that they don't dare transport him to us for the ransom money."

"This is bleak news indeed," the Duke of Breckenridge said

in his sycophantic way. He patted William on the shoulder, trying to support him as he rationalized his friend's behavior to the king. "The loss of a prince is always a great tragedy, but you've a loyal and stalwart soul right here."

"It's not just bleak," Lord Ellesworth replied, irritated, countering the absurd tribute to William. "It's a disaster. They know how valuable he is to us. They know they have the man who planned and executed the tremendous slaughter of their forces, especially when he unleashed hell on their rear guard. We'll be lucky to get him back in one piece. They'll charge us so much for the ransom that we'll be destitute. And they know it."

"I am sorry about John Paul, Father." William managed to look sorrowful. "I am!" he shouted, standing up and pounding the table. "For the love of stars above, he's my brother." He took a deep breath and swallowed hard as he composed his thoughts. "It's not cowardice as you suggest, my Lord Father." He tried not to sneer, but the attempt was not lost on those in the room. "It's logic and wisdom. John Paul was a fool. He should've saved himself from the dangers of the battlefield. He should've been on the ridge with me, delegating orders to his men. Leading, not fighting. Why should royals fight when there is no need?" William scoffed and shrugged impudently as he sat back in his chair. He crossed his legs and straightened his tunic. "I played the part you asked me to play, Father. I led and I extended mercy."

"To whom?!" the king exploded. "This draw leaves us in the same position we were in before the battle. When I said lead, I meant win. We had no other choice. It had to be a decisive victory. There is no other circumstance by which we can demand that they leave."

"I did my best, Father."

"Your best? You call this your best?" the king raged, his jowls quivering.

"They had an answer to everything we threw at them," William justified. "I knew it would be a draw as I watched."

"Yes, yes. You've already outlined your cowardice, which is truly shocking. Your behavior off the battlefield suggests that you'd be a vicious monster on it."

"Sire," he began more calmly, stung by the king's contempt, "we have intelligence that suggests the invader caught the assassins that killed Commander Burrage and one of his knights, and overcame them."

"You mean killed them in retaliation?"

"Yes, Father."

"So, we have a draw. Our wounded prince to their murdered commander," Lord Cronmiller declared, looking down. He grimaced as he interlaced his fingers.

"And all those men dead in the mud don't even go toward the tally," the king said sadly. "When will we ever learn?"

A courier quietly entered the council chamber, handed a note to the king, bowed, and left the room.

The king examined the seal, broke it, and read. His eyes transformed from anger and aggression to a dead stare, his face a ghastly white. He stood up and shuffled from council to his private chamber. On his way out, he tried to hand the note to Lord Cronmiller, but it fell from his hand onto the table. Cronmiller opened the note, read its contents, and rubbed his face hard with his hands.

"The Edmiran commander believes that John Paul is dead."

Meg felt her breath catch in her throat. She struggled to breathe. Uncontrolled tears welled in her eyes. As the horrible truth sank in on members of the council, her mind caught on a barb, just as if a thorn on a rose bush had snagged her gown as she walked by. "But what does it mean, believed to be dead?" she asked, trying to comprehend the explanation behind the words. "How do they not know for certain?"

Lord Cronmiller rose from the table and frowned, his dark clothes making his sallow skin look more yellow in the faint light. "He is no longer in their custody."

"What?" Meg cried in shock as the other ministers erupted into clamor and chaos. "Where is he?"

Cronmiller looked at the note as if he would burn it on the spot.

"It says here that John Paul was suffering high fever and infection from dreadful wounds, but now he's gone," Cronmiller whispered in confusion with a sad shake of his head. He's either been stolen out from under their noses or tossed into a ditch with the rest of the dead." Lord Cronmiller laid the missive on the table and pressed his lips together, his brows clashing with concern. "Aside from the terrible tragedy of losing a most beloved and valued prince, we must admit to ourselves that fighting no longer works. We're going to have to arrange a peace treaty, and that's all there is to it."

"Lord Cronmiller," William said. "Who signed the note?"

"A commander named Sheppard."

"What kind of imbecilic name is that?" William scoffed.

"Obviously a common one," Cronmiller replied irritably. "He may be nothing but a peasant to you, William, but he is a cunning commander who has King Caius's favor. The king agrees with the democratic selection of Sheppard by the men in the Edmiran army."

"That means they will follow him to the death," William said, contemplating. "This is an ill omen for us. I've heard of him. He's the brains of the operation and a bloody good killer, and now he's the new commander. He'd wipe us off the face of the map if he ever got the chance. We cannot bargain with cold-blooded killers. We've got to cut him down, draw him into battle. Once he's dead, they'll leave. You can take my word on that."

Meg practically vaulted from her seat and pounded on the table. "Just like the Edmiran army left when their last commander was killed? What a joke. Everyone knows they never left. And who would lead our men to battle? You? Stop before you embarrass yourself, William." Meg echoed the hurtful words her brother had said to her in the past. "We all know you were not part of the last battle. John Paul is the only one who could mastermind another." Meg shuddered and contorted her face in anger. "You make me sick."

"I slipped out to speak with your father and we will broker for peace," Cronmiller said.

"Not while I'm alive," William sneered.

"You will do what your father and this council commands," Cronmiller warned, pushing past William as he tugged on the lapels of his robe and straightened the links in his chain of office. "You are not king yet."

∼

MEG KNELT AT THE ALTAR IN FRONT OF THE ROYAL CHAPEL, bowing her head in prayer as she had for several days. Her mind wandered from praying to vivid memories of John Paul. It embarrassed her that she didn't have the strength of mind to stay in constant prayer, but the memories were too precious to push away.

Sometimes, Meg saw in her mind's eye her two brothers as boys forced to come to daily prayers. Dressed in their finest tunics, capes, and caps, they stood at the front of the chapel as her father led her to the altar to kneel, her tiny fingers wrapped around one of his. Meg never prayed during these times. She was too distracted by William and John Paul, who elbowed each other and whispered jokes. Inevitably, one of them would stumble out of line and receive a fierce glare from their father.

Her mind wandered to another precious memory of John Paul. He'd arrived in the practice yard just in time to see Meg clanking swords awkwardly with a young knight. The king had finally convinced someone to teach her how to fight.

"Just what do you think you're doing, Meg?" John Paul asked while walking toward them.

"I'm learning to fight," Meg said, wielding a sword that was too

heavy for her.

"Why?" John Paul asked, diverted by the preposterous training.

"Because father said I could."

"He says yes to everything you ask," he retorted, rolling his eyes at her.

"I know." She gave him a triumphant grin.

John Paul watched the 'fighting' with mounting frustration.

"You're not going to learn to fight if this gentleman is not willing to hurt you."

He stepped between them and stopped the engagement, which looked more like a silly country dance, the partners facing each other and skipping forward with blades in their hands instead of holding gowns and capes.

"Pardon me, sir," John Paul said, grasping the sword from Meg's partner. "If you don't mind, I'll take it from here. Thank you for your effort."

"I'm glad to be relieved of it, my lord." The young soldier exhaled and walked away, looking nervously over his shoulder before they could call him back.

"You see, she needs someone who's not afraid to knock her to the ground." He did so without ceremony.

"Why did you do that?" Meg snapped, her rump and ego smarting.

"Because you won't learn to fight properly dancing around daisies with men who would rather woo you," he replied, trying not to laugh.

"What are you talking about?" Meg asked as she got to her feet and swiped the dust from her behind. "He said he would be happy to help me."

"Of course, he did," John Paul shook his head, amused by her lack of understanding. "What man in the kingdom wouldn't?"

Meg scrunched her lips up, crinkled her nose, and scratched the side of her head, thinking. "Are you telling me that every man in this kingdom wants to woo me?" she asked, disbelieving.

"Yes," he said quickly and gave her a teasing smile. "If our father thought that any one of them was suitable for you, I don't know a single man who would gag at the thought of courting you."

"Well, I suppose if you put it that way..." Meg fluttered her eyelashes comically. She gave him a saucy smile, and then she slugged him. "That's a horrid thought, John Paul, to know that men think of me that way."

"Don't flatter yourself," John Paul smirked in his loveable way. "It's only because you're rich. Being pretty just makes it more palatable for them."

"You are insufferable," she said, offering him a reluctant smile.

"I know." He smiled and raised an eyebrow at her. "Now, if you want to learn to fight..."

Meg looked down at her clasped hands and smiled sadly. He did relish the opportunity to get out of worthless meetings with ministers and knock his sister flat on the ground.

"Poor John Paul," she whispered, coming out of the reverie. "Little good all that sparring will do now. How I wish I had you back."

Stars Above, I've been begging for days now. I know you can save my brother. I need him so much. We all need him. John Paul is the only one who can tame William and cause him to make proper choices without believing for a moment that he took anyone's advice. John Paul is clever that way. I need him more than you know. I live in terror of William. At times, when I am not in control of myself, I cry and tremble and have horrible dreams of him hurting me, of killing me. I do not think I can survive this world without John Paul. I know it's a selfish thing to ask, but please bring my brother back.

"My Lady Marguerite?"

She quickly wiped her tears, stood from the altar, and turned around.

"Come here, child, and sit with me." The bishop gestured to the first of the sculpted wooden pews near the front of the chapel.

"Yes, Father Elias," Meg replied obediently, but her eyes prickled from the pain while hot tears welled. "I have prayed and prayed for days. I can't reconcile this, Father. I just can't believe that my brother is dead. It hurts too much to consider." She stood up and paced, her fists balled tightly, her fingernails pressed into the palms of her hands. "Don't they hear me?" Meg wailed at the glorious depictions of sky, clouds, and stars painted on the ceiling.

"We don't always get the answers we hope for in our prayers," he consoled.

Lady Byron entered the front of the chapel from an aisle next to the nave. When Meg saw her, she turned from them both and sprinted down the center of the church, her gown and hair flowing behind her. She was so tired of talking. Pushing hard on the heavy wooden door, Meg looked behind her and saw the worried expressions on their kind faces before she dashed into her mother's garden, now covered in frost and snow.

Meg ran as far away from the chapel as she could, desperate to find a hidden spot where no one could find her. She couldn't face anyone just now. The snow crunched under her feet. Her tears felt frozen on her cheeks, tiny icicles of unbearable sadness. She vaguely registered when her fingers and toes grew numb. Her temples throbbed. Her heart felt as if it would burst from her chest and explode into tiny red ribbons right before her eyes.

Not comprehending where she stood in the garden, Meg turned circles in a panic as the landscape whirred past her. She stopped herself, caught her breath, and looked for her favorite gazebo. In warm weather, wisteria grew on the granite pillars, twisting and turning their tendrils, their beautiful blossoms swaying gracefully in the breeze. In honor of her mother, the royal gardeners always hung large baskets of flowers bursting with blooms and cascading over their rims between the columns. Meg found a familiar bench inside the gazebo and collapsed. Pulling her knees up to her chest, she folded her arms around her legs, buried her head, and sobbed. She rose from the cold stone bench, rubbing her temples as another prayer threaded through her mind.

Nicholas ... He's the only one left. I still have father, but he is so sad. Nothing makes him happy. The realization that pains me the most is knowing my brother and my mother are the only people who loved me and I will never feel their love again. And I can't love them back. I will never be able to talk to John Paul, just talk, make him laugh, see him smile, get mad at him for pushing me around, or invite him into my chamber for a meal and watch my ladies swoon over him. Or watch all the ladies in the kingdom swoon. He was the real prince. I'm not the only one who will feel his loss so much. Losing him will make the whole kingdom shudder to the bones.

I need Nicholas. I need him to wrap me in his strong arms, caress me, kiss my tears away, and tell me that everything will be all right. I need to lie in his embrace for hours, weeks, months. I need to wake up when all of this has gone from me. When the pain is not so grave and I can face people and talk to them without crumbling to the ground in a cascade of tears and misery. How can I get through this without him, without someone to help me stand tall?

Meg heard snow crunching under someone's feet. She hid behind a pillar until she spotted Lady Byron carrying her winter cloak.

"My Lady Marguerite," she called. "I'm worried to death. If you don't come inside and get warm, I'm afraid you'll get quite sick. Wouldn't it be better to mourn with the king? He asked for you not too long ago."

"I am quite well," Meg lied, stepping from behind the pillar.

"Good gracious, child. You look a fright." Lady Byron ran to her and covered her with the cloak, lined with extra warm fabric and trimmed with fur, but Meg let it fall from her shoulders.

"I don't want it."

"But you are already chilled. I'm not sure that you can sustain the shock of losing your brother, be out in this frozen air, and not get sick. We cannot lose you, too."

"I will go to my father," Meg said distractedly. "It was wrong of me to think of only myself."

"What if we walk back to the castle together?" Lady Byron suggested as she tried to place the cloak on her shoulders once more.

"I already told you I don't want it. Just leave me alone!"

And she ran to her father.

29

IN DREAMS

"Father?" she called quietly as she shut his chamber doors behind her, trying to focus on the room. A fire burned in the grate, and a few candles were lit throughout the apartment. Meg thought the king might be sitting in the chair that faced the blaze. "Lady Byron told me you've been asking for me," she continued, walking toward the chair. "I'm sorry I took so long to come. It was wrong of me."

The king was not sitting in his chair.

"Father?" she called a little louder this time. "Where are you?"

As she whirled around to walk in the direction of the king's bedchamber, she almost bumped into his personal groom who had not seen her, either. He carried her father's favored slippers, looking down as he fluffed the soft sheepskin.

"Oh, Daniels! You scared me to death!" Meg exclaimed as she put a hand over thumping heart.

"Forgive me, my lady. I was just ... just..." He couldn't seem to finish his thought.

"Tending to my father."

"Yes, my lady, trying everything I can think of to get his mind off this tragedy. Has there been any more news? Could John Paul live?"

"We may never know what has happened to him for certain. My hope is that he has used his cunning to escape and he'll come walking through the castle gate in a fortnight with his hair blowing in the breeze and that rakish smile on his face," Meg said, trying to sound more positive than she felt. She eyed the slippers. "They look very plush. I'm sure he will be glad to have them."

"It's always been my honor to serve the king, my lady."

"You've served him well, Daniels. How is he doing?"

"Handling the news as well as can be expected, I suppose."

"Which isn't well at all." She answered her own question. "None of us can accept this news. Where is he?"

"Perhaps just in his bed chamber. Allow me to—"

"No, it's fine, Daniels. Let me go to him," Meg insisted. She walked toward the door, but she turned back toward him. "I think..." She paused for a moment. "I think we need each other right now."

"Of course, my lady."

"Father?" she asked, not more than a whisper, as she opened the door to his bedchamber and stuck her head through. "It's me. I'm sorry I've taken so long to get here. I was out in mother's garden feeling sorry for myself. I should've come sooner. Forgive me?"

Meg walked to his giant four-poster bed with the thick ornate draperies open and found the bed empty. She looked around the chamber. Her father lived an austere existence. The few pieces of carved and brightly polished furniture he had were of the highest quality, but the room held no thick carpets or tapestries, just the monotony of stone floors and walls. One thing that stood out was the portrait of her mother set in a gilded frame, which hung on the wall opposite his bed. Meg tried several times over the years to convince her father to take it down and place it in the gallery.

Seeing it every day caused him to miss her all the more. Still, he stared into the young, beautiful face of his wife and never stopped being overwhelmed by the grief and sadness of his great loss.

Everything seemed in order. Another fire burning, more candles set about the room. The king's writing desk looked as it always did, with papers scattered about and the quill in the ink pot. On a large table near the desk were the usual assortment of maps and books. A few books spread on the bed, although it didn't appear that her father had been in bed today. Maybe that's what he planned. She was glad of it. Books would help get his mind off...

Forcing back her tears, Meg walked to the writing desk. As she shuffled through some papers, she found one that said simply, "Forgive me."

"What?" Meg knit her brows together as she gave the note a closer look. "Why is he saying this again? He always apologizes for the silliest things, as if he's the greatest disappointment in the world. Silly papa." She tossed the parchment back onto his desk and sighed. "Where are you?"

Then she saw him.

The king lay on his side, face down, in the small space between his bed and the wall.

"Father!" Meg screamed and ran to him. As she kneeled beside him, she turned him over to see his eyes wide open. His own dagger protruded from his chest, blood oozing from the fatal wound to his heart. Every moment that she'd seen her father melancholy over the years burst forth. Thousands of images raced through her mind, flashing behind her eyes, out of control. Meg did not doubt that her father had taken his own life. Losing John Paul was the last thread that unraveled his tattered existence.

Shocked, Meg scrambled back from him on all fours. Panting, she stood, her heart pounding in her ears and sweat bursting from her neck and temples. She felt horribly light-headed. Daniels burst through the door, yelling something that she couldn't hear. She saw only his lips moving. He had a look of overwhelming concern on his face and though he ran toward her, he seemed very slow. Meg remembered lifting her hand and pointing at her father.

Then, she fell, the pain in her head exploding, the castle reforming in a familiar, yet wholly unfamiliar way.

Meg found herself walking through the corridors of the castle, her home, but it was different. As she passed areas familiar to her, she realized the castle had transformed into something more shining and vibrant than it had ever been. The large bricks were brighter, glistening almost white. More windows than she remembered allowed the sunshine to warm and spread an amber glow into the rooms and great halls. Plants near the windows, around every corner, and vines clung to almost every pillar. They had a heady scent that reminded her of life, of renewal, that spring was coming.

The furnishings were different, too, and Meg wasn't quite sure what to make of them. Creamy in color, soft and plump, they looked much more comfortable than the dark, hard wooden chairs and tables she was used to. Fluttering in the breeze that wafted through the windows were sheer curtains that seemed to delineate each area for rest and conversation. Meg stepped between two couches and twirled with her arms spread out, inhaling the scent of sweet-smelling herbs rising from fresh rushes on the floor. When she passed through the curtains, something on her head got caught in them. As she raised her hands to feel it, Meg realized that she wore a veil that mingled with the curtains.

When the veil detached from the airy curtains, Meg adjusted it on her head. That's when she realized that she wore a most exquisite gown. With just a twinge of frustration, she wished for a looking glass. And there it was. A mirror appeared right next to the wall beside her and she saw her reflection. Made of cream-colored silk, with just a hint of buttery yellow, it fit her torso tightly. The gown gathered in elegant folds at her hips and trailed behind her into a long train. A thick sash was tied below a golden applique and touched her slippered toes. It was sleeveless except for the cuffs that hugged the top of her arms. The same sheer fabric as the veil, sewn to the cuffs, reached the floor, and sprawled to the same length as the dress's train. Gathering up the veil in one arm and train of the dress in the other, Meg twisted and turned for side views of the gown in the looking glass. She smiled brightly at herself.

And she ran to her father.

The king sat on his throne, as happy and healthy as she'd ever seen him. He wore his royal robes, his crown placed perfectly on his head, with a scepter in his hand. John Paul knelt on one knee before him on the dais in anticipation of his father's blessing, his thick blond hair mussed up as always. They both looked toward her as she glided into the throne room, her veil floating behind her, slow and soft as feathers falling.

"Come here, my child," *her father commanded, though he had a smile on his face.* "What a grand day for you, Marguerite Anna Louisa Longbourne. You shall be married to the love of your life. I was lucky in that, too, you know." *He raised an eyebrow and gave her a quirky smile that was so like John Paul, she almost cried.*

"I've missed you so much, Father." *She kneeled on the dais next to her brother. John Paul turned toward her and his eyes warmed. He smiled that dazzling, mischievous spread on his face that always got them both into trouble. He held his hand out for hers. When Meg placed her hand in his, John Paul gave her a squeeze and didn't let go.*

"There's not much time, dear girl," *her father said.* "You must go to the people and show them that you and your sweetheart can rule the kingdom better than it has ever been done before."

"I don't understand, Father," *Meg replied, confused.* "William will rule."

"You have my blessing, my darling daughter," *the king said as he placed a hand upon her head,* "in your marriage and in the ruling of this great land."

"And for an heir in the cradle." *John Paul winked at her and kissed the top of her hand.*

"Now, go," *her father insisted with a sweeping gesture of his hand.*

"He's waiting." *John Paul gestured with his head toward the hall that would take Meg to her chamber.*

To Meg's surprise, a glowing light appeared beside her. So much like the distant sun in summer, the orb floated in mid-air. She followed it from the throne room, through the corridors, into her bedchamber, and out onto her balcony.

And there he stood, waiting for her.

When Nicholas looked up and saw her, he walked toward her with a smile as wide as a rainbow and bowed. He took her hand in his and placed it through the crook of his arm, just like he did when they walked across boulders onto the lake. He led her to the railing of the balcony. With a loud roar of approval, the people, the entire kingdom it seemed, clapped and shouted and whistled and blew kisses as soon as they saw their princess. Touched by their expressions of joy, Meg waved, and smiled, and waved some more; it felt like hours. The spectacle was blessed with glories, shining rays of golden sunshine bursting through bright puffy clouds set before an azure sky. Nicholas took her in his arms and kissed her, dipping her in his embrace. The crowd became ecstatic once more. But Nicholas had given her that look, that passion in his eyes that told her exactly how he felt and what he wanted, and she had no desire to wave anymore.

When they turned away from the people and walked off the balcony, her bedchamber had transformed into her mother's garden, but not quite.

It was her mother's garden at night.

They had transformed, too. Nicholas wasn't dressed in his formal armor and cape anymore. He wore a pale blue brocade robe over beige linen pants. Untucked and unlaced, his shirt revealed a part of his chest she definitely wanted to explore. Meg now wore a dress, styled almost like her gown, but the thin, translucent fabric didn't fall into a train behind her. It had more of an iridescent, flowing quality. It was the clothing of lovers. She smiled at the thought.

As she held Nicholas's hand and took her first step into the garden, Meg noticed how warm and heavy-scented the air had become, filled with perfume and spice from plants and blossoms she was unfamiliar with. They saw her favorite gazebo, her mother's gazebo, and walked toward it. Illuminated from within, the light shone brightly and burst between the pillars to shine on the surrounding trees and bushes. From there, they strolled through trees in full bloom with long torches planted in the ground radiating light from beneath them, making the color of the flowers blaze more than in sun light. As they stood on a bridge, spectacular blooms of water lilies rose out of the water and showed themselves only to the moon. Still hand in hand, they meandered toward a fountain, light dancing on droplets like diamonds splashing into the pool. Just beyond the fountain, they walked to a patio with more curtains fluttering in the gentle breeze, sumptuous food spread on an elegant table, and many candles burning that led the way to a bed hidden deeper inside by more curtains.

Nicholas turned toward her and placed his hands gently on her shoulders. Gazing into his eyes, Meg saw desire burning them a brighter blue than she'd ever seen before, like the intense hue of the hottest flames. He pulled her closer, lifted her chin a little higher, and took her mouth to his, a kiss of love and longing that grew passionate. He lowered his hands from her shoulders to the small of her back and pressed her body to his. He pulled a comb from her hair, and it fell in a luxurious tumble to her shoulders and down her back. As he ran his fingers through her hair, Nicholas's kisses became fevered. He slowly moved his hands from her waist, along the side of her body, and touched the outside of her breasts with the palm of his hands. She gasped.

"I've been looking at these all night long, Meg," he said breathlessly as he delivered soft, sensuous kisses to her neck. "I don't think I can contain myself much longer."

"I thought we were looking at this beautiful garden." She smiled, flirting with him as he stopped his advances and gave her a wry smile.

"Well, my lady, while you have been looking at the garden, the moon has done a magnificent job of letting me see just how nicely shaped you are."

As she stepped out of his embrace, her head fell back. She laughed louder and more joyfully than ever before, pointing a playful finger at him.

"Do you know I've never heard you laugh before," he said, pulling her back to him in awe.

"Well, we haven't had the chance. To laugh, I mean." Meg wrapped her arms around his neck and kept kissing him, his whiskers soft against *her lips and cheeks. He lavished her back with long strokes up and down her spine and then returned his hands to the sides of her breasts.*

"May I?" he asked ever so softly and sweetly into her ear.

"I'd question your manhood if you didn't." She gave him a crooked smile and raised an eyebrow, teasing him.

His eyes widened in surprise and he laughed, a deep rumble in his chest, enjoying her little streak of wickedness. "That, my lady, you do not have to worry about." He picked her up with a heroic flourish that made her giggle. She wrapped her arms around his neck as he walked toward the bed.

"The great masters could not have done better, and you're all mine." He raised his eyebrows comically a couple of times and smiled down at her.

"I love you, Nicholas. I always have."

"I love you more, dearest, loveliest Meg."

30

DEFIANCE

"It's been three days," Meg heard someone say. Was it Father Elias? "I don't know how much longer the princess can lie unconscious without..."

"Dying?" A voice dripped with malevolence. Even with her eyes shut, Meg knew it was William.

"I think it's time to administer the last blessing for the parting of the soul," Father Elias persisted. "She's barely breathing. We don't want her to go to the other side without—"

"Don't say such things! I can't bear it," Lady Byron wailed. She sniffled and blew her nose.

"Nonsense," a man's deep voice boomed. It sounded an awful lot like Cooksey. "The princess is as strong as an ox, and she's kept the broth down that I made special just for her. Lady Byron has been dipping a rag in the broth and dripping it into her mouth. Her ladies have worked hard through all these long nights to keep her fever down. She's been delirious, half way in and out of consciousness. She'll pull through. You'll see."

Meg didn't intend to do it, and tried to stop, but her eyelids fluttered for a few seconds.

They seemed to have noticed. Voices murmured excitedly.

Feet shuffled closer to her bed. She couldn't believe they were all in her bedchamber.

Then, she remembered.

Everything came crashing back to Meg with the power of a toppling wave, her knees aching as she spent hours in the chapel praying for John Paul, the full knowledge of his disappearance and probably his death, running into the frozen garden, Lady Byron's desperate plea for her to come back inside, finding her father dead, and then ... falling.

How her head hurt.

How her heart rent into tiny pieces. Very little of it would remain if she kept dreaming of Nicholas, or of her father and John Paul. If only such a dream could come true.

Reliving the pain and longing made her eyes burn. Tears trickled down the side of her face toward her temples.

"Look at that!" Cooksey exclaimed. "See? She's crying. Oh, bless her."

Meg found that she was unable to take a breath and panicked. Struggling to catch her breath, she shuddered. She heaved herself forward and sat up, gasping, coughing, and crying.

Lady Bryon was the first beside her, swatting her hard on the back to improve her breathing and then gently patting her. Cooksey was there too, right in front of her, his thick hands on her shoulders encouraging her to gain control.

"Just breathe, dear girl. That's right. You've got it now."

Amid ragged breaths, she looked around her room, shocked to see so many people. Her brother William, Father Elias, Lady Byron and all her ladies-in-waiting, Cooksey and Tilly, her uncle Lord Ellesworth, Lord Cronmiller, and perhaps all the ministers from her father's council. It occurred to her that they were there to witness her death.

"I'm fine," Meg whispered hoarsely.

"Thank the heavens!" Cooksey exclaimed with tears in his eyes. He grabbed her into a rough hug, which made her cough a bit more.

"All right, Mr. Cooksey," Lady Byron said, guiding him away from Meg. "I do believe we've got our princess back." She beamed at everyone in the room.

"Let us thank the stars above," Father Elias said. A great sense of relief engulfed him.

"How long have I been here?" Meg asked.

"It's been three days," Lady Byron answered. She helped Meg scoot up in her bed with her back comfortable against the pillow, blankets smoothed out. Lady Byron combed her hair with her fingers, trying to make Meg look presentable even in her sick bed. "When you feel strong enough, we'll need to prepare for a grand occasion. There will be a coronation as soon as you're ready." She eyed Prince William nervously.

"A coronation?" Her brows clashed in confusion. "Oh, of course." Meg risked a glance toward William, but he just looked away.

"What about father's funeral? And some sort of memorial for John Paul?"

"We will give them a grand procession." Lord Cronmiller stepped up to speak. "And allow Asterians from all over the country to view your father's body before a solemn funeral. They will show up by the thousands. Your father and brother are much beloved."

"I don't understand," Meg said in a small, uncertain voice, furrowing her brows in confusion. "That's not what Father wanted. He always said he'd want something small and private, like he did for mother. He couldn't bear the thought of people who did not know his beloved wife just gawking at her. I feel the same way about my father." Meg took a great, shuddering breath. She tried to control the tremor in her voice. "I know it's belies tradition, but I think we should try to abide by his wishes. It's a time of war. His subjects will understand why his body is not on display."

"As usual, you're thinking when you're not supposed to," William snapped. He stomped to her bedside, his face screwed up in anger. "You don't have a say in any of this, Meg." He pointed rudely at her. "It is not your place, nor has it ever been your responsibility to decide any matter of state. I know Father was trying to include you, to teach you like John Paul did, but this is ridiculous. Nothing will stop me from giving my father and my brother every honor they deserve. We don't want the enemy thinking that we are weak."

"William." Meg sighed impatiently and brought a hand to her forehead as if she were warding off a headache. "It's clear to me that you never really knew Father. You've spent too much time defying him. If you had done a single thing Father had asked of you, you'd be..." She hadn't the focus to finish the thought. "I'm asking now, will you please do the one thing we all know he wanted?"

William raised his hand in the air to hit her. She flinched in anticipation of the blow, but Lord Ellesworth charged through the crowd like his fastest stallion and grabbed William's arm before it fell.

"I will not tolerate abuse of my niece," Lord Ellesworth reprimanded, his voice low and threatening as he held William back.

"Let go of me, you wretch," William snarled, trying to wrestle out of his grip. "I'm the king. I can do whatever I want."

"No, you can't," Lord Ellesworth snapped and dropped William's arm in disgust. "Unlike your father, there are now those who will keep you in check. You are not crowned yet."

William flushed and paced a few short steps, and then he stopped. He pointed his finger at Lady Byron. "Just make sure she's healthy before I send her off," he warned before striding out of the room.

"What is he talking about? Send me where?" Meg said, her voice barely a whisper as her gaze lingered on her uncle and Lord Cronmiller. No one had the courage to look her in the eye.

"My lady," Lord Cronmiller said, clearing his throat as he came closer to her bed. "I think Prince William is wrong in this.

You are the next heir. It is the duty of the king's council to preserve and protect the next in line to the throne."

"What?" Meg asked in shock and anguish. She forced her eyes closed, trying to shutter uncontrolled tears, and shook her head in denial. "It's not possible. It's just not possible. The law of inheritance has always been given to males only."

"Your father penned a new law on the night of his death, switching inheritance of the throne to lineal," Lord Cronmiller continued, "meaning that any of his children could succeed the throne, not just his sons. In my view, you should keep your place here in Tirana, in the heart of the country, so our people know that the line of succession is safe, that their leaders and government are secure. William has got to marry quickly and produce an heir. It would be simpler and easier to keep you here until that happens, but he sent envoys to broker a deal with Edmira. King Caius has sent out feelers in the past to see if such a bargain could be made. It's no secret that he admires you." Cronmiller paused uncomfortably. "William is waiting to hear Caius's official response. The enemy will withdraw its troops and leave this country for good in exchange for you. We will then become friends and allies. You would also have to produce an heir to keep their line going and their succession prosperous. They've not had good luck in this matter."

"You must know," Meg began, gritting her teeth in anger as she sat up straighter and steeled her resolve, "that there is no way on earth I will marry that hideous king, let alone go to his bed! I will die first. I promise you that. I will take my own life. I will truly be my father's daughter." She fell back onto the pillows, folding her arms defiantly across her chest, glaring at everyone in the room.

"Please don't say such things," Father Elias interrupted, alarmed. "You are just worn out from your illness. Consider the consequences to the people if you disobey, Princess. The enemy will not leave and they are the ones who will suffer. You must go and do the will of your brother the king, as soon as he is crowned. We will have peace at last."

"The will of an unrighteous, selfish..." Meg seethed.

"I am sorry, my lady," Lord Ellesworth said sadly. "William has wanted this for a long time now, to use you as the centerpiece of a treaty. You were his bargaining chip. It cannot come as a surprise."

"It's a back-handed betrayal," Meg flared at her uncle. "It's never what Father wanted. He doesn't even have the brains to convince the enemy to leave without using me as the main inducement. And what about Breckenridge? What does he get out of the deal?"

"My lady?" Lord Cronmiller queried.

"Don't play dumb with me, any of you," she fumed. "I know what's going on here. Breckenridge will get something."

"If I may, my lady?"

"Please speak, Uncle. Shed light on this foul scheme."

"It appears you are right. It's not official news, just rumors filtering in from my spies, but it appears to me that Breckenridge has been in contact with King Caius, interceding on behalf of William."

"I've never believed he was spying for William," Meg snapped, thinking of the day she saw the duke at the lake.

"Why is that, my lady?"

Meg opened her mouth to speak and then shut it just as quickly, thinking of what to say. "Maybe it's just women's intuition," she said with a shrug. "Maybe it's because I've never trusted him or anything he's said since the day he came into this castle. William trusts him too much. What will he get in exchange for being so loyal to William?"

"All of the southern reaches will be his. He will be a king himself."

"So, he's going to do it." Meg settled back into her pillow and clasped her hands in her lap. "I can't believe William would let those valuable lands and its people out of his hands, but I knew it. He's a fool. He'll parcel off his kingdom until there is nothing left. Does he really believe that Caius will stop his invasion once he has me in his filthy grasp?"

"I fear you are right. If I may be so bold, my lady, but how could you have surmised such a terrible plan?" Lord Ellesworth asked.

"It is my great misfortune to be good at guessing, Uncle."

31
AN ARROW AND A NOTE

Meg followed William behind the long train of his red coronation robe, emblazoned with gold at the edges, trying not to step on the ermine trim. When she lifted her gaze, she found it hard to ignore the curious stares of the people watching the procession. Like a tiger trapped in a cage, Meg felt as if she were on display for everyone to see. And yet, she wondered about them. Did they feel the way she did? Were they happy that William would be crowned king? Or did they grieve for her father? It seemed the whole country had shown up for his viewing, slowly passing by his body in despair, mournful eyes full of fear. Did they wonder what would happen to the country with William as their leader? Would he make the invader leave and eventually bring joy and everlasting peace? Or would he continue his reckless path to what he thought was glory? Meg was still convinced that he would lose the kingdom in the years to come. His promises to others would bankrupt him of his most valuable lands.

She forced herself to look up once more and found herself awed, even in her sorrow, by her view of the cathedral. Stunning in its beauty and grandeur, it almost made her weep. Lost in endless, soaring golden arches and carved, crowned pillars, she felt like she was looking into a mirror in front of her, reflecting a mirror behind her, and into the face of eternity. Royal blue stained-glass windows illuminated from behind by the bright afternoon sun seemed like enormous eyes looking down on her from above. She felt as if she were looking into the face of a glorious god.

William paused at the bottom of the staircase that led to the dais and the altar. Behind it, the archbishop waited in his tall hat and ivory robes, both ornately embroidered with brilliant gold thread. William closed his eyes and feigned prayer, but Meg knew he was making sure that he wouldn't misstep or trip on his robe. When he got to the top, he kneeled before the altar, bowed his head, and clasped his hands. That was Meg's cue to straighten the royal cape to perfection and continue her journey up the stairs to stand beside her brother and support him during the most important moment of his life.

Meg listened to the archbishop's words in an ancient tongue as he presented William to the people for their acclaim, her mind trying to puzzle out the exact translation. William smirked, as usual, especially when he stole glances with his old pal Bran, the Duke of Breckenridge, who stood behind Ellesworth and Cronmiller. She despised him for his irreverence. Why couldn't he be humble for once in his life? This was the pinnacle of his existence, what he'd been raised to do by their father — to rule the country.

William had promised with a satisfied smile, that after his coronation, he would send Meg to the enemy king in an apparent trade. King Caius promised to withdraw his troops and she would be forced to marry him in a hasty ceremony in full view of the marriage bed. There would be no beauty in the ceremony, no rejoicing of the people over their union, no pageantry of any kind. And none of her family would be there. Of course, no one remained, but not even her aunts and uncles, her cousins, or ladies-in-waiting would be there. William would make her not only a prisoner in enemy territory, but a hostage chained to a bed.

When Meg looked up into the bright blue windows once more, they reminded her of Nicholas, his blue eyes warm and loving. Thinking of him almost made her cry. How had she gotten into this dreadful situation? How had she fallen in love with such a wonderful man, only now to become a prize for an evil king? She naively thought that William would never defy their father's wishes, even in death. Her mind spun with the unfairness of it all.

The death of her father had shifted her whole existence from warmth and safety to dangling perilously on a broken branch as wolves circled the tree. How was it possible to lose everyone she cared about and everyone who cared for her in a matter of days? She'd always thought of herself as independent, but her father and brother had left her helpless in the face of two powerful kings who would use her to their vicious ends. She did not doubt that it would kill her. To her great dismay, she was a pawn in a complicated game of chess after all.

Nicholas was her only way out of this bleak situation, even though she knew a future with him was impossible. If she could just be in his embrace one more time, she'd gain the strength and clarity she needed to get through. Political problems aside, she wasn't sure he survived his wounds. John Paul had delivered a grim note to her before his departure. He couldn't find the man with the soft eyes or with the wounds she'd described.

The archbishop finished his incantation. William rose from the altar, turned, and faced a hushed crowd. He swore an oath to uphold the law and edicts of the church and kingdom, and then sat on the throne. The archbishop came forward and blocked William from view as he anointed his breast with holy oil. Father Elias brought the crown on a pillow to the archbishop. With the crown in his hands, the archbishop lifted it high above his head and extended his arms toward the magnificent arches and then slowly placed it on William's head.

Once the crown was situated, William stood and walked toward the end of the dais to face his people as king for the first time. They gave him warm applause. None of the ebullient cheering Old Addy said occurred at her father's coronation. She recognized some of Breckenridge's cronies, plants in the crowd, clapping much louder and encouraging the people to a rousing ovation.

In the din of the applause, Meg looked up once more to admire the colors from the stained-glass windows bouncing a rainbow of light onto the arches. A trick of the light, perhaps? A flicker of shadow emerged from behind a pillar on the top of the staircase opposite her and just as quickly slipped away.

When she looked back at William, he seemed frozen in form, his arm still holding the scepter locked in a square. He lurched forward and fell flat on his face, the sickening crunch of his facial bones smashing into the unforgiving stone stairs. To her horror, she saw an arrow sticking out of the back of William's shoulder. She looked in the direction the arrow had come and saw nothing except the nobles on the staircase panicking and rushing to get off the dais.

Meg got trapped and pulled by the crowd as dozens of nobles, ministers, and bishops rushed toward William. Smaller than the men but strong enough to bully through to her brother, she knelt by his side. She checked to see if he was conscious. He was, though just barely. He moaned in pain and tried to move his head. When she scanned his body for further signs of injury, she saw a piece of parchment sticking to his back, pierced by the arrow.

Two soldiers on each side of her pulled her up. She frantically grabbed the note, knowing that it could be the key to who had tried to kill William.

"Wait, what are you doing? Where are you taking me?" Meg demanded as she tried to get out of their grasp.

"Our orders are to take you downstairs, my lady."

"To the dungeon?" Meg bellowed, struggling against them,

her heels digging into the floor. "No, please. Take me to Lord Cronmiller. I've got a letter from the enemy." She waved it in their faces. "He must know of it as soon as possible."

The soldiers were deaf to her pleas as they pulled her down the stairs. The passage was lit by an occasional sconce, and she kicked and screamed. She even bit one of them, wildly trying to escape and run back upstairs. This was one of her worst fears, that she would be imprisoned for doing nothing wrong just because someone else wanted her out of the way.

Suddenly, the soldiers stopped and pushed her toward the waiting jailer. Meg caught her balance mid-way between them, shooting scathing glances back and forth. Had someone besides King Caius planned this all along, to jail her as William lay dying? Who in her own kingdom would want everyone dead? And who would be bold enough to assume that he had a claim to the throne? Her head spun with the possibilities.

"Your new accommodations, my lady," the jailer said. He pointed to a dirty cell with its door already open, his fat, greasy face anticipating delight.

Meg stood frozen. Her eyes bulged wide as realization dawned on her. She shook her head violently. "No, no, no! Please, no! I've got a letter from the assassin. I must talk with Lord Cronmiller about it this minute. We cannot waste a single second."

"Well, lucky for us you've got no choice in the matter," the jailer sneered.

One of the soldiers from behind shoved her so hard into the cell that she fell, scraping her hands and knees on the rough stone floor.

"It's for your own good," the soldier said, yanking the door shut.

Meg ran toward it, but she was too late. She pounded on the door until her fists were aching and bruised. Exhausted, she slipped to the floor and cried, her tears mingling with the filth on the floor.

Hours later, it seemed, Meg heard a key turn in the lock. She stood up from the stained, rumpled mattress and backed into a corner, not sure what to expect. John Paul and Nicholas had taught her to be prepared for anything, in any circumstance. She cupped a handful of shards she'd scooped up off the floor to use as a distraction or even a weapon if anyone threatening walked through that door. Lady Byron stuck her head through the opening in the doorway. Meg rushed to her and they grabbed each other in a tight embrace.

"Lady Byron, I am so relieved to see you!" Meg said, her eyes watering as she pulled away from her friend and searched her face. "Why am I here? And what on earth is happening out there?"

"William is close to dying," Lady Byron said, shaking her head in disbelief.

"But the arrow only hit his shoulder blade. I've seen men recover from worse wounds. It can't have been that bad, can it?" Meg tried rationalizing, but her heart told her otherwise. Never did she think or believe, until now, that William would die. Of all the people in her family, she always thought he'd be the last to pass on.

"Aside from the dreadful wounds to his face, the doctors believe that the arrow was poisoned with a toxin that doesn't respond to any of the familiar antidotes."

"This is the worst possible news." Meg's head fell into her hands. "We were never friends. There were times I knew he wanted to kill me if he could, mostly because I've spent my life trying to annoy him, but he's my brother. I never wanted him to die. Not ever!"

"I know, child."

She heard the click of leather boots on the stone floor and looked anxiously toward the door.

"My lady."

It was her uncle Lord Ellesworth and her father's prime minister, Lord Cronmiller.

"Why I am here?" Meg demanded as she stood defiantly. "What evidence do you have against me?"

"We have no evidence against you," her uncle replied. "We brought you here for your own safety, my lady."

"Wait a minute." Meg paced, thinking. "You knew you would imprison me before that slinking, shadowy archer shot my brother?"

"We suspected, but we did not know for certain, that something sinister would happen during the coronation. We heightened security for the sake of Prince William, but there are spies amongst us and those who know how to penetrate our defenses. We should've had guards looking up," Lord Cronmiller said, his gaze stern and immovable, a somber scowl etching his face. "We thought it best to protect our last heir to the throne."

"Well, someone could've told me before those oafs dragged me down here!" Meg snapped. "From the way he looked at me, I thought the jailer was going to lop off my head and throw the rest of me in a cauldron for supper. Why do you have such a disgusting pig in charge of the dungeon?"

"It is a difficult post to fill," Cronmiller said without apology. "Nevertheless, we are sorry to distress you, my lady. It was imperative to keep this action completely secret."

"Distressed? You think I'm distressed?" Meg yelled at them. "How could you do this to me? I thought someone had succeeded in annihilating my entire family, including me, and would waste no time in usurping the throne. I know who it is," she said acidly. "I have his letter."

She handed the parchment to her uncle. He leaned toward the light from the candle on the bedside and read the letter from King Caius out loud.

"I care not that you've not lost all your family, nor the pain it brings to bear. Before I'm through with you, you'll be so twisted and raked and enamored with pain, you'll beg for more. I will have you endure it with

pleasure. We will wet the linens with our blood and sweat together. You will rejoice when you and your country are mine."

"I am aghast at the filthy mind of this man," Cronmiller said, taking the letter from Ellesworth by the corner as if it had been picked out of the sewer. "At least this confirms our suspicions."

"He played William for a fool," Lord Ellesworth said disgustedly. "Caius would take his prize, and then plunder. He never planned to withdraw his troops. That much is clear."

"The question is," Lord Cronmiller said, tucking the note into his robe, "who works for Caius and what are we going to do about it?"

"Oh, I have a few ideas," Meg fumed, rubbing her temples.

"Perfect," Cronmiller whispered to Ellesworth. "Just what I wanted to hear."

"William would like to see you." Lord Ellesworth looked as if he would rather have taken the poisoned arrow himself than request this of her.

"Oh, dear. What can he have to say?" Meg stopped pacing. "William won't want to see me. He will be angry that I have survived. I think, when father died, Will planned on marrying and siring another heir. I was never a part of his plans to save the kingdom, except to use me as a bribe."

Meg never believed the mantle of leadership would fall to her. She felt enormous sorrow at the prospect, but she would take his place. How could she face him?

"I think you will be surprised, my lady."

32
A SPOILED-ROTTEN, WORTHLESS GIRL

William lay on his side facing the door to his bedchamber, propped up on pillows, the blankets covering only half of his body. Behind him, an army of physicians took turns examining the wound on his shoulder blade by candlelight, discussing possible treatment. The bishops hung back, whispering prayers and singing hopeful incantations.

But the stench of death hung heavily in the air.

Meg hesitated in the doorway. He looked at her with agonizing despondence. He knew he was going to die.

"Come here, Meg," William said with a weak, raspy voice. He held his hand out to her.

She walked toward the bed and knelt by his side.

"Meg, I know I've been cruel to you." His body convulsed when he spoke. He tried to control the shivers that came. "Take my hand, sister. I won't hurt you ever again, even if I survive."

She couldn't help but give him a small, sad smile at his attempt at humor. Meg slipped her hand into his. She noticed how cold it was and leaned closer so she could hear.

"You are queen now..."

"Wait, Will!" She tried to swallow the emotions that stuck in her throat, but a few tears rolled down her cheeks. "You need to know that I never wanted this. I always knew you would rule and that John Paul would be your most trusted counselor."

"Except that I blundered. I trusted the wrong person," he whispered savagely. "Now, everything I've ever wanted is gone from me and my sister, of all people, will rule my kingdom for eternity. Great stars, I couldn't be a bigger ass."

"That's not why this happened, Will," Meg argued. "This is the work of an evil, unrighteous, horrible monster."

"It's the work of Breckenridge."

"What?" She knit her brows in confusion. "I thought you were convinced he was loyal to you."

"You were right about him. I never allowed myself to believe it. He's been spying for me, which made his ruse believable, but he's also selling information about us to Caius. What I need to know, Meg, is how did you know about him?"

"Know what?"

"You knew something about him that I did not. What was it?"

"I should've told you when I confronted you in your chamber. You were too angry with me to listen to reason. I've tried to hide it from you, but I sneak out of the castle a great deal, William. I saw Breckenridge in a place he shouldn't have been."

"I knew it!" He whispered hoarsely and fell onto his back, wincing from the pain. He managed an ironic laugh that fluttered in his chest.

"It wasn't because I was bored or to seek adventure or to endanger the throne." Meg smiled through her tears. "I wanted to help. I wanted to find a way to win. That's when I saw him, and that's when I began to wonder about his loyalties."

"Spoiled-rotten, worthless girl," William wheezed and squeezed her hand. "You know you've got to kill him, and Caius eventually."

"Yes," she whispered, nodding her head. The duties of kingship already resting heavily upon her.

"Shove my dagger through his heart and twist it hard, will

you, sister? Tell him it's from his old pal, Will, and don't take it out until you see his hideous soul leave."

"I think we can manage to get the job done without the queen getting her hands dirty, Your Majesty," Lord Ellesworth said as he approached.

"I mean it, Meg!" Will gained strength and pulled her face very close to his. "You must be strong. You've got to muster the courage to do unsavory things."

Meg grimaced and swallowed hard, but she nodded as she stared into his fierce eyes.

"I have to admit that you just might make a decent queen," he said grudgingly. "The people already love you."

William shivered and coughed so violently that her uncle pulled her out of his grasp. He led her to the back of the room. "Take her away. She doesn't need to see this," Lord Cronmiller commanded.

But she did see it.

William gurgled up an awful foam. He coughed and choked on it, a torrent of blood splattering on the floor.

She would never have wished this on him. Never.

"I am sorry for your loss," Lord Cronmiller said as he rushed Meg away from William's chamber and walked toward the great hall. She kept looking over her shoulder, wondering if she should order him to let her go. Her brother was dying. Shouldn't she be there during his final moments, despite their feelings for each other? It was such an unspeakable and terrifying way to die. Meg could not change course. Lord Cronmiller had a steel grip on her arm. "I know words cannot describe your grief, especially with what is happening to your brother..." He paused searching her eyes with sympathy. "But let us speak frankly, shall we?"

"I have many questions, my lord."

"Your Majesty." He stopped in front of her father's throne. "By law, you are now queen."

With a sob and a torrent of tears, she gazed at the throne,

wishing her father still sat there, or one of her brothers. Even William would've sufficed as long as he didn't send her away.

"I know," she said. Her throat constricted as she shook her head, tiny tremors of agreement.

"There is the matter of the coronation ceremony, but I think we can delay for a time. We need a period of mourning for the king. I believe it should be small and private with key figures as witnesses. We will then post notices throughout the kingdom."

"That's a relief, because I don't want one, not with what happened to William. I wouldn't want to invite any more threats close to home."

"Exactly. If you don't mind, Your Majesty," he said pleasantly, "please follow me to my chamber where we may converse in private. Or we can use your father's council chamber as I'm sure those rooms will be prepared for you."

"No! Please, no." Meg yelped without thought and stopped abruptly. "Please tell the stewards and chamberlains that I won't be able to work there. It would be a constant reminder of him. I would rather work with you and the other ministers here for my governmental duties, and out of my own chamber with my ladies about me for my private duties. That part of the castle is my home."

"I understand, Your Majesty," he said, an empathetic look on his face which was foreign to her. He always frowned when she was present and tried to ignore her. Meg spent years trying to gain access to the man. He would have none of it until now.

With guards stationed outside his door, Cronmiller gestured for her to sit down in one of the chairs around a huge council table. He took the chair opposite her. Stained in deepest mahogany with ornately carved spires in the middle and at each end, the chair resembled a miniature throne. It served as a vivid reminder of who governed the kingdom, especially while her father declined.

He leveled a hard stare at her. "Who are your enemies? Whom must we defeat?"

Her eyebrows shot up. Meg had not expected such candid conversation so soon.

"You heard King William say it himself, that you would have to do unsavory things as queen," Cronmiller warned. "There are more threats to you and this kingdom than you could know, or will ever know. They always lurk, waiting for weakness to show itself, for a spy to tell them what evil to do and when. We must keep you safe. You and this country are one. You have become our only hope."

Meg swallowed hard at his honesty. "King Caius appears to be the greatest threat, and Breckenridge. I've always believed that he sold information about us to Caius and then somehow convinced William that he was spying for Asterias. William said as much, just a moment ago." Thinking of William made her pause. Her eyes watered and she looked down, trying to compose herself.

"Take your time, Your Majesty."

Meg pressed her lips together and swallowed hard, trying not to think of her brother's body convulsing or the bloodstains on the floor.

"I think he's trying to weaken both sides so that he can pick up the pieces and rule his own kingdom. I'm wondering if that's what Caius has promised him, his own realm in the south, and if Breckenridge believes that evil king will keep his pledge."

"My sentiments exactly," Cronmiller said as he gazed at her over the top of his steepled fingers. "They are the most immediate threats. I will send out a team of spies to track down Breckenridge. We must discover what he knows and make him answer for what he's done. I do believe he's responsible for more than we think. Now, about Caius..."

"How can we get him over a barrel?"

Cronmiller's eyes practically twinkled. "I know his grasp on the Edmiran throne is tenuous."

Meg chewed on the inside of her cheek as she furrowed her brows in thought. "It doesn't matter that he is the oldest son and has inherited his father's throne. He has too many brothers who are not loyal to him. Our spies in his household report that there have already been attempts on his life. I've heard rumors that King Colestus died of a poison that caused his heart to stop. There's no way to prove that, of course, but how do we negotiate with men who conspire to treachery? Two of Caius's brothers are already under arrest."

"You are right, Your Majesty. They are not unified, but they have wealth and means, more than we do. How could they have sustained their fight in a foreign country for so long otherwise? They have a great desire to incorporate Asterias into Edmira, as it once was hundreds of years ago. And I think you play into their desires as well."

"Well, they can't have me," Meg whispered fiercely. She set her back against the chair, corrected her posture, and smoothed her gown. "You forget, Lord Cronmiller, that I am a wealthy woman. I have inherited the fortunes of all my relatives. While the royal treasury is lower than it ever has been, I have access to personal assets. I can fund the government's expenses for the foreseeable future. I cannot think of a better investment."

"We will pay you back, Your Majesty."

"That does not concern me right now, Lord Cronmiller. Now, about Tirana and my people. What can we do?"

33
A WOMAN UNDER A PILE OF DEAD MEN

They circled overhead, a huge black cloud of them, cawing, crowing, and landing, picking at the dead. Accursed vultures. Nicholas stood watching them, hands on his hips, thoroughly frustrated. It was an insurmountable job, tending to the dead after a battle.

The outcome of a battle was always sobering, but this one was staggering in the sheer number of lives taken and hellish in its aftermath. It would take a long time to sort out where all these bodies needed to go. He had crews on the field, men as well as boy soldiers gleaning, pulling bodies out of the mud and hauling them onto carts, whipping the poor mules as they struggled through the mud. He would have to recruit more, he thought, when he saw Luke stomping toward him, his features clashing in turmoil.

"Just what am I supposed to do with women who fall to the ground and weep on my muddy boots when they see the bodies of their sons?" Luke stood with his arms crossed, the parchment he carried dangling precariously as he glared at his commander. "Why did they come, anyway? Don't they send stewards or servants for this awful duty?"

"Not all those wagons are helmed by the servants of wealthy families," Nicholas countered. "Some of them are mothers and fathers looking for their sons."

"Says the man who doesn't have to deal with the tears face to face." Luke flipped his hand in the air and lost grip of the stack of parchment he held, the names of the dead who'd been taken home. "Ah, grant me patience, dear Mother Earth," he groused as he bent down to pick up the dozens of papers rolling through the mud. Nicholas helped him gather them up until he spied a knight on horseback at the edge of the battlefield. When Nicholas looked closer, he recognized the bald head and burly build of the Duke of Breckenridge. Nicholas sighed and cursed. He was going to have to deal with this man sooner than he intended.

"Luke, I need you for this job," Nicholas said as he handed him some papers. "I know it's difficult if for you, that it tries your patience, but the people need to be consoled by a leader high up the chain of command. You know I'd be doing it were it not for the death of Commander Burrage."

"A strangely fortuitous circumstance that worked out well for the army."

"I'll not hear slander coming from you, Luke," Nicholas warned as he walked toward the figure on horseback. "You never know who's listening."

"I'm not afraid of King Caius's spies."

"Maybe you should be."

Nicholas walked toward Breckenridge, his mind racing with all the intrigue. Nicholas knew from intelligence reports that King William had died from a poisoned arrow. Even the attempted murder of Prince John Paul and subsequent suicide of his father, the King of Asterias, seemed like part of a plan. What was intended? What was happenstance? And how did the events play into King Caius's hands?

Breckenridge realized he'd been spotted and retreated into

the forest. Nicholas followed him. He had no qualms about meeting this man in an isolated location. There was no doubt in his mind that he'd been the author of these heinous deeds. He would send him to his maker if necessary, but first he would find out what the man knew.

Breckenridge dismounted his horse, tethered the animal, and unpacked food from his saddlebags by the time Nicholas caught up with him. In a small copse of woods, he found himself staring at a pair of beady, malevolent eyes, tufts of fat rising above his armor around his neck and chin, and a large balding head. He was shorter than Nicholas, but bulky and strong. He would be a worthy opponent.

"I hope you don't mind," the knight said, gesturing to the items he'd taken out of his saddlebags.

"Mind what?"

"If I eat."

"What are you doing here?" Nicholas demanded gruffly, ignoring the pleasantries. "I've seen you in Asterian and Edmiran territory several times now and I can't help but wonder who you work for."

"You don't know?" the man smirked, amused.

"I've got some theories, but I prefer to hear them from you."

Nicholas leaned against the large trunk of a tree, folded his arms defiantly across his chest, and waited for the man to start talking. The knight used a dagger to cut cheese into smaller chunks. It had an ornately carved and curved handle. His mind flashed to the murder of Commander Kane, and the handle of the dagger protruding from his chest.

It was clear to him now.

This man had killed Kane, something Nicholas intended to do himself to shorten the war. The murder and the ensuing battle did not affect the situation as Nicholas thought it would. The politics between the two countries little changed in the aftermath, horns still locked like two angry rams. Breckenridge was a knight for Asterias; he had proclaimed his loyalty to King William and offered him a mountain of gold, men-at-arms, and a new royal fleet. Besides trying to purchase the queen, a woman promised to King Caius through a failed treaty, why would he do it?

"I'm Breckenridge, duke of all the great lands of the south, and I'm on the king's payroll."

Nicholas almost laughed out loud. "Which king?"

"Yours, of course," Breckenridge sneered. He popped cheese into his mouth and chewed, his eyes twinkling in savage delight, as if he were a hunter who'd just shot an arrow through an elusive buck.

Nicholas glowered but said nothing.

"It's true, but I've also been known to work for King William as well."

"Spying for both sides." Nicholas sighed, his suspicions confirmed, and nodded his head. "So, what do you get out of this?"

"I will rule my lands without deference to Asterias since poor King William ran into a tainted arrow. I doubt the new queen could take it from me."

"That's what Caius has promised you?" Nicholas raised his eyebrows in feigned shock. "Do you trust him to keep his vow? He wants this region for himself, just like his ancient ancestors. I suppose he could call you a king, but I have no doubt that he would be the lord of the land."

"*Tsk, tsk*, commander," Breckenridge said as he tossed more cheese into his mouth, chewing with his mouth open. "Spreading lies about your own king. That's treason. Those words could send you to the gallows."

"It's not treason," Nicholas scowled, justifying. "King Caius holds no secrets about his desire for Asterias. Although, I doubt he will be king for long. His brothers are just as lusty for the throne as he is."

"Perhaps he should find a commander who is not so outspoken."

"Perhaps," Nicholas agreed as he narrowed his eyes at the man. "Was it your plan all along to murder the entire Asterian royal family so that it would be easier to overtake the kingdom?"

"The queen is still left, but Caius hopes she will see the light and decide that she is better allying with him."

"Through marriage."

"Of course."

"Am I to understand that the queen has said no, again, to the king? First to Colestus and now to Caius?"

"She will pay dearly for such a decision. And after Caius tires of wooing her..." Breckenridge tried to smile, but it was an eerie attempt. He feigned thoughtfulness with his hands behind his back. "Well, we both know his idea of it is to compel her. Then I will simply take her off his hands."

"I see," Nicholas grimaced. "The plan is to force this woman to her knees and take her kingdom? That sounds more like pillaging to me. Not what I would call honorable warfare."

Breckenridge raised his eyebrows comically. The idea of honor meant nothing to him. He walked back to his food, made a tiny sandwich out of the bread and cheese, and nibbled on it. "Oh, I'm not going to take her kingdom. Caius can do that. I'll just take her to mine."

"If I were a sick git like you, I could understand why you thought the deaths of Commander Kane and King William were necessary, but why Burrage, the younger prince and his father, the king?"

Breckenridge scowled a little and then shrugged as if he could not have cared less. "Those deaths were unintended, but not surprising. These are the consequences of war but fit nicely into the overall plan."

"I suppose you were also responsible for the attack on me. At the moment, I can't quite see how my death would fit in your overall plan, since you see me as someone who would thwart Asterias."

"No, I can't take credit for that stroke of brilliance. That was William's idea because he wanted to level the playing field, and I can't say I discouraged him. Although, I am surprised you survived the poison," Breckenridge added indifferently. He took another bite of his sandwich, crumbs clinging to the hard, unforgiving line of his mouth.

"I have the antidote," Nicholas enunciated clearly.

"Humph. I didn't know there was one."

"You're a strange man, Breckenridge, working at such odd angles and making such strangled alliances, all to put people in their graves."

"It suits me," Breckenridge shrugged, still preoccupied with the morsel in his hand.

"I can see that," Nicholas nodded, despising the man.

Breckenridge put the last of the sandwich in his mouth, wiping the crumbs from his mouth with the back of his hand. He grabbed his dagger from the rock on which it lay, held it up to the light, cleaned it with the bottom of his tunic, and sheathed it. He put the food back into his saddlebags and sloughed the tiny morsels off his hands. He walked toward Nicholas as if to get closer to engage in the conversation more easily, but Nicholas recognized the ruse.

"I don't see this new queen giving in," Nicholas said, widening his stance. He lowered his hands to his sides, his leather gloves crackling as he balled his fists. "By sins of commission and omission, you have killed her entire family. She will never give up her kingdom. You have given her reason to fight to the death. I think you and Caius have underestimated her."

"And you, Commander, where do you stand regarding the queen?" Breckenridge stood so close that Nicholas could feel foul breath on his face. "Do you pity her? Poor Queen Marguerite Anna Louisa Longbourne has lost all her heroes, all the men who would fight for her. It's all the more pitiable since she is the most exquisite woman I've ever seen myself, and quite spirited. I think she'd make an excellent bedding partner. There's nothing quite like seeing desperation, fear, and pleading in a pair of beautiful eyes."

His eyes lost focus for a moment and he flicked his tongue, enjoying the perverse fantasy.

"Will you turn your back on your country and fight for her? You seem to think that King Caius has unworthy goals and uses evil men to secure his desires. What will you do, Commander?" Breckenridge cocked his head and stared, laughter rippling in the black pools of his eyes.

Nicholas thought he was ready, but Breckenridge surprised him with the speed of a charging boar. Powerful and dangerous, Breckenridge slammed his shoulder into Nicholas's ribs. They tumbled to the ground. Punching him brutally in the face and torso, Nicholas muscled his way through the pummeling. He gripped the man by the upper arms and threw him aside. Breckenridge lost balance and fell on his back. Nicholas jumped to his feet, sword in hand, and rushed forward, slashing at the man on the ground. Breckenridge parried the blows above his head, to the sides, and even protected his legs. When Nicholas went for the kill at the torso, Breckenridge rolled away and got to his feet.

"Fire and brimstone!" Nicholas shouted as his sword hit the ground.

He repositioned his fighting stance, determined to put the man down. They engaged in a dance of dizzying strikes and parries that took them through the length of the forest glen, around trees, behind rocks, over fallen logs, and across a stream. When Breckenridge stepped out of the water, he slipped on a rock and fell. His sword dropped out of his reach, clattering to the ground. He was up fast, dagger in hand, swiping the air. Breckenridge lunged a few times. Nicholas swayed out of its lethal reach.

Breckenridge charged again and slammed Nicholas into the trunk of a tree. As he lost hold of his sword, the back of his head exploded with pain and he was sure he'd cracked a few ribs. The hand flew fast. Nicholas barely saw it in time. Breckenridge raised his dagger for the kill, ready to plunge it into his neck. Nicholas grabbed onto his wrist and held the weapon back. They struggled for the dagger, breathing hard, working to keep control of it. Nicholas pushed Breckenridge's back against the tree and ruthlessly pounded the hand holding the dagger into the trunk. As Breckenridge uttered a foul oath at the pain, the knife fell from his grip.

"It looks like it's just man to man from here," Breckenridge spat. He rounded his large hands into fists and shifted his weight from foot to foot. He struck first, landing a mighty series of blows to Nicholas's face. Nicholas fought back hard, but his hits landed on Breckenridge's torso. He only wore leather armor, but it didn't seem to have an impact. The man was a brick wall. Nicholas maneuvered and landed a brutal backhand across Breckenridge's chin. A tooth and flew from his mouth. When he faltered for a just a moment, Nicholas kneed him in the nose. Breckenridge staggered back and bent over. In that moment of weakness, Nicholas deftly turned the man away from him and snapped his neck with his bare hands.

"In answer to your question, Breckenridge, what will I do?" Nicholas said, trying to catch his breath as the man fell to the ground. "I am not sure, but I won't have to look at that ugly face ever again."

~

"And who is the dumb son-of-a-whore who thought he could best you in a wrestling match with a dagger?" Luke asked after he'd been summoned to Nicholas's tent. "The foolishness of it is staggering. Does he not know who you are?"

"He knew me, all right," Nicholas replied, trying to sit still for the camp physician, who wrapped long strips of cloth around his torso. The back of his head had been bandaged but still throbbed abominably, along with the other bruises and abrasions.

"So, you got him. Good." Luke rounded the table and picked up a missive. "This letter has just come from the king. I suppose you should read it before long."

Nicholas took the letter from Luke, read it, and threw it to the ground. He sighed heavily. Ignoring the physician's pleas to finish, he dismissed him.

"What does he want now?" Luke asked.

"This is madness."

"What?"

"He wants us to usurp, Luke," Nicholas fumed, tapping his fingers impatiently on his knee. "To attack Tirana, occupy, enslave the people, and kill all of the ministers but spare the queen if she'll agree to marry him. I guess if he has the last vestige of Asterias, that somehow makes his claim to the country legitimate."

"How does he expect us to do that? Clearly he's not been sitting in the trenches."

"Clearly." Nicholas shot him a scowl. "Have you ever noticed, Luke, how there is always a woman under a pile of dead men? Always a woman motivating men to murder and mayhem whether she means to or not."

"The queen, you mean."

As soon as Luke uttered the words, his mind raced back to the day he sat with Meg on a giant boulder in the middle of a lake at night, the full moon casting a silver, ethereal glow on everything. Nicholas had teased her about being like a woman of legend who had incited a war. He delighted as her eyes bulged with surprise when she understood his meaning, that a woman might be the reason for the hostilities. He sighed, yearning for her. How he missed her. What he'd give to stare into her eyes just one more time.

"Yes, well," Luke continued, "she seems to be a motivating factor for Caius."

"And Breckenridge. He figured he could skim her off the top of the spoils after Caius got tired of her."

"Poor girl."

"I'm afraid her problems worsen by the day," Nicholas grimly agreed. "As for King Caius, I suppose I will have to tell him that we don't have a large enough force to usurp. Hell, we'd be lucky to penetrate the city wall, let alone engage their army inside the city to overtake the castle. And occupy and enslave? Great Goddess Above, what is he thinking? They're in bad shape, but they still have a more sizeable army than I do."

Nicholas picked the letter off the ground, about to tuck it away when something about it caught his eye. He examined it more carefully.

"Did you break the seal on this letter?"

"What?" Luke thumbed through a thick book that sat on the table and had not heard the question. "Did I do what?"

Nicholas waved the king's letter at him.

"The seal. Did you break the seal?"

Luke shrugged and then frowned. "I thought I did." He looked back down at the book distractedly before he shot his glance back to Nicholas and locked eyes with him.

"Luke, are you sure?"

"It looked fine, but it didn't snap when I opened it, if that's what you mean," Luke said defensively. "You've asked me to open your letters if you're not here and to act on the orders if possible. You've told me a hundred times that we are of the same mind. Does this mean what I think it means?"

"That Asterian officials know King Caius's orders? It's possible."

"I'll find the courier," Luke said just before he left the tent. He paused at the exit. "What are you going to do, Nicholas?"

He placed his elbows on the large wooden table that belonged to the former commander, still strewn with maps, figurines, books on strategy, and writing utensils. He shook his head, rested his chin on top of his clasped hands, and peered over his fingers at Luke.

"If we could just chat for a few minutes. The queen and I both have good reasons not to fight." He tapped his fingers nervously. "I don't know..." he sighed, shrugging. "Give them all the appearance of following orders, and then..."

"Something will come to you, lad, no doubt in my mind."

34

A WITNESS REMEMBERS

Meg began riding on the plain almost every afternoon, accompanied by guards. The only horse left in the stable that Hopkins thought suitable for Meg was her father's beautiful white and grey dappled charger. The king had named him Shadow. Bred for use in the cavalry and eventually selected by Hopkins for the king himself, the stallion's speed surprised her. A proud, swift horse, her father would've enjoyed riding the animal very much if he'd ever taken the opportunity. She shouldn't have, because it seemed disrespectful to him, but it was the most exhilarating thing she'd ever done in her life, except for the time she'd spent with Nicholas.

Not even the fresh air or the horse speeding across the grass at breakneck speed could compare to that, she thought as she rode through the castle gate into the courtyard. When Meg dismounted and walked toward the castle, Lords Cronmiller and Ellesworth awaited her near the grand entryway to the castle.

"My lords, you surprise me. To what do I owe this reception?"

"There has been a delivery, Your Majesty," Lord Ellesworth said, his mouth twisting into a grimace.

"What is it, Uncle? You seem out of sorts."

"If you will just follow me." Lord Cronmiller turned and walked toward a grassy corner created by an outcropping of the castle wall.

Cronmiller gestured toward the object of concern.

"Who sent this?" she demanded, pointing at the decapitated head. Her eyes bulged and brows arched in shock. She fought back the bile that rose in her throat.

"It is a special gift to the new Queen of Asterias from Commander Sheppard," Cronmiller said, pressing his lips tight as he gave her a look of sympathy.

She forced herself to look at the head of the Duke of Breckenridge, the bloody burlap bag opened enough to show his face. His final expression did little to show how he'd died; it was merely frozen in surprise. Meg grew angry at the realization. She hoped he'd die an excruciatingly painful death. He deserved it more than anyone else she'd ever known.

"What's this?" Meg bent over and pointed, spying an object mostly hidden inside the bag.

Lord Ellesworth cut a piece of fabric with his own dagger from a clean part of the bag and used it to pull the object from its bloodied, damp spot.

A dagger with a curved handle.

Meg stared at it for moment, her eyes blinking furiously as her mind worked to retrieve the memory.

"Your Majesty," Lord Ellesworth asked, slightly alarmed. "Are you unwell?"

"I am well enough," Meg said, the brutal realization of the memory hitting her hard. She had watched Commander Kane die. How could she have missed seeing his executioner? "I am convinced that this knife matches the one that we found in Commander's Kane's body. Breckenridge must've owned a special set to accomplish his foul deeds."

She sighed heavily, her face wrenched in concentration as a barrage of questions came to mind. "What is this new commander trying to say? Is he trying to misdirect us because our scouts intercepted his orders? But how could he know for certain? Did he kill Breckenridge himself? Why would he send me this dagger along with his head? Does he mean to brag, to tell me that he caught Kane's killer?" Meg pressed her fingers to her temples. "Why would he do it? Why would an enemy commander try to help me understand the reason for the assassination of Commander Kane? It doesn't fit with what his motives should be."

"Pardon me, Your Majesty." Lord Ellesworth stood in front of her, placed his hands gently on top of her shoulders, and looked into her eyes. "I found a note inside the bag from the commander himself. Perhaps he can answer your questions." Meg recognized the warmth in his voice, urging her to calm down and think things through. The answers would come. At that moment, her uncle sounded just like John Paul, said something her brother would've said to her. Meg nodded and smiled, just a bit, remembering her wonderful brother. The realization didn't make her cry. Today, it made her more determined to save Asterias.

"Would you mind reading it then, Uncle?"

"To the new Queen of Asterias, from Sheppard, commander of the Edmiran army. I've taken care of a mutual enemy as a gesture of my good will to you. In return, would you be willing to meet? We have much to discuss."

"That's it?" Meg cried and grabbed the note from Ellesworth, baffled by its shortness and lack of clarity. "I could never meet him myself. He's too dangerous."

"I think it's possible that he's trying to tell us that Breckenridge was a spy," Cronmiller said with a weary sigh.

"We've always known he was a spy," Meg said in exasperation. She placed her hand on her forehead to ward off a headache.

"Yes, but we've never known for whom he was spying. I think it's quite possible that this new commander is telling you that Breckenridge was a double agent, working to get both sides to fight as they collapsed in the middle," Cronmiller elaborated.

"It's stunning. Truly stunning." Meg shook her head and took a deep breath. "But why would he tell me that?"

"I think it's likely," Lord Ellesworth offered, "that Commander Sheppard got Breckenridge to talk before he killed him and wishes to tell you in person the perplexities of the intrigue, including all the murders, and perhaps who ordered them. Maybe he really is just a soldier trying to get out of a tough spot."

"How could it be so simple, Uncle? Caius is behind all of this. I'm convinced of it," Meg hissed as she folded her arms and shook her head angrily. "Who else has the money and motivation to hire an expensive spy like Breckenridge? He would not have done such a thing at any cost to himself. If I learned anything about the man when he spent time with William, it's that he didn't do anything out of the goodness of his heart. I guess he was fool enough to think Caius would keep his end of the bargain. Frankly, I think Caius would promise anyone anything and then turn his back and scoop up all Asterias for himself. He just wanted Breckenridge to help dismantle the kingdom first."

And that he has done, she thought. Everyone was gone save herself.

"What on earth are we to do with this hideous head?" Meg shuddered. She looked at Breckenridge one last time, still puzzling over how he'd died. He may not have died in considerable pain, but at least he had been caught off guard. That was some small form of justice.

"Put it on a spike along the city wall, right where it belongs," Cronmiller said stoutly. "Plenty of soldiers would consider posting it an honor."

"Commander Sheppard is helping me, my lords, but shouldn't be. I feel like he's pulling me in somehow, trying to get me to trust him. It's got to be a ruse. I just don't know what this man is going to do," she lamented before walking into the castle.

∽

MEG SAT IN THE CONFERENCE CHAMBER BEWILDERED AND distraught as her ministers fought amongst themselves about which plan for negotiation they should adopt. Cronmiller had told them about Commander Sheppard's invitation. That he left open when and how they should meet caused nothing short of a ruckus. Over the last few days, she and her ministers agreed on nothing. Meg stalled, waiting to hear news from her uncle who had not yet returned from Breckenridge's lands. He hinted that he'd formed a plan, but it hinged on his discoveries in the south. She expected him back within a week. Her ears constantly strained to hear the clatter of hooves in the courtyard.

"Gentlemen, please," Meg said with a bit of a teasing in her voice. "I can only hear one of you at a time. I am well aware that our kingdom is on the brink of extinction and that we face an immediate daunting challenge — getting through the next few days alive."

A few of the men chuckled uncomfortably.

"We have been through this before, for generations now, have we not? We're here to adopt a final plan, to decide upon what will happen when this new Edmiran commander shows up for what he presumes will be a surrender. Why else would he be so brash, so bold?"

"Thanks to our stalwart scouts, we know that King Caius has ordered his new leader, Commander Sheppard, to usurp," Cronmiller began, standing up from his chair to stretch his back and crack his knuckles. "That's an impressive word to use in this situation, but can the commander succeed given what we know about his great losses in the last battle? Does he have the strength of force and a promising battle plan?"

"We have not yet discovered his battle plan," Lord Parrish, the minister of war, replied. "He'd have to have enough men to penetrate both the city and castle walls to follow his orders. We have a strong force inside the city. I don't believe our citizens would serve up their beloved queen without fighting themselves."

Meg thought he looked quite old, his face dark and wrinkled from spending years in the sun. His eyebrows and beard were white, thick, and bristly, but he stood straight and appeared strong. He had been her father's most trusted confidante when they fought in the field together. His presence on the council was essential, though he was often brusque and formidable. "Can Tirana be taken?" she asked, alarmed by the idea. She'd always believed that the city was impregnable due to the wall.

"The city has never surrendered itself to our enemy, but that doesn't mean it could not be taken under the right circumstances," Parrish said bluntly. Everyone shrunk under his menacing glare. "Edmira would need a tremendous force, one much larger than ours, and we know they don't have that."

"Why would King Caius order a plan that cannot succeed?" Meg asked, trying not to furrow her brows. "Is he testing Commander Sheppard?"

"I think it is quite possible that Caius is testing the loyalty of his new commander." Lord Cronmiller walked around the table, his arms folded across his chest with one hand propped under his chin.

"You mean King Caius doesn't actually mean for him to attack?" Meg asked, confused.

"No, Your Majesty. The more likely answer to his confusing strategy is that he doesn't appear to be in his right mind," Cronmiller explained. "Reports from our spies indicate he goes through drunken and violent fits of rage followed by collapses in which he does not speak to anyone. If these rumors are true, if Caius is mad, of course he thinks he can win and has the resources to do it. The only thing he and his advisors may not fully comprehend is how depleted his forces are. That might be a little something we can add to the tally in our favor."

Her uncle Lord Ellesworth burst into the chamber, conferred with Cronmiller, and walked toward Meg.

"Your Majesty." He knelt before her and handed her a note.

Meg scanned the contents and looked up into the curious faces of her ministers.

"My Lord Ellesworth has arrested three members of Breckenridge's family for consorting with the enemy. They confessed to betraying me and have shed light on troubling circumstances in Edmira."

"What circumstances?" Parrish asked.

"There is civil war," she said, stunned at the news. "King Caius's brothers have led a rebellion against him and many of his subjects support the brothers. He is presently holed up in his castle. He could last there for a year. Sieges are a long, discouraging business. Perhaps their kingdom is crumbling now. How many brothers are left vying for the crown?"

"Four remain," Ellesworth answered. "Breckenridge's two brothers and a sister, caged in the dungeon, claim that they will support the oldest of them if he breaks off war with Asterias."

"And the two that are imprisoned?"

"They are believed to be dead."

"Four out of seven," Meg said sardonically. "What a shame. Brothers killing brothers. How do they feel about Commander Sheppard negotiating for them?"

"As far as we know, only Caius is communicating with his commander. The surviving royal brothers don't seem to have any interest in him unless he comes back to Edmira. As you can see, gentlemen," Ellesworth said, standing to address the ministers. "The commander can't enforce the demands of his king. We already know from intercepting a courier that Caius has not called him off and the king is daft enough to think he can win. I propose," Ellesworth continued, offering Meg an exuberant smile, "that you meet Commander Sheppard on the plain, face to face, to cease hostilities and begin negotiations for withdrawal of the Edmiran army."

"We cannot send out our last heir of royal lineage like a lamb to the slaughter!" the nearest minister shouted in the din of instant uproar.

"She does not yet have the negotiating skills to bargain for peace!" another blustered loudly.

"I will not let the future of my family and its nobility hang on the ability of a nineteen-year-old girl!" wheezed the oldest of them all, a frail, cranky creature who could barely stand and almost stumbled to the floor.

"We should be willing to go in her place. We are expendable!" Lord Parrish clamored, pounding his fist on a nearby table in righteous indignation.

Meg jumped up from her chair as if a bee had stung her and yelled over the commotion. "I am not afraid of meeting Commander Sheppard and I am not afraid to die! I hope it doesn't come to that," she said more softly as the room quieted. "I can think of a thousand reasons why I want to live. One of them is to keep Asterias out of King Caius's grasp. If it is decided that I should go myself to negotiate, then so be it."

"Gentlemen, please," Ellesworth said, gesturing calm. "I have full confidence in the queen. Unbeknownst even to herself, she's been training for this moment her entire life. Trust me, we won't send our only heir alone. We know his orders are to attack Tirana. That's a tall order in the face of his dwindling army, but we can assume he'll move forward with that in mind. To do that, he would have to post his army on the plain. Isn't that so?" he asked, searching the faces of the advisors. "I think we should line our forces up to meet his on the plain outside the city. We should make a vigorous attempt to look like we can engage him in a very serious battle. We should make every effort to play the part, make sure our nobles are suited to perfection and that their banners snap in the wind. There would be thousands. We still have far greater numbers than Caius. If he comes expecting a surrender, he'll be very surprised, indeed."

"That's a dangerous ploy, Ellesworth," Parrish warned, shaking his head in disagreement. "It could easily invite a battle."

"I agree with Lord Parrish." Meg tapped her foot under the table, trying to hide her nervousness. "He had a smaller force in the last battle and look what damage he did. He's still very dangerous, despite his fewer numbers and irrational orders from his king."

"He didn't have to deal with you in the last battle," Lord Ellesworth countered. "I think he would hesitate as soon as he got close enough to see you." He offered an embarrassed smile, while some of the ministers smirked into their napkins and goblets.

Meg glared them all into silence. "A seasoned warrior would never fall for that," she snapped in irritation. "What is the point of lining up his army if only to move it out again? It has to be there for a reason."

"The point of lining up the armies is to intimidate, a show of force that can be rallied if negotiations fail," Lord Ellesworth answered. He paused for a moment and swallowed nervously. "It's not something we've discussed yet, but we may very well have another battle on our hands. No one wants that, of course. I've got to think that even Commander Sheppard doesn't want it, given the state of his army and the coming of winter. Seeing you could soften his resolve," Lord Ellesworth continued, undaunted. "You know this to be true. The men in my companies and many others in the Asterian army carry your banner. And not just because they think you're..." He sheepishly glanced away from her as he chose the right word, "angelic, but because of who you are and what you have become. You are now the symbol of this great country. I say we should use your legend to our advantage, against the enemy, and for our men. They love the idea of fighting for you."

"Men can't be moved by so little," Meg said tiredly, rubbing her hands over her face.

The whole idea sent her plummeting into sadness. Nicholas had warned her. It seemed ludicrous at first, but the more she thought about recent developments, the more she realized that he could be right. The Edmiran king wanted her. The men in her own army would fight to the death for her. She loathed that she had become the object over which men fought in war.

"I've been searching the military gallery for days trying to find some new treachery that we could use on him." Meg turned her thoughts to strategy. "If I meet this commander on the battlefield, although I'm still not certain that's the right move," she said with emphasis as she glowered at them, "I want him to understand, through ruse or reality, that he faces tremendous slaughter of his forces. We must give him no choice but to back down."

"Then we will most certainly find something to force his hand." Lord Cronmiller rocked back and forth from heel to toe, his hands clasped behind his back with the barest hint of a smile.

35

THE PLAIN

"This is your idea of a little chat?" Luke blinked his eyes and shook his head in wonder. "I know we sent the army ahead to assemble early. Holy Mother, Nicholas, I had no idea. Our small numbers look pretty big when they're spread out on the plain."

Nicholas reined in his horse as he and Luke emerged from the forest, stopping to watch the scene unfold before them. Pawing at the ground, their horses seemed intent on following the thousands of men and horses onto the vast plain outside Tirana. Amidst rolling hills, tufts of leafless trees, and an occasional outcropping of rock, both armies continued to form lines facing the other below a long, steady hill that led to the colossal wall surrounding the city.

The queen's forces had already presented themselves in perfect order. Some companies took positions on hilltops overlooking the enemy with great interest as they assembled. They stood at the ready, their armor polished, their capes billowing, and their thousands of colorful banners fluttering beneath a leaden sky. And those were just the knights. She stationed foot soldiers with javelin and pike on the flats. Her archery force stood on surrounding hilltops.

A fine set-up with an impressive array of soldiery, he thought. This queen and her ministers knew what they were doing. Of course, he expected nothing less. The pounding of blood raged through his veins. He would present this new queen with a few ideas on how to end the war and get his men home alive. He sat up straight in his saddle, stretched his neck, and cocked his head. He was ready.

He gently nudged his horse. As he moved forward to flank the back of his army and take his position at the head of them, masses of peasant folk arrived to see what the day would bring. They huddled against the cold, bundled in thick shawls and coats. Some fashioned hoods out of blankets. Others wrapped many layers of rags around their hands and feet. He felt for them. He had always felt deeply for them regardless of what country they called home, maybe because he was one of them. These people were the reason he was willing to sacrifice his own life if necessary, to bring peace so that their lives would be better.

And then there was Meg.

His darling Meg. Could she be here today? She had a great sense of adventure and talent for slipping away without notice. As he scanned the crowd, he offered a silent prayer to the Goddess, the great protectress in love and war. Meg was definitely here today. He could feel it, his skin tingling from the jolt of realization, and he would find her. After this business with the queen.

∼

"You cannot meet him looking like that!" Lady Byron reprimanded as she kept pace with Meg. "It's improper and you will give him the wrong impression. You are not a warrior queen. At least try to look royal."

Meg rounded on her lady in the stone passage that led to the courtyard where her horse awaited. "Lady Byron, if I cannot inspire your confidence, then I would ask for your respect. Last time I checked, I am still your queen."

"I beg your pardon, Your Majesty," she said, her eyes cast down. She gave Meg a shallow curtsy. "I am worried for you."

"As always." Meg smiled as she met Lady Byron's gaze.

She ignored the effort of her ladies-in-waiting, who had spent hours reworking a gown from the royal wardrobe for her to wear upon meeting the commander. It was regal, majestic, and had more jewels sewn into it than remained in the treasury. Stiff and prickly, Meg would be unable to move quickly in it, so she rejected it outright. Meg didn't plan on being caught in a gown that bound her to immobility in case Commander Sheppard tried something. Her dreams had been inundated with him killing her in the most violent, morbid ways, so she pulled out the chainmail and thick leather armor, reinforced bracers and greaves she'd secretly commissioned while the army was away. Underneath she wore her most comfortable breeches and a tunic that flowed to mid-thigh, along with her tall riding boots. The beautiful purple cloak her ladies had fashioned for her would cover the rest. Upon seeing her dressed like a man, Lady Byron fumed like steam escaping from a covered cauldron.

"I'm worried that if this commander sees you dressed for battle, he will assume that you plan to summon your forces against him. You must dress for the part. You will send him the wrong message if you wear armor."

"I'm wearing it," Meg said flatly as she pushed past Lady Byron. The waiting guards pushed the door open for her.

Meg expected her horse to be saddled and standing near the mounting block, her royal guard nearby donned in their best armor holding her banners. She expected to see her grooms and squires darting about to make sure everything was in order. She even expected to see her ladies holding the purple cloak they'd made, anxious to adjust it to their grand visions. What she didn't expect was the entire royal household and all her ministers to show up. They stood before her in awestruck silence.

"They love you, Your Majesty," Lady Byron whispered in her ear as she stepped quietly behind her. "You can see it in their faces."

"Why?" Meg's breath caught in her chest. "I'm afraid that I will disappoint them."

"You are risking everything for them and they know it. They are praying to the stars above for your success."

"Well," she choked on a nervous laugh. "I will take all the help I can get."

"You must speak to them before you go."

"I don't know what to say. I didn't prepare for this."

"You have watched your father do this very thing since you were a little girl. Mount your horse and search their faces. It will come."

The crowd parted. Hopkins stood by the mounting block ready to assist her. Three of her ladies stood at his side, holding the luxurious purple cloak. Meg walked toward her ladies. They placed the cloak on her shoulders, tucked her hair in, and tied it in front. Father Elias came forward with her crown and placed it on her head. It was the crown of a princess, now of a queen, forged in a circlet of thin gold and delicate pearls, the same one that reminded her of white daffodils in her mother's garden.

Meg turned toward Shadow and swept a hand along the horse's jaw as he nuzzled her. Giving him one last pat above his nose, she stepped onto the mounting block and settled into the saddle. Her ladies made sure that the cloak fell perfectly off the animal's back and sides, trailing almost to the ground. As she grasped the reins, a dream remembered flooded her consciousness, like water escaping the dam, surging, flooding all in its path.

Framed in purple, the hood surrounding her field of vision, her hands graced in leather gloves trimmed with fur clutched Shadow's long, beautiful mane on a cold, winter's day. It was all here, just as she'd seen it before. Meg never would've believed a dream would foretell that she would one day be a queen going to meet a conqueror. That she would step out onto the plain that led to the mountains, the forests and the sea, all boundaries for her country, and negotiate, perhaps even fight for her kingdom.

Blinking out of the vision, Meg lifted her face to the crowd. She searched the souls of her people.

"We all know that meetings such as these have most uncertain outcomes." She gave them a tense smile, trying to swallow the lump in her throat. "While I do not know what will happen, I can promise you that I have done everything in my power to protect you. I will meet Commander Sheppard on the plain, and I will tell him Edmira can go to hell!" Her horse whinnied nervously. Holding the reins tighter, she flung her fist in the air as her horse got agitated and pranced around. Some members of the crowd clapped and repeated her phrases.

"We may have to fight for our freedom this day, for I will not have anything else for my people except liberty. Caius would take that from us if he could. We've always been a free people. We will stay that way. I will not allow Caius or his commander to push us into slavery. It has never been done and it will not be done today!"

The members of the royal household were now exuberant, chanting, clapping, smiling, and waving to their queen and her entourage as they left the safety of the castle courtyard and began their journey through the meandering stone city.

Meg swallowed hard and closed her eyes as she listened to the Captain of the Guard bark to the gatekeeper to raise the portcullises.

This was it. Today would bring a new dawn ... or ... she couldn't think about it.

Meg drew a deep breath and clucked at her horse. She exited through the gate, not as a girl in disguise, but as high queen of the realm.

And then it began to snow, fat, almost fuzzy crystals sparkling for the briefest moment before landing. Meg held out her hand in wonder to catch a few flakes and brought them close to examine their delicate shapes. She delighted in the heavens opening to deliver the light flakes floating by. Even the sounds of the men and animals on the plain were muffled, almost as if they weren't there. All she could feel were her own lungs breathing deeply, her own heart beating purposefully, as if nature itself blessed her with courage. Maybe this was the sign she'd been praying for, that something good would come from this day.

"Let's see what Commander Sheppard has to say, shall we?" Meg said out loud as she raised her hood and covered her head, nudging Shadow forward.

"After you, Your Majesty," Darrion said, her Captain of the Guard gestured with his hand.

∽

"Well, here she comes, laddie. She's got quite an entourage," Luke said casually, as if he were describing the onset of rain. "I don't think you'll get a good look at her wrapped up in that huge purple cloak."

"I don't care what she's covered in, Luke. She and I are just going to talk, that's it, to see if we can find our way out of this mess."

"What if she's got something deadly hidden under there?"

"She may have, but it's snowing. Of course she'd wear something warm."

"And she wants to show you who is queen."

"And I intend to show her who is high commander. What she wears has no effect on me."

"We'll see," Luke muttered and stifled a smirk.

Nicholas couldn't bear the thought of wearing shining armor to meet this queen, although several of his advisors swore it would be disrespectful if he didn't. He didn't care about what message his attire sent. He wore his usual clothing, although he agreed to newer versions of them, and he got a squire to clean his leather armor. To set him apart from the rest of his troops, he allowed his aides to prepare the former commander's scarlet victory cloak. Like the queen's, it was a grand thing that fell off the rump of his mount. His wolf skin trailed on the outside, dangling far down his back. She would know he was the Wolf Knight and the commander, one and the same. He pulled the hood over his head as the snow fell.

Nicholas nudged his horse forward and walked the long line in front of his troops toward the queen. She was still quite far away and flanked by her guards and entourage, but he could see through a slight opening in her cloak that she wore mail and leather armor. She seemed prepared to do more than chat if circumstances arose. He would do his best not to provoke her. As he scrutinized the city, the great wall, the plain, the armies, all the people who'd come to witness events of this great or terrible day, he swore that he would get his men out of this alive.

He searched the faces of the peasant women and servants, hoping for just one glance of Meg. Seeing her bright eyes and smile would galvanize him and give more purpose to what he must accomplish this day. Nicholas would not let circumstances get out of his control. When he heard the crunching of hooves in the snow, and the two horses touched noses, he finally pulled his gaze toward the queen.

She sat on her shifting mount for longer than he thought necessary. He still couldn't see her face, hidden under the folds of fabric, but he could tell that she trembled. The captain of her guard advanced, but the queen held up a hand and signaled for him to leave her alone. Dismounting easily, she held onto the reins and patted her horse longer than he thought was appropriate for such a situation. But he would spare her some dignity. Nicholas dismounted and waited. As she walked under the animal's huge head, wisps of long blond hair escaped from under her cloak. Something about the way she handled the horse seemed familiar, how she patted the creature with delicate, yet strong and steady hands. Then she turned toward him and reached up to pull back her hood.

36
RAPTURE

His steps faltered upon seeing her, brief and inconspicuous, but Meg noticed. Why would he be surprised? Had they met, maybe seen each other before? Narrowing her eyes, she studied what she could see of him from under his hood. The shadow of it kept his face hidden. They stepped closer to each other, still a few feet apart, and he pulled back the hood from his head.

Meg's eyes widened, her breath caught in her throat, and her heart hammered against her ribs. She shook her head in denial, sure that if she looked away for a moment, Nicholas would not be standing in front of her.

He couldn't be, he just couldn't.

Nicholas was in her father's army, not her enemy.

By the stars ... he was her enemy, she sighed.

Meg and her advisors had spent hours on an inducement that would encourage Commander Sheppard to leave her and her people alone. She'd been so caught up in devising her own plan that she hadn't thought of all the tricks that the Edmirans could play on her. This had to be one of them.

When Meg met his gaze, her stance wavered. In a small, stricken voice, she said, "I thought you died."

"I almost did," he whispered. He looked at her with agonizing softness and took a step toward her, but stopped knowing that he could not approach the queen first. "I think you may be what brought me back ... although I had a fine surgeon." Nicholas shrugged and cast a side-glance to Luke with his typical swaggering nonchalance and gave her a hopeful smile.

"Don't believe who he is for a second, Your Majesty." Lady Byron shot arrows with her eyes at Nicholas and Luke as she stomped toward Meg. "It's a foul scheme. King Caius somehow knows about your secret meetings with this man — if you can even call him that. It has been his plan all along to send this pretender to tug at your heart strings," she spat, her eyes slit as she glared at Nicholas. "I once believed he loved you and had your best interests at heart, but not today. He is here to trick you into surrendering. Demand to see the real commander."

Meg glanced between them, uncertainty rising like an arrow shot from the bulwarks. Even if she wanted nothing more than to throw herself into his arms, she owed it to her people to find out exactly who he was. It was a necessity. She must separate her heart from the task at hand.

"I'm inclined to agree." Meg stood taller, swallowing the turmoil she felt inside. "What are you doing here, Nicholas?"

"I've not been honest about my true identity. I couldn't..." His voice trailed off quietly as he handed the reins of his horse to Luke. "I am the real commander. Nicholas Greenwood Sheppard at your service, Your Majesty," he said, walking forward. He bowed. "I can offer proof if I must." Meg folded her arms crossly upon her chest. "And it looks as if I must."

Nicholas removed his gloves and clamped them tight under his arm while he fished for papers inside a pocket in his tunic. "Don't worry," he said to Meg's approaching guards as they positioned themselves between the two leaders. "Just parchment," he waved the papers so the guards could see, and they backed off. "I have a number of official orders from King Caius, including the one your scouts copied." He shot Meg a knowing glance, brow raised. "I'm sure if you compared the two, you would see that the message is the same, word for word. You can also question any soldier in the army." He made a sweeping gesture of his arm toward the plain, "for the veracity of my identity. They will tell you true. They elected me commander and my king approved."

"Any soldier would say as ordered," Lady Byron scoffed, the corner of her mouth askew, like a gnarled tree bent from the wind.

"Lady Byron," Meg said, weary of her lady's rancorous dissent. "Go back to the guards."

"I won't do it," she said, clamping an arm tight around Meg's waist, staring furiously at Nicholas.

"I must do as I see fit."

"I'm trying to protect you. Can you not see?" Lady Byron implored.

"And I have an entire nation to protect," Meg said through gritted teeth and sighed, straining for patience. "If he leads me to a path where I can keep them safe, I cannot turn away. Lady Byron, please, go."

At last her caring expression fell and Lady Byron's eyes deadened along with a pinched, sour twist of her mouth. With a huff of disapproval, she tromped back to the Asterian entourage.

Nicholas stepped closer. "Just a moment," Meg cautioned, raising her hand, and walked toward her Captain of the Guard. "Darrion, go to Lord Cronmiller and tell him he must find the message the scouts copied. He'll know which one. Bring it back to me. Make haste!"

"Yes, Your Majesty!" he yelled, spurring his horse into action.

When Meg turned around, Nicholas was leaning against his horse. Arms folded, one foot crossed over the other, he looked amused and irritated, as if this were a game he did not wish to play.

"What proof can you offer me, Meg?" he asked with a barb on his tongue, a stinging emphasis on her name.

Meg knew he had the right to ask the question. Neither of

them had been or could be completely honest with the other regarding their true identities. She pulled the dagger from her belt, the one sent to her along with Breckenridge's head, and studied it. She had cleaned the curved handle but left his blood on the blade. Anger at the man before her, the man she loved, lingered with moments of anguish. Why couldn't he just have been a shepherd boy who fought for John Paul?

"Perhaps this will convince you." Her graceful moves grew lethal as she threw knife toward him. It landed at his feet but not before Luke drew his sword and the men in the front lines of the Edmiran army erupted into discord and fury. Their eyes locked in a dangerous embrace for a moment. Nicholas smiled and signaled to his men with an upheld hand. His army shut down fast, silence echoing. "You too, Luke," Nicholas warned. "Meg, my darling," he said, maddeningly composed, "if you want these two armies to start fighting, this is a fine way to do it."

Shuddering at her own foolishness, her eyes prickled with hot, angry tears. "How dare you play with my heart?" She slapped him hard across the face. "How am I to do what's right for my people when you tempt me with those eyes and that smile, when you seduce me so?" Meg quickly swiped at the tears that threatened to fall, trying to gain control. "I assume this was delivered properly to the Queen of Asterias?" she said caustically as she gestured toward the dagger.

Nicholas bent down to pick up the dagger. After a quick examination, he handed it back. "Perhaps these circumstances offer proof after all. We are both of a similar fate, Your Majesty. You are angry and think that I've come to deceive you. Why else would you throw a knife at me except out of frustration?" Nicholas offered a sad, ironic smile. "Yet, I can't help but think that this is a ploy. Asterias has somehow discovered the Wolf Knight's one great weakness."

"You're the new commander and the Wolf Knight?" Meg's chest heaved again as she noticed the wolf pelt for the first time. Her head spun with all the stories she heard of that horrible menace inflicting death and sorrow upon others. "Where is my brother?" she shouted, lurching at him. "What happened to him? You killed him, didn't you? I wouldn't put it past the mighty Wolf Knight." Her bright eyes narrowed, slit with anger, fists clenched with fury.

"No!" Nicholas shot back, grimacing ferociously. He shook his head in denial, hands held up in surrender. "I swear to you. Commander Burrage tried to kill him out of spite and revenge because he did not win the battle. He and one of his cronies were on a murderous rampage and killed many prisoners that terrible day. I begged him not to do it, should've killed him myself to prevent it. John Paul was badly injured and I thought he would die. Even so, he has disappeared, Meg. As commander, I would know if any of my men had taken charge of John Paul. I do not know what has become of him. By all the rules of war, the prince should've been ransomed ... and you would not be alone."

"Truer words could not be said," Meg said as she looked onto the vast plain, her face threatening to crumple into despair. "I have dreamed of throwing myself into your arms and losing myself in your soul, just so I would not have to feel so alone as I travel through this unbearable pain. But I don't even have that anymore."

Meg looked back toward Nicholas, his face awash in agony. Weariness, wretchedness, and uncertainty rested on the faces of the thousands of men on the plain. Both armies had been fighting for too long. They missed home, missed sleeping in the arms of their loved ones. She could see it in their eyes. This godless, unholy war ... she thought with a sigh. Restless rustling and the stamping of anxious hooves surrounded her as crystalline flakes settled in her long hair. She searched Nicholas's face for a reason to believe he hadn't hurt her brother. His expression was so genuine and pure. She'd always felt it in him, his innate sense of honor and decency. It didn't bring her brother back, but she believed him.

Just then, Darrion pulled his horse to stop in a spray of dirt and snow, dismounted, and walked toward her with a piece of parchment in his hand.

~

MEG READ THE MISSIVES AS NICHOLAS STOOD NEARBY. She folded the letters and motioned for Darrion to take them back. When the Captain of the Guard walked away, Nicholas whispered covertly, "You didn't understand the meaning of my declaration when I said Asterias has somehow discovered the Wolf Knight's one great weakness."

Meg smiled in response, a pained, anguished smile that brought to bear all the love she felt slipping through her fingers, like trying to keep water cupped in her hands when she dipped them into a basin. With snow dancing around them, Nicholas turned toward her and searched her eyes. Hesitantly, he grasped her hands in his.

"I've seen you in my dreams, my lady. I wanted to believe you were like me, from a humble background. But you are a most extraordinary woman. I should've known you were something much greater."

"And I've seen you in mine, but…" Meg looked down at his hands holding hers. She shuddered and let go, glancing back at him. "I cannot yield to you, Nicholas."

His brows clashed. His lips pressed in disappointment, but he gave her a curt nod. He stood apart from her, placed his hands behind his back, and looked off at the distant mountains.

"I don't know where to begin, Nicholas. I suspected you could be someone of more importance than what you pretended."

"You pretended, too, Meg. We had to protect ourselves. Offenses like ours are easily forgiven." He swept his hand toward the armies. "We have far greater problems to solve."

"I even asked John Paul to check on you," Meg lamented,

feeling foolish over her request. "To see if he could find you in my father's army."

"But he could not," Nicholas finished for her. "I'm sorry, Meg. I'm sorry for your sorrows. I know there are many. I would do anything to heal them right here and now. Would it do your heart good to know that I've wondered a thousand times how I could find you and just slip away?"

He reached out to touch her, the back of his fingers lingering on her cheek, like he'd done the day they'd met, the day he was brave enough to speak to her. It made her breath catch. His touch always did. Meg brought her hand to his, pressing it tenderly to her cheek, closed her eyes, and wished that she could be any other woman in the world.

"You are the only woman who ever made me want to abandon my duties," he said, impassioned, "and walk away from the army. In my dreams, you and I live someplace far away from the hell of war ... but here we stand. I owe it to my men to see this through. That has been my torment, loving you and being unable to walk away from my men. Now that I see the sacrifices you are willing to make for your own people, I know you could never disregard them."

"This is hard, Nicholas," Meg began. Her emotions raw, she fought to keep her tears in check. "I can feel my heart. I can almost see it before my eyes, beating erratically for love of you and watching it rip to shreds and fall in tiny droplets on this perfectly white snow. You have no idea how it feels to love my people almost as much as I love you, and know that I must choose them over you."

"You want to be with me? You still love me?" Nicholas asked, his voice cracking. He took a step closer to search her eyes once more.

"I could never stop loving you, Nicholas." Meg stifled a laugh through her tears.

"Then what we talk about next has changed."

"Nothing has changed," she said with steely resolve. She swallowed her emotions and took a step back. "You have to leave, Nicholas. Take your army and go."

Nicholas scanned the plain. The armies had grown restless. The eyes of thousands of men fell on them both, each waiting for hand signal or a simple nod that would begin another battle.

"I had a feeling you'd say that, but I have my orders, Your Majesty. This is not a game I wish to play," he sighed with a shake of his head. "I'm here to force you into surrender. I have been commanded to smash through the wall and take the city. I am to reclaim Asterias, fly the Edmiran flag over your castle, occupy the city, enslave the people, and kill anyone who resists. King Caius's orders include a particular request for the head of the queen, since you have refused his offer of marriage."

"How interesting." Meg raised her brows in surprise, smiled tightly, and nodded. "I have John Paul's archers mounted on the wall and throughout the plain. There is no way you'll ever get near that wall. I know how they devastated your forces in the last battle."

"The battle would be a draw, Your Majesty, just like so many battles before. If you are determined to fight once again, we all lose."

"I've sent spies to Edmira," Meg said casually, changing the subject, dropping the trick she held up her sleeve.

"Oh, I know," he replied, smiling after a moment of hesitation. Meg knew him. She'd caught him off his guard. "I even know who they are."

"Do you, indeed? You must also know, then, that Caius's brothers are on my payroll. Your king is holed up in his castle and cannot escape. I'm funding the siege."

"You've bribed them," he corrected her.

Meg shrugged. "I had to have something that would send you running back to Edmira. I'm sure King Caius would welcome your support. On the other hand," she said mischievously, tapping her cheek with her forefinger, "your king has left his new commander and army in a foreign country with no support while civil war rages. His brother's forces might see you as loyal to Caius and a threat to them. It seems to me that you and your men are considered the enemy regardless of what country you are in. It's quite a dangerous spot, if you ask me."

"Trust me," Nicholas said, inching closer to her. "I'm aware of the narrow corner my king has backed me into. It comes down to us, Meg, and what we do today. We both know that a battle would not be decisive. No one can win. The determining factor for this day must come from our hearts. Whatever we decide between us is exactly what will happen to our armies. This is much bigger than just the two of us."

"I know," she whispered, refusing to make eye contact with him. "But I don't know how it can be done."

"Don't you?" he asked. With a warm calloused finger, he lifted her chin toward his face.

∽

As the snow drifted down, covering them all with fat, fluffy flakes, Meg realized that fate had smiled upon them. When she sat with her father on the balcony and listened to the whispering stars, she had no idea what to look for. She just knew she had to do something. Admittedly impulsive, she assumed that Commander Kane would be her answer, or she would discover through Kane what she could do for the king. Meg considered herself naïve and gullible on this point, but she knew, just knew, that she could find a way to win. She would deliver that great gift to her father.

Watching Nicholas smile at her, his eyes alight with hope for the future, Meg realized she hadn't followed the stars quite right. She had taken a long, circuitous route, one filled with darkness and danger, looking for a treasure for her father in all the wrong places.

The stars pointed in a different direction.

They pointed to Nicholas.

Shaking her head with wonder and smiling at the realization, Meg knew the stars had guided her to him. Spending time with him, loving him, allying with him, was the only way to get out of this predicament alive. Together they could win the war. By the grace of god, Meg and Nicholas stood together on a snowy plain, in front of Tirana with thousands of witnesses. They had to make something happen. They would never have this chance again.

"We can do much to secure the safety of our armies and our people ... together." She reached out to take his hands.

This time, he hesitated. "Indeed?" Nicholas raised his brows. "What did you have in mind?"

"We should unite our forces. It will take a bit of persuading on both ends." She smiled just a little, emphasizing the understatement. "But I believe it is something you and I can accomplish together. My ministers won't like this decision, but they will have to live with it. Now and in the future, it will be in peace because we love each other."

"Yes, we do love each other." He stepped forward, closing the gap between them. He took her hands into his once more. Searching her eyes in his reverential manner, he said, "I was hoping you'd arrive at this conclusion. As soon as I realized you were the queen, I thought of it. I'm trying to save my men and deal with a mad king and you are..."

"Just trying to keep everything in one piece," she said a little shakily and gave him a nervous smile. "There is a history of bad blood between our countries, but it is not of our making. It is now up to us to chart a new course. Edmira and Asterias have inflicted terrible misery on the people and there is much bitterness that will be difficult to overcome. Luke has lost his family..."

"And you have lost yours," Nicholas soothed, rubbing the top of her knuckles with his thumbs. "It is always the sad reality of war."

Meg took a deep breath, trying to gain courage to ask the one question for which she was not sure of the answer.

"Nicholas?"

"Yes, Your Majesty?"

She swallowed hard and cleared her throat. With a bold, loud voice, she said, "Will you abandon your king and his ill will for my country and my people?" The strength in her voice belied the weakness she felt as painful waves of nausea churned in her stomach. Her knees felt watery, as if she would collapse. Voices around them hushed, and the plain grew quiet. "Will you fight with me?"

As she stood before Nicholas in her great purple cloak, gentle flakes of snow dancing all around, Meg waited for his answer. She never took her eyes away from his and watched the concern on his face grow. Sighing deeply, he rubbed his mouth with his hand and raked his whiskers tiredly, but he never looked away. The silence on the plain echoed all around her as time ground to a halt. Just when she began to wonder if he might turn his back, give his soldiers the signal to capture her and begin the fighting, his love for her the greatest ruse of all…

"Yes," he shouted and gestured to the men on the plain. "For the good of our countries and the safety of our people, I will fight with you." Nicholas knelt before her on one knee, his head bowed.

Confused murmuring erupted. Shouts of victory grew behind Meg while Nicholas's soldiers stood in stunned silence. "Thank you, Nicholas," Meg said, placing a hand on his head in blessing. "Now, please stand. You are not my servant and I wouldn't want anyone to think so." She grasped his hand and helped pull him up.

He smiled and whispered in her ear. "I would do anything for you."

Relief washed over her as she stepped into his embrace and wrapped her arms around him.

"As you've pointed out so poetically," he said, looking into her face with his charming crooked grin, "my band of men and I don't have a safe place to go except the mountains, which is what

I was prepared to do. I would've officially called it border patrol. No one in or out of Edmira."

"I see," she said, suppressing a smile.

"I hate to interrupt your whispering sweet nothings to the lass." Luke stomped up and cocked his head playfully. "Shouldn't we get a move on? These forces need to know what's really going on."

Nicholas chuckled and shook his head. "This is what's going on!" he shouted with arms wide open to the men on the plain. Facing the Asterian army, he strode in front of them, swagger in check. He took his sword from its sheath and raised it triumphantly. He pumped his fist into the air several times, roaring with each successive shake of his hand. Though confused at first, the men in Meg's army recognized the gesture for victory and began pounding their pikes into the ground and hammering their shields with their swords in thundering support. When the roar grew deafening, Nicholas planted his sword in the ground and raised his hands in victory.

Meg's soldiers knew there would be no fighting today.

He turned to her. Meg needed to offer a symbolic gesture that would show Nicholas's men that they had come to an accord. Instead of leading them in a cry of victory, she beckoned her banner men forward. When they stopped in front of her and knelt on one knee with their heads bowed, she took one of the flagpoles. Raising the pole with both hands, she faced Nicholas's army and waved the banner. The Edmiran army responded with a low rumble of voices that grew into a booming furor. Meg planted the pole in the ground before them. The banner rippled and fluttered triumphantly in the breeze. Nicholas then grabbed her by the hand and raised it in the air along with his. Soon, both armies raised the pitch to a thunderous explosion of approval.

Turning from the wild adulation of the armies, Nicholas called to his second in command, "Luke!"

"Yes, sir." Luke grinned and stood at attention.

"I would have you command the men to fall out. Order them

back to camp. Have the riders tell them an explanation is soon to follow. They will want to know what happened here."

"Aye, sir." Luke backed away with a nod.

"I would have you give the same command to my Captain of the Guard," Meg said, smiling at him.

Luke cocked an eyebrow and grimaced as if it pained him to accept a command from her, but then he winked and walked to Darrion to deliver the order.

Meg and Nicholas stood together arm in arm and watched the messengers on horseback race to company commanders to deliver the order to stand down. Nicholas kept her hand in his, as if he would never have the chance to hold it again. Then he turned toward her, grasped both of her hands, and gazed at her with utmost tenderness.

Nicholas slipped his left hand under her hair onto her neck. Sliding his other hand down her back, he grabbed her by the waist and pulled her closer. As Meg stood in his arms and searched his face, his eyes penetrating, as if he were looking into her very soul, she couldn't help but think back to their first kiss. It had been unexpected. They were both in shock and he was wounded. Meg didn't know if Nicholas would survive through the night, let alone through the next several months. Panicked for each other, their pulses pounding, they kissed each other wildly, clinging to each other, kissing through the tears and pain.

Meg could hardly breathe as she waited for him, the desire in his eyes heating her blood. Her eyes shifted from his fiery blue eyes to his full lips, aching for them to touch hers. He leaned down and kissed her once, ever so softly. Ripples of delight shot through her. She smiled. He noticed the smile and pulled back. He brushed her lips with his thumb and kissed her again, this time longer and more deeply. It felt like a charge, a powerful sensation that shocked her body to life, as if everything she'd felt up to that point paled in comparison, almost as if they had not occurred at all. She found her mouth moving with his, his breath warm on her face, his musky scent overwhelming her senses.

For a dizzying moment, he stopped. He cradled her head in his arms so close to his heart she could hear it thumping madly. He looked into her eyes as if he would devour her and plunged his lips to hers. He swung her to the front of him once more, still kissing her, his hands cupping her jaw, her hands clasped the back of his neck entwined in his hair, their foreheads touching.

"I never believed that we'd get through the day without a fight," she whispered.

"Believe it," Nicholas said breathlessly and crushed his lips to hers again. It was so glorious, so overwhelming that they fell to their knees in the embrace. They wrapped purple into red and red into purple, the fluffy white wolf skin fluttering in the breeze. As they kissed, their tears of joy mingled and fell into the snow.

Nicholas stood up and pulled Meg to her feet, his hands still holding hers, the look in his face tender but mischievous. He dropped her hands and wrapped his arms around her waist and lifted her up so that her head was above his own. He spun in the snow, slipped and almost fell. She shrieked with delight, their cloaks twirling, mixing, and fusing. Meg felt so overjoyed that she threw her arms up in the air and lifted her face toward the heavens.

And then she laughed, a deep-throated, uninhibited, joyful laugh.

Nicholas suddenly stopped twirling, looking at Meg with wonder. "I've never heard you laugh before." He put her down but still held his hands on her waist, staring into her eyes. "I've dreamed of it, you know," he said with a devilish grin. "Hearing you laugh, of one day making you laugh."

"I have, too." Meg tried to stifle an outburst of giggles and bit her lower lip. She wrapped her arms around his neck and put her forehead to his. "I'll tell you what, my handsome warrior," she began in her most sultry voice. "You can do whatever it takes to make me laugh."

Nicholas threw his head back and chuckled.

"I can assure you, my lady. That is not going to be a problem."

"I love you, Nicholas."

"I love you more."

He kissed her again and Meg did not want it to stop, ever.

She could still feel his lips on hers when he pulled away. Her gaze lingered on his eyes, something about Nicholas that always shook her existence to the ground, like an earthquake. There he stood, still holding her hands and smiling at her, while gentle flakes of snow fell all around him, his glorious blue eyes exuding enough warmth to melt all the snow on the plain. He put an arm around her shoulder as he turned toward the thousands of men leaving the plain, his eyes wide with wonder as the armies received the news to stand down.

"I can't believe I'm seeing it with my own eyes. I prayed for a peaceful resolution before we met on the plain, you know. I had no idea that it would involve the two of us," he said a little sheepishly and cast her a nervous side-glance. "Watching these two armies leave the plain without a fight is nothing short of a miracle."

"It's stunning," Meg sighed in agreement. She turned toward Nicholas, holding his eyes with her own. "I know we must part ways soon to enforce this alliance, which I can hardly bear the thought of, but will you come to the castle first for a short time? We have a few things to discuss." She raised a brow and gave him a seductive smile, the one she knew he couldn't resist.

"I'd like nothing more than to have you all to myself," Nicholas answered with a wicked grin. He took her hands in his. "But I think this order to stand down is going to require a more thorough explanation from both of us. Our men need to understand what has happened here today, and they do, too." He glanced at her nervous guards and advisors. When Meg turned around to see them for herself, Lady Byron still looked as if she were a horse behind a gate, chomping at the bit to run and rescue her. "Besides, if you and I enter a room alone, Lady Byron will surely think that I'm a pretender with nothing more on his mind than debauching the queen."

"She already thinks that," Meg quipped and rolled her eyes. "Even though she and Luke are witnesses to our very chaste relationship."

"Perhaps we can reinforce her thinking," he said with laughing eyes as he kissed the top of her hand. "Lead the way, Your Majesty."

37
JOYFUL

Malcolm Cooksey was the real hero. In his typical, unflagging confidence in the queen, he knew that Meg would conquer the day and arranged for a quiet celebration before she even left the castle. He made sure that the antechamber opposite the great hall, the one that everyone reveled in, was ready for her and a few friends to take a drink and nibble on the kitchen's best store of bread and cheese in front of a blazing fire.

It was a welcome relief. The wind had picked up as they journeyed through the city. By the time they entered the castle gate, a blinding, howling blizzard had settled over the countryside. Meg shuddered at the thought of it and took another swallow of the warm fragrant mead, enjoying the pungent spices that wafted to her nose. She stole a glance between the chairs to Luke and Lady Byron who sat on opposite sides of the room, trying to ignore each other. She couldn't believe that the two of them would not let her and Nicholas out of their sight. That's how it was going to be until she and Nicholas gained the trust of their aides and advisors, politically and personally. Infuriating as that was, she was not going to deprive herself of this moment with Nicholas.

They laughed about meeting by accident in the castle all those months ago, about how he thought she'd scream for the guards but saddled with him a babysitting job instead. Nicholas smiled as he relived a secretive jaunt through the castle kitchens, sprinting in the shadows of the castle wall to a dilapidated tunnel. Once Meg had closed the door to the tunnel, Hannah tried to run away from him through the entire journey. She screamed and cried, even scuffled with him. He gripped her by the arm to keep her going in the right direction, dragging her through the dirt while he trudged on, holding the torch. He finally slung her over his shoulder like a bag of potatoes. At least that way, he could avoid her kicking his shins and biting his fingers. It wasn't until they emerged from the tunnel that she believed he would see her safely home.

"Mother, give me mercy," Nicholas sighed with a laugh. "That child was a trial."

"You see," Meg said smiling as she sipped from her goblet. "I knew there was a reason I could trust you."

"You could trust me with anything since the day I first laid eyes on you."

"Love at first sight then."

"Definitely." Nicholas leaned back into the luxurious cushion with his eyes closed. He rested his head on the top of it as he stretched his long legs out in front of him, hands clasped on top of his chest. She'd never seen him look so comfortable. "What of your enterprises, then?" he asked, opening one eye to gaze at her.

"I'm afraid my father only allowed me a certain amount of surplus grain. The rest had to be saved for the army."

"But you are queen now. Certainly, you can make arrangements for the grains to be used again for the people."

"As long as I know I'm not going to be attacked," Meg answered cheekily and took another sip of mead. "I think I can work that out."

"Ah, we come to the dreaded subject at last. No, Meg," he said as he leaned forward and rubbed his hands together, holding them closer to the fire. "You're not going to be attacked, not by me, and not any time soon. Another battle will come, though, one that we must fight," Nicholas said with a note of somberness in his voice.

"It won't come to that," Meg said stubbornly and stood to pace in front of the fire, gnawing on her thumbnail. She whirled to face him and gestured with her hands. "I've stirred up too much trouble in Edmira for King Caius to overcome it."

"You have spurned him and I have taken control of his army," Nicholas replied patiently. "If he is in his right mind, Caius will not sit by and watch it happen."

"Is he in his right mind?" Meg asked in a tiny, fearful voice. "I've heard rumors from our spies in his household."

"I don't think so. He's not the same man I've known over the years, even before he was crowned king. If he is, he will not be denied revenge."

"I thought we had him running with his tail between his legs." Meg turned toward the fire and slumped, wringing her hands.

Nicholas stood and turned her toward him, hands on her shoulders, smiling in his reassuring way. "We do, for now."

"Oh, Nicholas," she whispered and fell into his embrace. "I've been through so much. We've been through so much. If I have an uncertain future, more darkness hanging over me, I want to be with you. You're the only who makes me feel strong." He had removed all his outer garments, including his cloak and leather armor, and dumped them in the corner. When she wrapped her arms around his waist and laid her head on his chest, crying just a little, she could feel just how gloriously proportioned and muscular he was. She closed her eyes and breathed him in, the musky scent of him, making her feel at once relaxed yet nervous, every cell in her body calling to him, desperate for his touch.

"I'm afraid I must leave soon." He looked especially

mournful as he put a finger under her chin and raised her face to his, searching her eyes.

"Where will you go?" Meg asked, although she wasn't sure she wanted to know.

"Back to our encampment deep in the forest. And I intend to keep them there, to keep them away from your army for a while. I will convince them that we have nowhere else to go, that this is our only option. I will lay out for them the treachery in Edmira."

She tightened her hold around his waist and squeezed.

"I am forever grateful for your willingness to yield, Nicholas. It was brave. You are the one who avoided bloodshed today."

"I would've done anything for you, today and always." Nicholas kissed her forehead and looked lovingly into her eyes. "I think you know that."

"Yes, I do," Meg said, offering a warm smile.

He shot a glance toward Luke and Lady Byron and a mischievous smile spread across his face. He bent down to whisper in her ear. "Do you suppose you could escape your chaperone and meet me some where tonight, after all the excitement has died down?"

"You intend to debauch the queen after all, is that it?" she replied and quirked her brow.

"Not at all. I wouldn't do so unless invited by the queen herself or had her in my marriage bed, but I'd like to give her something to remember me by."

"I can tell you with full authority that the queen would like that very much," Meg said. She put her arms around his neck, resting her forehead against his. "Shall we meet in the alcove then, the one hidden in the vestibule? You remember it, don't you?"

"Aye, how could I forget?" he whispered huskily. "I remember how much I wanted to be alone with you. Maybe I would've remembered to ask your name if the lass hadn't been sniveling." He gave her a sweet lopsided grin and a warm soft kiss that made her tingle all over. He let go far too soon for Meg's liking and picked up a loaf of uncut bread. He examined it for a few seconds, turning it over in his hands. "Luke," he hollered and tossed the loaf of bread toward his second-in-command who caught it deftly. "For you, my friend." He said to Meg loud enough for Luke to hear, "Now maybe I won't have to hear him grumble about not getting any fresh bread."

"It's about time. Do you know how long I've waited for this?" Luke said, thrusting the loaf playfully at Meg. "I've worked my fingers to the bone on your enterprises, shoveled manure, climbed city walls with nothing but dreadful rock fields below."

"My ancestors built the wall near them for that purpose, Luke."

"Slogged through deep mud in battle," he continued his tirade, "fought with swords back to back with my mate here, nursed him back to life, and have endured his infatuation with you enough to drive me mad. Somehow, I lived through it. This…" he said, smelling the bread and rolling his eyes into the back of their sockets, as if he died and gone to heaven. "Is long past due."

Meg felt Nicholas convulse with laughter. He picked her up and whirled her around, giving her a good, hard kiss.

"Shall we join the party then?"

Luke stood by the table cutting a piece of bread for himself, looked up, and smiled. Lady Byron, however, emerged from the back of the room, walking slowly with a frown on her long, taut face.

"Lady Byron, all we need is a little trust," Meg implored, waiting for a sign from her head lady-in-waiting. She had been more than that over the years, more like a mother to a headstrong, willful, adventurous young girl. She was protective, comforting, a voice of reason, and wept when she thought Meg was going to die. As the war worsened, the king entrusted Lady Byron with the safety of the princess. She took it seriously, eventually traipsing the countryside with Meg to keep her from falling victim to her own foolishness or to someone with malicious intent. Lady Byron had made unwilling sacrifices, but kept her silence as well as Meg's secrets.

"I've always said you're either the smartest girl I know or the luckiest. The stars smile upon you, child. You move through life with the sheer force of your resplendent personality, your aura, bending people and circumstances to your will. How could anyone say no?"

"Thank you, Lady Byron." Meg rushed toward her lady and pulled her into a rough hug.

Nicholas opened the door with more force than he intended. It bumped against the wall. He laughed and held out his hand to her. Meg rushed to his side. The brightness of the great hall burst into the room. Although constricted by the walls and the doorway, its golden glow seeped into the room, inviting them to join in joy and celebration. All the inhabitants of the castle had been waiting for them to emerge. They clapped and whistled and cheered.

Meg smiled and walked into the light, holding Nicholas's hand.

ALSO BY SHANTAL SESSIONS

See how the story begins and uncover a secret!

Get The Runaway Queen (prequel novella to The Entangled Princess) for FREE by signing up for Shantal's newsletter.

Come hang out for fun banter, exciting book deals, exclusive giveaways, new releases, and freebies.

https://mybookcave.com/d/4d40ad16/

-Shantal is also a writer of Swoonworthy, Heartwarming, Happily-Ever-Afters-

Where falling in love unfolds in the most beautiful places in the world!

Paradise Beach: A Sweet Second Chance Romance (Book 1)

She thought she was over him. His tour of duty matured him. Will their heart-breaking history stand in the way of a happily-ever-after?

Paradise Shore: A Sweet Second Chance Romance (Book 2)

The gorgeous Italian Riviera. A couple with a chasm. Thrown together again in Italy, will it be more than the sun making them sizzle?

Paradise Cove: A Sweet Second Chance Romance (Book 3)

Maya thinks she knows what she wants. Until she travels to America to follow her dreams. And unexpectedly find the one man she thought had walked away forever.

ACKNOWLEDGMENTS

Some amazing people had a hand in helping me develop my story. Thanks to readers of early drafts, Heidi#1 (Thornock), Heidi#2 (Wilde), great ladies who have become good friends. Thanks Wendy Knight, a total "sweetling," the author of *Fuedlings* (and so many more) who first agreed to read my story; Camelia Miron Skiba, who insisted my lovers meet sooner; Sarah Hiatt, who loves a good romance; and Deanne Cummings, who always encouraged me because she enjoys the way my words flow.

Thanks to my sister Juli Caldwell who is a gifted writer and editor. I couldn't have done any of this without her help. Her advice, stories, writing style, and spunky narrative voice are an inspiration to me.

Thanks to Silviya Andreeva for designing absolutely the most beautiful cover in the world! I would never have believed she could capture a moment that rendered my princess and her motives so well. She's an amazingly talented artist, in addition to being professional and kind.

And most of all, thanks to my guys — Gene, Daniel, and JC for putting up with all the hours I spent glued to my computer monitor. The series has been years in the making and you've been over-the-top loving and supportive. I must've heard this a thousand times: "Just publish your book, Mom!" They light my world.

ABOUT THE AUTHOR

Shantal adores reading and writing gorgeous, feel-good, heart-warming romance. She enjoys many genres as long as there is a happily-ever-after. Originally drawn to writing Medieval romance, she's since written in a variety of genres, all of them sweet and clean.

A native of southern California, she moved to Utah when she was 16 and hasn't looked back. Living in the foothills of an impressive mountain was the perfect place to marry her king and raise their two princes. A little princess (her first grand baby) joined the royal ranks in the summer of 2020.

When not reading, writing, or watching costume dramas or romcoms, she enjoys gardening in the summer, skiing in the winter, and makes the most delectable pumpkin chocolate chip cookie ever.

To keep up-to-date with her writing adventures and more, follow Shantal at these sites.

Printed in Great Britain
by Amazon